DREN

SECRETS AND LIES SERIES BOOK 4

B J ALPHA

BREN

Secrets and Lies Series Book 4

Copyright © 2022 by B J Alpha

All rights reserved.

No part of this book may be reproduced in any form or by any electronic or mechanical means, including information storage and retrieval systems, without written permission from the author, except for the use of brief quotations in a book review.

This book is a work of fiction. Characters, name, places and incidents are a product of the authors imagination.

Any similarity to actual events, locations or persons living or dead is purely coincidental.

Published by BJ Alpha

Edited by Dee Houpt-Proofreader

Book Cover Design by Katie Evans

 Created with Vellum

BREN

Secrets and Lies Series Book 4

BJALPHA

DEDICATION

To Kate, for giving me the confidence to bring you Bren.
Thank you.
Forever.

AUTHORS NOTE

***WARNING:** This book contains triggers. It has sensitive and explicit storylines such as: human trafficking, strong sexual violence, sexual scenes with dubious consent, graphic violence and strong language. It is recommended for readers aged eighteen and over.*

PLAYLIST

Lewis Brice - It's You (I've Been Looking For)
<u>Bren and Sky's Song!</u>

Forest Blakk - Fall Into Me
Gracie Abrams - I miss you, I'm sorry
Cian Ducrot - All For You
Timbaland - Apologize ft. OneRepublic
GABRIELLA - Goodbye My Lover
Forest Blakk - Fall Into Me
Clinton Kane - I Guess I'm in love
Gone West - I'm Never Getting Over You
James Bay - One Life

ADVICE FROM BJ ALPHA...

Bren is a Dark Romance book and contains TRIGGERS!
Please heed the **warning**.

This book also suggests a **Survival Kit**:
Water – because you're about to become dehydrated from those steamy scenes.
Batteries – in case your partner isn't available or making the cut. Your battery-operated boyfriend will be required to be on hand and may possibly want to participate in recreating said steamy scenes.
Defib machine – This is not a necessity, but should you struggle with breathing issues its probably wise to make sure its nearby.

Author does not accept liability in any event that may occur due to you choosing to read on… Please be warned.

PROLOGUE

Bren

I sit back lazily in my chair, watching and listening to my brothers' banter, a warmth spreading through me.

Tossing another chip in my mouth, I almost choke from Con's words, "Soon as me and Will are married, I'm knocking her up." He grins to himself like the cat that got the cream.

Finn chuckles. "You should just fuck off to Vegas like Angel and I did. I don't know why the fuck you need to spend a shit ton of green on one fucking day."

Con visibly exhales. "Because, dipshit, my woman wants a proper wedding, so I'm giving her what she wants." He shrugs.

I scoff. "Please, that's the biggest load of shit I've ever heard. You wanted the fucking big elaborate wedding, not Will. Will couldn't give a shit less; the poor fucking woman is just going along with whatever you want so you don't have another fucking meltdown." Because let's face it, Will is prepared to bend over fucking backward to keep Con happy. I've never known a woman so dedicated. Apart from my ma, that is.

Con all but glares at my analysis. "What the fuck ever. So what if I want to show the world who owns Will? Let some fucker try to steal her, see how far he gets." He lifts a shoulder as though what he's saying is normal. As though he doesn't sound like a possessive asshole. How the fuck a man can feel so hungry and desperate for one woman is beyond me.

I laugh back at him, fueling his little tirade. "You're getting married because you want people to know Will is yours? Do you have any idea how deranged you sound right now?"

Con sneers at me childishly. "Don't fucking care." His eyes hold mine. "You just wait, Brother. One day you're going to be as possessive as us." He waves his hand around in Finn's and Cal's direction.

I choke. Is he serious? There's no way in hell I'd hand a woman my balls. It makes you fucking weak, and that's one thing I'm not.

Nah, I'm good sticking my cock in a bunch of randoms to get off. I sure as shit don't need tying down. "Fucking doubtful. I just need a hole to empty my load into, not all this other shit." I wave my hand around the table.

"How noble of you." Oscar sneers in my direction. My brother has a problem with my womanizing ways, but what the fuck does it have to do with him? He pays for sex for Christ's sake.

I sit back in my chair, staring back at Oscar. "About as noble as you paying for sex." I cross my arms over my chest, waiting for an argument to erupt. I taunt Oscar further by raising an eyebrow in his direction.

Finn clears his throat and shuffles on his chair, clearly sensing the tension.

His voice turns deep and serious. "Are we any closer to figuring out who the Mexican guy is that attacked Angel?"

Finn's now wife, Angel, was viciously attacked and brutally raped by our uncle and two other guys. Our uncle and one of those guys are now dead, the other still unaccounted for. We have no clue who he is. To make matters worse, it transpired our uncle was the head of a sex trafficking ring and had planned on shipping Angel somewhere unknown.

Oscar sits straighter. "Not exactly. I'm working through Don's computer files. There's…" He goes quiet for a moment, swallowing harshly. "A lot of fucked-up shit on there." He winces on his words.

My gut clenches at the thought. We've since learned Uncle Don dealt in the skin trade of children too. My fists clench beside me and the muscles in my shoulders tighten to the point of pain.

"What about Teddy?" Cal asks, his voice full of concern. The room is deathly silent, and we seem lost in our own thoughts. We recently discovered the truth that our Uncle Don had raped our mother years ago too. He was a fucking monster, and we had no idea there was a viper in the nest. She gave birth to his son and later put him up for adoption, but before we killed Don, he taunted us with words eliciting to him knowing about his son, Teddy. We owe it to our ma to track Teddy down, if only for all of us to know he's safe.

"I'm getting closer." Oscar sighs. Oscar is the technology whizz but also a bit of an oddball. He doesn't like to be touched and has a shit ton of other issues. Since we learned that Cal has a teenage son, Reece, who is high functioning, it's really brought light to Oscar's own struggles. We certainly haven't supported him in the way we should have. But now we know and we're all trying really hard to be there for him. The pressure he's under to get us answers into our uncle's dealings must be immense.

"Maybe we should leave it alone," Finn says flippantly.

Cal sucks in air and spits out, "He's our brother, Finn!"

Finn glares in his direction with hate in his eyes. He's one fucked-up guy, that's for sure. "Like fuck he is. He's that fucking rapist's son. Probably fucked in the head, just like him." He points his finger toward his temple with emphasis. His eyes drill into Cal's, begging for an argument.

The fact that Finn is so against us finding Teddy pisses me off. We've all accepted Angel's daughter, Charlie, as our own, knowing full well how and who she was conceived with. I jerk my head up and I stare at Finn. "Like Charlie, you mean?"

Finn's eyes drill into me with intensity. I hold my hands up not wanting to cause another argument. "Just fucking saying, Brother. He's biologically Charlie's father, the same as Teddy." Yeah, the sick fuck left a physical lasting impact on Angel in the form of her little girl, Charlie. My brother Finn has taken her on as his own, for that I'm truly proud of him.

His eyes gleam in malice, not leaving mine. "She's fucking mine."

I nod in agreement. "I get that. But she's innocent, same as Teddy. What about Ma, huh? You think this is fair to her? She deserves to know her kid, Finn, just like Angel got to know hers." Finn's expression changes as if realizing I'm right. He drags a hand down his face and exhales loudly. "Get it," he spits out reluctantly.

My cell phone ringing cuts through the tension in the room. The word "Warehouse" dances across the screen. I mouth it to Oscar, knowing we've probably got an issue with the shipment due in tonight; I knew I should have stayed behind.

"Put it on speaker," Oscar clips out in annoyance, probably thinking he has enough going on.

"Sir, this is Paul. We have a crate here that isn't the correct weight."

My eyebrows furrow in confusion. That's odd. If anything, I'd expect one to be missing. It's happened in the past, too many times. But it's probably easier to take one than it is to actually open one up and try to steal something from the inside without being detected.

"Have you opened it?" I snap back at him, annoyed as fuck.

"No, sir. I don't think it's one of ours. It has a blue sticker on the side." My spine straightens and I look to Finn. Angel was being transported in a crate with a blue sticker on it. The tension in the room is now so thick you could cut it with a knife.

"Give me a full breakdown of the situation." Oscar leans forward, his assessor head now on.

"The shipment came in on time, sir. But this crate stood out because when we weighed it, it was under the weight requirement."

"By how much?" Oscar's eyebrows knit together deep in thought.

My heartbeat thumps against my chest and my muscles are coiled tight as I wait for his answer.

"The crate weighs seven hundred and twenty pounds, sir."

All in an instant, our eyes go to Oscar, who is staring at the phone. He blinks rapidly, as if something is registering in his head.

"We'll be there in fifteen minutes. Do not touch the crate. Do you understand?" he snaps.

"Yes, sir."

The line goes dead.

I watch Oscar and wait for him to speak. I feel like a time bomb waiting to go off. Anger bubbling through me. "I think it's a person in the crate," he admits quietly. *What the fuck? Where the hell does he get this shit from?*

"What?" Cal gasps.

"What the fuck makes you think that?" I spit at him.

"An average crate is five hundred and fifty pounds, average person is one hundred and seventy pounds, coupled with the fact it has a blue fucking sticker on the side, I'm pretty damn sure there's a person in the crate." His voice rises with a hint of panic.

"Jesus!" I scrub a hand down my face, my stomach plummeting at the shit show we have facing us next.

"What we gonna do?" Con asks while standing with the dog tucked under his arm.

I jump up and attach my gun holster. We need to get to the bottom of this shit. "Gonna go check it out. Oscar, keep the feds off our back." Oscar nods at my request and begins to furiously type on his tablet.

"I'm coming with you," Finn tells me.

My back snaps straight. *Is he capable?* Given what happened to Angel, it's probably not a good idea. We don't know what the fuck we're going to find in there. "You sure you can handle it?"

My eyes meet Finn's. He swallows hard. "Of course." I nod back at him.

"You need me too?" Con asks while looking down at the dog as though it's a baby in his arms. Damn pansy ass.

"No, fucking stay here with Oscar."

Cal is already out the door with me hot on his tail.

My fists clench with determination.

Determination to sort this out once and for all.

CHAPTER 1

Bren

I drive us to the warehouse in complete silence, racing through the backstreets of New Jersey, eager to get to our destination. Cal, second in command, sits beside me, and Finn is in the back. You can feel the heat and anger radiating off him.

"He might have it wrong." Cal's voice cuts through the air, his tone laced with uncertainty.

I scoff at his analysis. "Doubtful. Since when has Oscar ever gotten anything wrong?"

I glance in my rearview mirror. Finn sits forward, his knee bouncing with nervous anticipation. Finn's tone is clipped. "We need to do something, Bren. Fucking human trafficking? Coming through our turf?" He shakes his head in disgust, his voice rising higher on each word.

My head pounds and my temple pulsates in fury. Damn fucking right we need to do something. I tighten my grip on the steering wheel, my knuckles turning white. "We'll get some answers. If someone's in that fucking crate, you can torture it out of them, if need be." I meet his eyes in the mirror and he nods in approval.

I turn into the warehouse parking lot. The guards on the gates have them wide open for us. The gravel churns under my tires as I speed through the roller door, pulling up sharp beside one lone crate.

I jump out of the SUV and register the sound of my brothers slamming their doors behind me. I pull off my suit jacket, throwing it to the floor. Taking my time, I roll up the sleeves of my shirt. I sigh when they won't go any farther up my thick arms; the muscles straining my shirt.

I scan the room. Under the darkness, the warehouse lights barely illuminate the interior unless we put the flood light on, which we won't do. We sure as shit don't want to draw any more attention to us.

I scan the room and register the open roller door. "Drop the door," I snap at the idiot standing beside it. I shake my head at their stupidity.

Paul stands off to the side of the crate with a crowbar in his hand. I gesture for him to pass it to me. Cal walks around the perimeter of the warehouse, and I notice the men are vacating the room, only Paul remaining.

Snatching the crowbar from him, I step up to the wooden crate. It's about four feet high and three feet wide. Sure enough, there's a blue sticker on the side with the letters G.O.D. Cal snaps a photo with his phone, no doubt sending it to Oscar. I dig the crowbar into the nook of the crate and put my entire bodyweight into it, pressing down with all I have. My shirt is stretched over my back so tight I'm surprised it doesn't tear.

The sound of the crate opening echoes through the room. Pulling it open, I drop the crowbar and force the front of the crate down, letting it fall with a slam to the ground.

My eyes focus on the crate and then I see it…

My heart plummets. A small naked body curled into a fetal position. The smell from the crate makes me wince. Finn stumbles backward in shock, no doubt thinking of Angel in this very same position. Long, filthy, matted hair covers the body, completely laced in dirt.

My head drops forward. We were too late. The heaviness of the situation feeling unbearable, a foreign feeling of sickness welling in my stomach.

"Jesus." Cal sighs solemnly, his hand shoving through his hair as he turns his back.

The room is deathly silent, an eeriness to it, the heaviness of the situation palpable.

A faint scratching noise makes my head dart up in the crate's direction, my eyes lock on to movement from under the hair, sensing Finn moving forward, I spring into action. Crouching into the crate, I reach out to the mass of tangled hair, moving it out of the way and meet the face of a young woman. Her terrified, bright-blue eyes startle me as much as I do her. My heart seizes in my chest. She blinks slowly, as if asking if this is real.

"Jesus, she's alive!" Finn puffs out in relief.

My throat goes dry, and I'm frozen to the spot, my heart thumping hard against my chest. I've never had a reaction to anyone like this before, the thought both intrigues and startles me.

Her slight frame begins to quiver and I scan down her

body. Naked. Completely fucking naked. My teeth grind and my neck pulsates in anger. How dare someone treat her like this? I'll fucking kill them.

Her dry, cracked lip wobbles and a pained whimper leaves her mouth. The action makes me swallow thickly, overcome with emotion. I don't want her to fear me. I gently move the rest of her hair from her face and trail my fingers down her cold cheek. Her eyes dart toward my hand, watching the movement with caution. "Shh, it's okay, sweetheart, I'm not going to hurt you. We're here to rescue you." Her eyebrows furrow in confusion, and then sluggishly move over to Cal and Finn. She closes her heavy eyes slowly, as if she's struggling to keep them open.

"Bren." I turn my head to meet Cal's eyes. His Adam's apple bobs slowly, showing he's just as affected by the sight. "She's chained man." He nods toward her feet and my eyes follow, only now realizing her feet are cuffed and linked with a chain to her hands. She's been cuffed into this position. The bastards. I close my eyes to rein in my temper, determined to keep control and not scare her any more than she already is.

"Paul, get the cutters," Cal bites out.

Finn is sitting against the car with his fist in his mouth, his legs outstretched. He looks heartbroken, no doubt comparing the scene to how Angel must have suffered.

Paul hands Cal the cutters and Cal crawls low. I try to move out of the way, but the look in her eyes is a plea for me to stay. The brightness in them consumes me, my heart beats rapidly as our eyes stay locked on one another.

The air fills with a sharp snap of the chain, followed by a thud when they fall to the floor. "Get me my jacket." I gesture toward my suit jacket on the floor, my eyes never leaving hers.

Paul hands me the jacket. And I drape it over her small body. It completely covers her like a blanket. "I'm going to move you, sweetheart. Take you somewhere safe and warm, okay?" Her lips move, but nothing comes out. "Shh, it's okay. Don't try to speak."

On my hands and knees, I scoop her up and hold her close to my chest. Backing out of the crate, I hear Cal barking orders.

"I'm going to stay here and sort this out. I need to make sure nobody knows about this," he tells me as he follows me to the car.

Finn has now moved around the car and takes the driver's seat. But I can't take my eyes off the girl with the brightest blue eyes staring back up at me. I hold her tighter, her weightless body molds against me, her small fist clutches my shirt.

"Bren!" Cal snaps. "Did you hear me?"

I turn my head in annoyance and glare at him. "Yeah."

"I'll call Oscar and make sure he has Dr. Yates waiting." His forehead furrows. "Are you okay?" I'm quiet, not raging. Not me.

I glance back down at my girl, her innocent face watching me for a reaction. "Yeah, I'm good."

Cal opens the door for me, and I climb in with the girl, holding her in my lap, nestled tightly against my chest. Cal dips his head into the car and hands me a bottle of water with a nod in the girl's direction. I grab it from him before he slams the door shut.

Finn starts the engine, the rumble making her whimper. "Drive fucking careful!" I spit at him.

He nods in understanding. "She okay?" His voice is low as if cautious, and I'm grateful for that.

I glance down at her and notice she's watching me. "Yeah, she's okay." A fierce protectiveness fills my body as our eyes lock on one another, making my heart thump harder. Faster.

What the fuck is wrong with me?

CHAPTER 2

Sky

I watch the man with the blue eyes, too scared to blink. If I do, he might disappear and it'll all have been a dream. I need him. My fist tightens on his shirt. I didn't think I had any strength left until I saw him.

There's something about him.

The man watches me as much as I watch him. His hair is cut short. The women at the compound would say it's been shaved at the sides, but it is a little longer on the top. He has piercing blue eyes that make me feel like I can see his soul. His eyes crinkle at the sides when he smiles and his shoulders are so big, I don't think I've ever seen a man so broad. He smells fresh and of cologne. I know what that is because some of the men that visit the compound wear it.

He maneuvers me to sit up slightly but it hurts. Everything hurts from being in the same position for hours, maybe even days. I can't help but whimper.

"Shh, it's okay, sweetheart. I'm going to give you some water, okay?" I part my lips as he brings the bottle to my mouth. Desperate to quench my thirst, I struggle to swallow it. The water spills out of my mouth and down my chin.

The man talks, his voice deep, but he's trying to talk low and soft as if trying to make me feel comfortable. "Shh, not so fast, baby. Nice and slow." I dip my head in understanding and take another sip, my fists not leaving his shirt. "Good girl," he praises, making my heart flutter at his words.

I drop my head into the crook of his arm, feeling completely exhausted just from drinking. I watch the man; his eyes never leave mine.

"Is she hurt?" the one in the front asks.

The man doesn't reply, his eyes holding mine, almost entranced.

"Bren!" the man snaps.

The man, Bren? His head snaps up toward the voice in the front. "The girl? Is she hurt? You checked her?" His voice is lower this time.

Bren glances back down at me, he scans my face, then my huddled body, it's completely covered in his jacket. He swallows thickly, then meets my eyes. "Baby, just going to check you. Make sure you're not hurt anywhere, okay?" I try to nod but whimper, my head hurting with every movement. My body drained.

Bren moves his hand and unfolds one side of the jacket to scan my body, I shiver from the cold and being completely naked, but I'm beyond caring. I watch his face closely, his jaw ticks, then his Adam's apple bobs when his eyes land on my breasts. My body is so cold I'm covered in goosebumps that have my nipples peaking. His eyes briefly lock on them, then quickly dart away before coming back up. A small noise leaves my lips, making his eyes jump to my ankles, and then slowly back up as if taking in every inch of me, only now fully taking in my complete nakedness below.

A faint "Jesus" drops from his lips before he stares forward and quickly covers my body again with the jacket.

He chokes the words out to the one driving, "Yeah, she's good."

My stomach gripes with hunger pains, causing my hand to tighten on his shirt, his eyes dip down to me in concern. "Shh, it's okay, baby. We're almost there."

His blue eyes soften and scan my face. "My name's Bren. What's your name, sweetheart? Can you tell me?" One of his hands caresses the side of my face, comforting me. His warmth seeping into my skin makes me close my eyes, relishing in his touch. My voice is low and not as strong as I want it to be, almost like a whisper. "Red Seven."

Bren stares into my eyes. I try to talk a little louder, my throat scratchy and sore. "My name is Red Seven," I repeat my name once again to him. His eyebrows knit together in confusion.

"Gonna call you Sky for now."

I must look confused, because he chuckles a little at my reaction. "Sky, the color of your eyes." His eyes light up playfully, leaving me desperate to touch the crinkling of his skin around them. I can't help but smile back at him, my lips painfully cracking as I do.

"We're here, man," the man in the front informs us.

CHAPTER 3

Bren

I pick Sky up bridal style, nestling her against my chest for both warmth and protection. Her eyes are closed, but her chest moves faintly up and down, so I know she's still alive.

Finn scans his hand on the elevator security pad, and we step inside. Focusing on Sky's face but wanting to check on Finn, I ask, "You okay, Brother?" My voice choked up with emotion from the evening's events.

I flick my eyes toward Finn when he doesn't respond, his meet mine. Finn shakes his head. "Nah, man. How the fuck can I be okay with this?" He waves his hand toward Sky and my arms tighten around her. "That was Angel, man." His voice breaks slightly before he glances away to compose himself. "How am I gonna tell her, Bren?"

Not so long ago, we discovered that Finn's childhood sweetheart had been brutally raped and trafficked by our uncle, a man we trusted for years. When Finn discovered Angel after years of pining for her, a whole bunch of secrets and lies were discovered that led to Uncle Don being outed as her attacker. The same scenario we are seeing now, Angel had been placed in a crate to be trafficked somewhere. It sounds like the crate had the same sticker on it, something I remember Angel saying when she relived the ordeal to us.

I shudder at the thought and stare down at the small woman in my arms, vowing to protect her with everything I possess.

"Wait until we have some answers," I reply gruffly. I side-eye Finn and he responds with a firm nod.

The elevator door opens, Oscar is standing in the entryway ready to greet us with the door to my apartment open. His signature tablet in his hand, his eyes narrow in on my jacket. "Dr. Yates won't be long." Dr. Yates has been our family doctor for an eternity and knows everything there is to know about our family. We pay him well enough to keep his mouth shut. The only downside is he's so fucking old he looks like we've dug him up. Oscar glances at the tablet. "He's just parked his car, so approximately three minutes." I nod at Oscar's preciseness and make my way down the corridor toward my master suite.

Opening my bedroom door, I step inside and walk toward my bed. Tugging back the duvet, I gently place Sky inside it, still wrapped in my jacket, her dirty hair splays out over my pillow. I stare at her face for what feels like an eternity before I hear voices descending into the room.

"Bren, Dr. Yates is here." Oscars, no non-sense voice cuts into the room with an air of urgency. I startle back, reminding myself of why he's here, he wants to assess Sky, which means touching her; over my dead fucking body will he have his hands on her. Turning on my heel, I step in front of the bed, virtually blocking his view as he enters the room with a briefcase in hand. My hands have balled into tight fists, causing my knuckles to ache from the pressure.

"Ah, Oscar, nice to see you again, my boy." His voice is cheerful in his greeting to my brother. I watch the interaction closely. My brother dips his head with a faint smirk forming on his lips, the equivalent to a smile for him. Oscar has always had a lot of "issues" growing up, and therefore spent a lot of time in Dr. Yates's company.

"Tell me why I'm here." He glances back and forth between me and Oscar.

Oscar straightens his spine and raises his head. "We found a girl in one of our crates."

The doctor jolts, his eyes narrow on me, then back at Oscar. "Human trafficking?"

Oscar nods in confirmation. "We believe so."

"Show me the girl."

I broaden my shoulders and stand taller; no fucking way is anyone touching her.

"Bren, let the doctor see the girl," Oscar snipes the words out like I'm being ridiculous.

I glare at my brother. "Not gonna happen."

Oscar steps forward, clearly annoyed with me. His voice dips low so the good doctor doesn't overhear. "Don't be so fucking ridiculous, Bren, the girl needs to be seen. She needs medical treatment, you idiot."

I drill my eyes into his, making sure we're crystal clear on the matter. No fucker is touching her again.

He steps back with a sigh, knowing I won't budge.

Dr. Yates chuckles. "Not to worry, Bren. Why don't you show me the girl and I can tell you what needs to be done?" He talks placidly to me, like a fucking child, making me lift an eyebrow at him for attempting to ridicule me. He needs to watch his fucking tone; I could squeeze the cunt's head in my bare hand if I wanted to. He gulps harshly, as if reading my mind.

"Bren, she might fucking die," Oscar snaps.

My body freezes and my heart skips a beat. Before I know what I'm doing, I'm turning around and walking over to Sky, standing beside the bed with fists clenching and unclenching beside me, my feet set apart as if ready for battle.

The doctor scans Sky's face before clearing his throat. "I'm going to need to…" He motions with his hand at the duvet cover.

My jaw grinds and my eyes flick back up toward Oscar when he sighs in annoyance. "Get the fuck out," I snap at him.

His eyes shoot up to meet my own in confusion. "Out!"

"Bren I…"

"Oscar, either get the fuck out, or it's on you." If anything happens to her, it's on him. He either leaves or the doctor doesn't see her fully.

As his hand touches the door, it's pushed open, almost knocking him off his feet. Lily, Cal's wife, comes barreling into the room.

"Oh god, Bren, Cal called and told me what happened. What did the doctor say?" Her words are fast as she approaches the other side of the bed toward Sky.

Oscar scoffs from the doorway, causing me to glare in his direction. He shakes his head and leaves the room with a click of the door.

I meet Lily's eyes and they're wide, waiting for me to answer. "Ain't sorted her yet."

Lily's eyebrows narrow in confusion before glancing down at Sky. They soften, with sympathy oozing from them. "Can I stay?" she asks softly, gently stroking Sky's hair from her face.

I fidget from foot to foot. Not at all happy with the idea.

"Wonderful idea, Lily, you can help with the more—" The doctor pauses and looks away from me. "—delicate areas."

I mill the words over in my mind, "delicate areas." As soon as they register, my spine jolts straight, over my dead fucking body. "You ain't touching her pussy!" I snap at him. The pulse in my temple throbs, my face feels hot, and my chest vibrates with anger. I grip his shirt in my fist.

The doctor's wide eyes look panicked, flicking between mine and Lily's as if pleading with her for protection. Fucking pussy.

Lily chuckles awkwardly. Her voice is soft. "Bren, I know you want to protect her, but she really needs to be seen. Look at her, Bren," she coaxes. "Please look at her."

I flit my eyes sideways and take in Sky, her small struggling body rising up and down from under the duvet. Her frail face deathly pale, her lips are split, and her eyes have black circles under them. If I didn't see her chest rising, I would assume the girl was dead. *Jesus*, I scrub a hand down my face. "The doctor needs to make sure she hasn't —" Lily swallows, emotion creeping into her voice. "—been raped. Hurt like Angel, Bren." My stomach roils and my breath hitches in a panic. Please no. I scan her body, wishing she'd always been cared for and under a duvet, tucked away safely.

If someone's hurt her like that, I'll make them live a lifetime of suffering. Our uncle got away too lightly, not again. The sick fucks will pay for their sins in flesh.

CHAPTER 4

Bren

I relent at Lily's harsh words with a firm nod, knowing it's essential I let the doctor assess her. He drags back the duvet and grimaces. Her small naked body shakes, and in the light of the room, it's easy to see the bruising marking her pale skin.

Emotional rage clogs my throat as I struggle to remain standing in the same spot, keeping myself from covering her to protect her from the scrutiny of their assessing eyes.

"I need to get her an IV drip set up and get some fluids into her. She's clearly dehydrated and malnourished. I'll start a course of antibiotics too." He begins to work around Sky, taking items out of his briefcase. Lily's eyes are locked onto Sky's face, her hand gently stroking her cheek in a soothing motion. I root my feet into the floor, willing my hands not to snatch her intrusive hand away from Sky's face.

The doctor lifts Sky's eyelid and shines a flashlight into her eyes. No response comes from Sky at all. Worry wells inside me, an unknown feeling brewing. "I want her fixed!" My finger points at Sky, my blood boils at the thought of losing her. "Fucking sort her!" I bellow, rage seething at my words.

The doctor exhales loudly. "I'm working as quick as I can." He doesn't lift his head to respond. His hands working over Sky's body send me into an internal frenzy.

"Bren, why don't you step outside and have a drink or something?" My eyes snap back toward Lily's. I glance back to Sky, vulnerable, defenseless. "I'll stay with her, make sure she's okay and well cared for." She nods encouragingly. "It's for the best Bren, just until the doctor has assessed her properly."

I almost lunge at the doctor when he lowers his hand toward her ribs, near her—

"Go!" Lily screams, pointing at the door.

My throat clogs and I stare back down at the girl in my bed. *Mine.* My body swells with pride. She's mine, I found her, I'll protect her.

Mine.

I turn on my heel and pull open the door, slamming it closed for emphasis.

Walking into the open-plan living area, all my brothers' heads shoot in my direction. Cal stands and makes his way over to the bar in the corner of the room.

"How is she?" Con asks. Now without his rat-bastard dog.

I scrub a hand through my short, cropped hair and sigh. "Not got a fucking clue. Doctor is working on her," I clip out.

Oscar sits straighter. "Perhaps if you'd let him do his job, instead of acting like a neanderthal, we might have some progress."

"Perhaps if you worked on that fucking tablet instead of talking, you might get us some fucking answers!" I snap back at him, pointing at the tablet.

He sighs and straightens his shoulders, never one to be deterred by me. "What would you like me to work on first, Bren? Uncle Don's shit? Ma's missing son? Finding Angel's other rapist?" Finn's spine straightens at the use of Angel's name. "The human trafficking ring we're embroiled in somehow? Oh, and let's not forget the demands I now have to deal with from Marianne's father because you've been fucking her about." He points back at me. Why I thought it was a good idea to sleep with the chief of police's one and only fucking daughter, I'll never know. Now the woman has turned into a full-blown bunny boiler, determined to make me her husband so we can "rule the city" as she puts it. Not. A. Fucking. Chance.

"Do you have the wedding adjustments on that list? Because I swear to fuck if I don't get that band at the wedding, I'm not gonna be happy." Con laughs to himself, causing me to glare in his direction. *Is he fucking serious right now?* He shrugs with a grin on his face, amused with himself for breaking the tension between me and Oscar.

Cal hands me a glass and I down the whiskey in one gulp and hand the empty glass back to him.

I throw myself down onto the couch and lean forward,

putting my head in my hands. I close my eyes, but images of Sky's soft smile and pale-blue eyes invade me.

"We got you, Brother." Finn's hand squeezes my shoulder, my head raises to meet my brother's concerned gaze above me.

I sigh. "You best go home. Tell Angel what's happened."

"I think perhaps we should wait until we know if she's been tampered with?" Oscar suggests.

Tampered with. His words play over in my head. Jesus, that's screwed up.

"Yeah, wait." I nod.

Finn steps back. "Gonna get going anyway. She's been blowing up my phone." He chuckles. "She wants a fucking burger brought home to her." Angel is only a few months pregnant but he waits on her hand and foot.

I vaguely hear my brothers saying their goodbyes, but it's hard to concentrate on anything other than the thought of Sky, her delicate body and the damage someone has potentially caused to her.

CHAPTER 5

Bren

The click of the door and footsteps approaching has me jumping to my feet. My brothers follow suit.

The doctor enters the living area with a grim look on his face that has my heart pounding, impatience already bursting from my veins.

He shakes his head, causing me to step forward threateningly. If she's hurt any worse…

He holds his hand up, stopping me in my tracks. "She's fine. She's going to be fine." My shoulders sag in relief at his words. "She's clearly a very abused young woman. Her wrists and ankles are infected because of her restraints." *Fucking restraints.* My fists clench. "She has bruising all over her body, possibly from transit, but I'd most likely say rough handling. There are, undeniably, palm prints on her skin." *Fucking palm prints? I'll kill them, rip their fucking flesh from their bones.* "A small incision on her arm, most likely a form of birth control." My spine straightens; that means… As if reading my mind, he shakes his head. "No. No rape." He fidgets anxiously, causing my muscles to twitch. I can tell he wants to say more and he's withholding something that's not giving me the relief I should feel after hearing him utter those words. He sighs dramatically. "I think she was precious cargo. I'd say she was being shipped because of her virginity being intact."

I am attempting to process that information before I say, "She's a virgin?" My eyes narrow at him. She's been through hell and trafficked but remained a virgin?

"She was being sold for her virginity," Oscar surmises beside me, his finger strokes over his lip deep in thought.

The doc nods. "I came to the same conclusion. I've given her a sedative. At some point her ribs were broken and they're still on the mend. I've wrapped them and given her pain relief. She'll be out of it for the next few days, but I'll be sure to check in daily."

Cal shows the doctor out.

I spin to face Oscar. "I want some fucking answers! How the hell did she end up in our warehouse and who was she being sold to?" He tips his head in acknowledgment.

"We'll know more when the girl wakes up," Cal muses, trying to placate me.

"Sky."

"Huh?" Con chides in.

I can feel myself getting irritable with them, calling her girl as if she doesn't have a name. As if nobody fucking cared to give her one. "Sky."

"Her name's Sky?" Oscar steps forward in hopes of new information.

"Dunno what the fuck her name is, until she says it, I'm calling her Sky."

Their eyes dart to one another's as if having a secret conversation. Well, fuck them and their dumb silent words.

I turn and walk over to the bar, pouring myself another drink, relaxing as the warm liquid flows down my throat before turning around and marching down the corridor toward the bedroom, ignoring my brothers' questions and comments along the way.

As soon as I step foot into my bedroom, a sense of calm comes over me. It's a strange feeling I'm not familiar with, but it's welcome, nonetheless.

Lily smiles up at me from the bed, where she was wiping Sky's forehead with a damp washcloth. "I was just trying to clean her up a little."

I nod my head in thanks and cast my eyes over all the medical paraphernalia on display. A stand with multiple bags of fluid, tablets, and creams on the bedside tables.

"It's not as bad as it looks, Bren. It's only for a few days. She'll be over the worse, and then we can look after her, right?" Her hopeful eyes meet mine, and once again, I nod my head. Damn fucking right I'll look after her. Nobody will touch her again.

"Bren, I'm going to get going. I've left Chloe with Reece, and although he's capable, he's also pretty determined Chloe is going to smash milestones she can't possibly meet yet." She sighs loudly. "Can you believe he's trying to get her to write her name? She's more interested in chewing the crayon than holding it. And then he's teaching her to say Pussy in every language possible." She shakes her head in annoyance. "He'll be teaching her how to extort money before she's in kindergarten." This makes me chuckle, because Reece, Cal and Lily's teenage son, is a child genius. Off the fucking charts, clever. The only problem is, he expects everyone else to be too.

Lily's hand touches my arm. "You'll get them, won't you, Bren?" She stares back toward Sky.

"Of course." I stare into her eyes with determination.

Lily smiles tightly. "I'll round the boys up and leave you to it. Let me know if you need anything else."

She turns and walks away, my eyes not leaving Sky's. "Lily?"

I glance over my shoulder at her, her hand on the door handle.

"Thank you."

A huge smile spreads over her face and she chuckles, pointing at me playfully. "You've fallen, Bren O'Connell. It's going to be so fun to watch this."

My eyebrows knit together in confusion as she leaves the room. I swear my family is insane.

I rid myself of my clothes, throwing them on the nearby armchair, stripping down to my boxers, then stop with my hand on the waistband. Is it inappropriate to be in bed with her naked? The doc did say she's out for the count for a few days. I grimace at the thought of having to think about someone else, when I'm used to it just being me. But then a soft whimper escapes Sky and I have to refrain myself from diving onto the bed to protect her.

Climbing onto the bed, I drag the comforter back and slide underneath. Lying on my side, I track every inch of her petite features. The way her small pink lips are open slightly, but they still look pouty. Her nose frames her face perfectly, and I narrow my eyes to count the freckles splayed across it. Twelve, twelve small freckles.

Her fair eyelashes bat and twitch as if she's dreaming, and I wonder what's going on inside her mind. Does she realize she's been rescued? Her faint eyelashes make me wonder what color her hair truly is, is it as blonde as her lashes? I touch her matted hair, it's thick with grime but I've touched worse things. A bit of dirt doesn't bother me. Stroking it between my fingers, I'm convinced it's going to be a lot lighter when I finally wash it.

Me, I'll wash her hair and care for her. I don't want anyone else touching her. Never again.

Sky's hand trembles as she sleeps, it's small with short nails, much cleaner now than before. It makes me realize how much Lily has done for her already. I rest my hand over the top of hers, mine completely encompassing hers. She's cold to the touch, and sensing my hand, she turns hers over and gently takes hold of mine.

Her soft, steady breathing hitches slightly, causing my heart to stutter when she finally releases a gasp. I lay my head down beside her, determined to stay awake and watch her through the night.

CHAPTER 6

Bren

At some point during the early hours, I'd fallen asleep. When I woke, I realized it was the first time I'd fallen asleep with another woman in my bed that I hadn't had sex with. *Strange.*

I had a raging hard-on from not having sex for a few nights in a row, so I went straight into the shower and tugged the beast, with my other hand propped against the shower wall, coming so hard I almost face planted into the tiles. When I'd closed my eyes, innocent blue eyes shone back at me, the color of the fucking sky, I roared my release, letting it wash down the drain along with my filthy thoughts. The entire experience made me feel all sorts of weird. I mean, I'm essentially masturbating to an innocent, trafficked girl. *Jesus*, I had to wash that shit down and get the hell out of there before I was tempted for round two. My cock sure as fuck was open to it.

The next couple of days I worked from home, in case Sky needed me or woke; she never did. The doctor came three times a day, even though he was insistent on once being enough. Lazy bastard.

Lily has spent most of the time over here caring for her, talking to her and shit, Will too. They brought her toiletries and women's shit for when she wakes and cleaned her up a little more. She now sleeps in one of my t-shirts, I can't wait to see her in it fully when she wakes.

Angel has kept her distance, which I understand. Finn said it really fucked with her head and she wasn't sleeping well again. He's now refusing to leave her side, which is another fucking problem, seeing as I need the extra support at one of our clubs.

I run a hand through my hair, annoyed that it's been four days since we found her and still, she hasn't stirred. I decide to go and check on her breathing again because it's quickly become one of my favorite things to do. Watching the soft rise and fall of her chest calms the storm inside me. Knowing she's in my bed safe, better still.

As I approach the door, I can hear movement. I rush toward the door and swing it open so fast it accidentally hits the wall and ricochets off it. I wince. It's probably left another dent in the wall. My ma always says I'm like a bull.

My gaze latches onto the bed, Sky is sat bolt upright tugging on the drip. Shit.

"Sky." I keep my voice low as I approach her, slowly stalking toward her.

Her eyes find mine and stop me in my tracks, my heart hammering out of my chest at the connection between us. I hold my hand up, and she stops her movement, removing her hand from the drip. She's now oozing blood from taking out the IV, but she doesn't so much as wince, her soft eyes never leave mine.

"Do you remember me?"

She dips her head slightly in acknowledgment.

"Do you remember my name?"

"Br... Bren." Her voice is low and wavers a little, but she doesn't look away. She doesn't appear remotely scared that she's woken up in a strange room with a giant standing over her.

I give her a faint smile and move toward the bed again. "Good girl." Her pupils dilate ever so slightly at my words. I've been trained to read people, so I don't miss a fucking thing, like the bit of flush traveling up her neck or the fact she swallows and quickly darts her eyes away but brings them back just as quick, feigning confidence.

I crouch down beside her. "Do you want me to clean you up?" I nod toward her arm.

She licks her lips. They're still on the dry side. "Are you my owner now?"

My eyebrows furrow at her question. Before, the fact that she was found in a crate hits me like a sledgehammer. *Owner? She thinks I bought her?*

"Baby. I didn't buy you. We rescued you; me and my brothers found you in a crate. A crate you shouldn't have been in."

She smiles, like she's dismissing everything I just said to her. "Sebastian put the wrong sticker on." She lets out a breathy sigh like she's a little annoyed at the fact. "He said he was saving me and sending me somewhere safe."

I scan her face. "Who's Sebastian?"

Sky moves her hand toward my face. The moment her fingers touch my skin, I flinch at the contact, causing her to stop. I give her a slight nod and have to tell myself to relax. She begins to explore my face, gently gliding her fingers over the scars and down my jawline.

"Who's Sebastian," I repeat.

Her eyes never leave my face. "He works at the compound."

"Compound?"

"The one where I came from."

My mind works over her words, and I pull my phone from my pocket, informing my brothers that Sky is now awake.

"Are you hungry, baby?"

"Yes, please." Her good manners hit me in the chest, and I stand to look down on her. "You stay in bed until I get back, okay? I'm gonna give the doc a call, get him to check you out and remove the catheter." I nod toward her legs, and she follows the movement before giving me a slight nod.

Forcing my feet to turn away from her, I walk toward the door.

"Bren." I turn on an instant. "Thank you for rescuing me from my owner."

Anger bubbles inside me, but I don't want to scare her so I simply just nod and continue to walk away.

When I find out who the fuck bought my girl, I'm going to kill him and any other fuckers involved in this fucked-up shit.

CHAPTER 7

Sky

I sit, fidgeting with my hands, scanning over the room. It's like one you see on television. It has furnishings, and the bed is enormous. The covers are gray and soft to the touch, on both sides of the bed are dressers with lamps on them. On the one beside me is a bottle of water, I glance at the door in front of me and nibble on my lip, unsure if Bren will get mad if I take a drink without asking. Swallowing down my nerves, I decide to go for it. He seems different from the keepers at the compound. He has a softness about him I haven't come across before in a man. One I like and want to keep for myself. I glance around the room again for a sign of a wife. *Will he keep me too?*

There's a door beside me that I'm pretty sure is a restroom or maybe a shower room?

The door ahead creaks open and Bren walks in

carrying a tray. His whole body fills the doorway with ease. He definitely houses muscles, I can see them from under his shirt that stretches as he moves; I want to explore them with my fingers, trail them over the ridges he's sure to have. I don't understand why he would stay covered up in his own room. "Do you own this room, Bren?"

He chuckles at me, and I'm not sure why. "I own the apartment, baby. It's my home."

I crane my head past him to try and see where else he owns.

"When the doctor has been to see you, I can show you around if you want?" He places the tray down on the bed before sitting down next to it.

Bren brushes a hand through his short hair and then explains to me why he's uncomfortable. "I made you a sandwich, it's the only thing I know how to make since I can't cook so…" His eyes meet mine with a look of vulnerability to them.

Growing up in the compound, you learn to watch people's faces to gauge a response of how they're going to react. The very last thing you want to do is to be sent to the blue zone. A shudder works through me, but then I remind myself how far I've come by behaving and doing what is expected of me.

"Doesn't your wife cook for you?" I question, tipping my head to the side to study him.

Bren laughs loudly and throws his head back. I can't help but smile in response, knowing I was able to get such a reaction out of him.

"I don't have a wife, baby."

My eyebrows pull together in confusion; I work my eyes over his body again, looking for any obvious reasons as to why he doesn't have a wife. The man is beautiful, and I'd love to have sex with him, but maybe he's not into women?

"Do you prefer to have sex with men?"

He drops his head and bites on his lip as if stifling another laugh. "No, I'm not gay, if that's what you're asking." He raises an eyebrow at me.

Now I'm confused. He isn't married and doesn't like to be with men? I'm lost in my thoughts when Bren suddenly prompts, "I got you a juice too and some vegetables." He points toward the tray, and I nod and wait for him to give me further instruction. My stomach groans causing me to shuffle uncomfortably.

"You going to eat it then?"

"I'm waiting for permission."

The muscles in his face tense and his jaw ticks, making me shift back on the bed.

He panics at my response. "Shit. Sky, don't move away from me, baby. I'm not going to hurt you. Fuck, I was just… just a little angry."

"Why?" I watch his face for the truth behind his words.

"You said you were waiting for permission?" I nod in agreement. "Fuck, it angers me you think you need permission to eat." As I watch him, I try to understand what he's saying.

"This is like what I've seen on television. Where you get to do what you want." I nibble on my lip in excitement, always on the outside looking in, wishing I could live like they do on the TV shows.

I shuffle forward slightly and take one of the sandwiches, biting into it under Bren's watchful eye.

His phone rings and he stands before walking toward the door, then he stops, turns around, and points to my plate. "Eat." He smiles at me before leaving, a warmth fills my stomach at his playful wink. If Bren doesn't have a wife, I'm pretty sure I'd like to be his.

I finish the meal Bren provided for me and wait for him to return, placing the tray on the dresser beside me.

When he finally comes back into the room, an older man follows behind him. I watch their movements. Bren sits on the bed, his voice low as if he's trying to soothe me. "This is Dr. Yates, baby. He's going to check you out and clean you up, okay?" I look from Bren to the doctor warily, unsure about him checking me out. I nibble on my lip, causing it to sting again. As if sensing my thoughts, Bren holds his hand out for me and tilts his head as if gesturing toward himself, I let him pull me from under the covers. Without giving him a choice, I crawl onto his lap, keeping ahold of his hand, his arm now tightly around my middle.

Bren sucks in a breath, and I swell with pride that I can make him have such a reaction toward me.

The doctor goes over a few medical things. All similar to the ones at the compound, after I received a punishment. He tells me I need to eat more, then he explains to us that he needs to take out my catheter. Bren's body tenses at this. His shoulders go stiff and the veins in his neck bulge, even his jaw is locked tight. I shift into position, straddling my legs over Bren's, his arm banded around my waist. Leaning my head back onto his chest, I stroke his jaw line gently to reassure him. His eyes dart down and lock onto mine. They're bright blue. A contrast to my soft blue eyes. But they're filled with warmth, and I melt into his response to me. Below me I can feel his hardness digging into my ass, and as desperate as I am to see it, I don't think Bren would be happy showing me since the doctor is here. My ass rises slightly as the doctor dips between my legs. Bren winces on my behalf, but I don't feel a thing, I'm far too entranced by his gaze. I press my lips to his jawline, his heart hammers against my spine, and a rush of love fills me. I want him to love me and care for me like he owns me. Because he does. He might not realize it yet but I'm his. I was born to be his, even though he doesn't like to be called my owner, that's what he is. He owns all of me. With that realization, I smile to myself, *how lucky am I?*

"There, all done." The doctor breaks the trance between us, causing both our heads to turn toward him as he snaps off his gloves.

"She's all good. Free to have sex when she's ready."

Bren instantly freezes. The doctor senses a change in him too. I use this moment to graze my finger over his jaw. "Shh, it's okay, Bren." He looks down and gazes into my eyes, pressing a kiss to my forehead before scooping me up and moving me back into the bed.

"Just gonna see the good doctor out, baby." He moves off the bed, following the doctor out of the room.

CHAPTER 8

Bren

I stride down the corridor, following the old prick who referred to my girl as a sex item. He knows damn well about how she came to be here; insensitive prick will learn some manners. He scurries toward the entrance faster when he hears the click of my shoes on the marble floor. Gripping him by the shoulder, I spin him around and slam him against the door with a heavy thud. My hand moves to his throat and I squeeze, causing his face to turn red and his eyes to widen in a panic. I dip my head down low to speak to him, my voice deadly. "Speak about Sky like an object again and I'll slaughter you, you old cunt. Don't push me, old man, you've seen what I'm capable of. I'll make sure to send your family your fermented brain."

I let go, and he almost falls to the floor; the gasping noises he makes give me reason to smirk with pleasure.

The doctor straightens himself and tugs his tie back into place. "My apologies, it won't happen again." He dips his head toward me while fumbling to open the door. The moment he leaves, my shoulders sag in relief.

I make my way back down the corridor toward Sky. Opening the door, her eyes light up in greeting and her smile widens, causing me to smile back at her, something I don't normally do often.

"You want a shower? Or a bath? My brothers are coming over soon, and I thought you'd like to clean up first?" I ask her, tilting my head to the side.

I can't help but smile at her reaction, her eyes bug out. "You have a bathtub?"

I point toward the door next to the bed. "Yeah, bathroom's through there. You can use it anytime you want, Sky."

She stares back at me with uncertainty, making anger bubble within me. "You weren't allowed to shower when you wanted?"

Sky lowers her head down to her hands that are clasped together. "No."

I walk over to the bed and lift her chin with my finger. "You can use anything in the apartment, anytime you want, Sky." She doesn't react, and I sense she's looking for the truth behind my words. Holding my hand out, I coax her, "Come, let me show you the bathroom." Her hand is small in mine as I lead her toward the bathroom. Her eyes widen when she realizes how big the room is. A countertop with two sinks lines the left-hand side with mirrors above. The toilet directly in front of us, to my right is a huge walk-in shower, enough for a party, and beside it in the corner is an enormous tub.

"Do ya want a shower?"

She shakes her head, her eyes locked on the bath. "You want me to run you a bath?"

"Yes, please."

I bend and turn the taps on, her hand still in mine. I chuckle at how attached to me she is, but I'm also conscious of how much I like it. Something I'd normally find annoying, I'm finding pleasurable. "My brother's wives dropped some women's shit off for you." I wave my hand toward the bag on the counter. "Do you want to check them out?"

She lets go of my hand and I watch her walk over toward the counter. I take in the length of her legs; my shirt hangs down past her ass and my cock twitches at the sight. I rake over her slim body before my eyes lock onto hers in the mirror and she breaks the stare and scrutinizes the box in her hand, her face twists slightly in confusion. I stalk over to her, willing my cock not to harden any more than it is already, taking the box from her and realizing I'm holding a box of fucking tampons in my hand.

Jesus. I scrub a hand down my face. While eyeing the little fuckers. "You use these?" I hold the box up.

Sky gently shakes her head. "No." I slam the little fuckers into the bin beside me.

"Good, don't fucking touch them." I sure as shit don't want her shoving anything unnecessary into her pussy.

"Yes, sir."

Holy fucking shit balls. What the?

I fidget from foot to foot. I've never had a woman say that shit to me before, let alone a pint-sized little hottie like her.

I glance up at her face, there's worry etched over it. As if I've received a punch in the gut, I wince. "You have to call someone sir where you came from?"

She nods, gently. "Ain't got to call anyone here sir, Sky. You understand me?"

"Yes, thank you."

"Good girl." Her eyes flare again at the sentiment. My girl likes praise, that's for damn sure, and for the first time in my life, I'm liking giving it out.

"What if I want to?" She nibbles on her bottom lip, causing me to stifle a groan as my cock bulges in my pants uncomfortably. Her head dips down, and she eyes the obvious bulge, she slides her tongue over her lower lip. *Holy shit, is she flirting with me?* I've never done the whole flirting thing, never had to. Usually, I just fuck 'em and chuck 'em. I watch her closely, unsure if she's even aware of what she's doing. Her breath stutters and I'm pretty damn sure if she was wearing panties, they'd be soaked.

As if on cue, she rubs her thighs together and slowly raises her head to meet my eyes, mine boring down into hers.

"Do you?" she breathes out her words faintly.

I swallow past the lump in my throat. "Do I what?" The air is thick between us.

Flush creeps up her neck. "Want me to call you sir?"

My heart hammers in my chest and my cock oozes pre-cum from the tip, no doubt leaving a wet patch on my boxers like a god damn teenager.

Annoyed at my reaction to her, I shake myself. My voice comes out gravelly, "Maybe stick with Bren for now?" I don't miss the flash of disappointment behind her eyes when she nods and turns back toward the sink and continues unloading the items from out of the bag. I watch her like a useless sap, unsure how to make it right.

I sure as hell don't want to be like one of those pricks where she's from. I don't want to force the girl to call me sir. And, fuck me, I didn't even know it was something I would want until she said it.

I turn and roll the sleeves of my shirt up my arms. My forearm muscles make it impossible for them to go very far, but I need to check the water in the tub. I'm about to throw some sweet-smelling shit in for good measure, but my eyes spot my shower gel. The thoughts of her washing in my shit makes me feel primal. If I can't have her, I sure as hell can make her smell like she's mine.

I squeeze a good dose of the gel under the tap, reveling in the potent fragrance. Nobody will mistake who she belongs to now.

CHAPTER 9

Sky

I watch Bren closely in the mirror. He's bent over the bath testing the water. His broad shoulders almost rip open his shirt with how muscular he is. I want to run my hand along the ridges and feel them tense under the tips of my fingers.

"You ready?" Bren turns to face me, and I spin around and put the skills to use I've been trained to have. Before he can bat an eye, I lift his huge shirt over my head and drop it at my feet. His pupils dilate and his lips part, but I don't pay him any attention. I stroll toward the tub and dip my foot in beside where he's knelt, making sure to give him a full display of my body, then I lower myself into the tub. I stifle a smile at his shocked reaction, loving his eyes on me.

He quickly stands, almost in a panic, brushing his huge

hand over his short, cropped hair. "You, er... you need anything?"

His eyes dart around the room, looking everywhere but at me.

"Yes, please."

He stills, then meets my eyes. They quickly dip to my tits that are sitting just above the bubbles before darting up to my face. "Could you wash my hair for me, please?"

He sucks in a breath. "Your hair?"

I nod gently. "Yes, please, Bren."

"Fucking Jesus," he grumbles and then grabs his shampoo. Kneeling again, he turns the small shower head on. I tip my head back slightly to allow him to wet it.

The sensation of the water and Bren's fingers working through my hair is amazing. I can't help but groan, and this causes Bren to release a tirade of expletives under his breath, but I still catch them.

I can't wait to feel clean again.

Bren lathers my hair up numerous times before rinsing it off. "Jesus, Sky, your hair looks a different color, baby." I open my eyes to peek at him.

"It's really blonde. Do you like it?" I watch him hopefully.

Bren chokes a little. "Yeah. What's not to like?" He shakes his head at himself.

"Have you washed yourself?" Bren nods toward the loofah and body wash.

I take it from the side of the bath and squirt some of the liquid onto the loofah. "Wash your body, baby. Give yourself a good clean." He swallows thickly, watching me scrub over my neck, down my chest, and over each breast slowly. "Wash your pussy and ass." I move up onto my knees to get into a better position, I gently wash myself between my legs, then do the same around my ass. I can feel the heat of Bren's gaze on me the whole time, and I can't help but release a breathy moan under his intense stare.

As if snapping out of a trance, Bren jumps to his feet. His shirt is dripping wet from washing my hair for me, making his muscles even more prominent. I squeeze my legs together, desperate for some relief.

Bren grabs two towels and motions for me to get out of the bath. He stares at the wall while I wrap the towel around my body. His words come out choked, "Go sit on the bed and dry yourself off. I'll be out in ten." I watch his face for a reaction, but he continues to look past me, so I do as I'm told and leave the room, a little disappointed but unsure as to why.

BREN

Watching Sky pull the shirt over her head shocked the hell out of me. If I thought she was going to be a timid little mouse, I was fucking wrong. She's a brazen little vixen, and I'm pretty damn sure she realizes it too.

The door clicks shut, and I make quick work of my belt and zipper, desperate to alleviate some of the building tension in my aching balls.

Tugging my boxers down slightly, I tuck them under my balls and release my angry-looking cock with a moan, pre-cum oozes from the tip, and I grip it roughly in my palm, closing my eyes at the relief my touch instantly gives me. I grip the counter with my other hand, holding my cock over the sink.

I relive the moment Sky strutted over to the tub and lifted her leg, giving me a flash of her bare pussy. What I'd have given to lift her leg over my shoulder and tongued my way through her slick folds.

My hand works faster, and I already feel on edge. I grip myself tighter, annoyed at how wound up I am. I work my hips, forcing my cock in and out of my hand.

The image of Sky washing herself makes my heart beat out of my chest and ignites a fire in my veins. The soft moan and parting of her lips as her hand worked between her legs has me racing to the finish line, squeezing tighter with each stroke.

As if sensing something, my eyes shoot open and lock straight onto Sky's through the mirror. She stands in the doorway watching me, her mouth parted in awe. Her tongue darts out and she licks her lower lip, causing me to lose control and fuck my hand harder, my cock pulsates without warning, causing thick, warm cum to shoot onto the counter and over the sink as I imagine it landing on her beautiful, innocent face. I glance down at the mess and my chest heaves up and down before my eyes dart back up, expecting Sky to have turned away, but she stands there watching me, waiting. My pulse quickens instead of slowing down.

I release my cock, but it's still hard, knowing it needs another release that only she can give me. Running my clean hand frustratingly over my head. "You see a man come before?" I keep my eyes locked on hers for a sign she's not okay with what she's just seen.

"Yes." She swallows harshly.

Her breathy voice sends a shiver down my spine, and her words cause my jaw to lock. "Did ya wanna?" My heart hammers, waiting for a reply, hating the fact not only has she witnessed this before but with another man, nonetheless.

She shakes her head from side to side, her wet hair dripping into the towel wrapped around her, my eyes zeroing in on every motion.

My shoulders tense at the thought that she was forced

to watch this before. Does she think that's expected of her here too?

"You know you don't have to do anything you don't wanna here, right?" I tilt my head toward her to prompt her.

"I wanted to."

My shoulders sag in relief at her words, then my mind replays them. *She wanted to.* My cock twitches, *fuck*.

I clear my throat. "Go wait on the bed, Sky. I'll get cleaned up and be out in a minute." She nods in response and turns.

Dropping my head, I grimace at the mess I've created. It's been a while since I shot a load this big. Then again, it's been awhile since I last fucked, so it really shouldn't be a surprise. Of course it has nothing to do with the little beauty waiting in my bed.

Fuck, I'm so screwed.

CHAPTER 10

Sky

I wait on the bed patiently for Bren to return, going over the image of his face when he was pumping his thick cock into his hand and finally when he locked eyes with me in the mirror. I felt the lust radiating from him, and I wanted nothing more than to reach out and touch him, stroking the tips of my fingers all over him.

The door opens and Bren walks in with the hairbrush in his large hand. "Scoot up, baby." His gravelly voice sends a shiver down my spine as I do as he asks, and I shuffle my butt forward for Bren to sit behind me. I'm acutely aware of his huge, solid frame.

I turn my head slightly and I catch a glimpse of him out of the corner of my eye. He has one leg tucked under the other, a giant next to my small self. He wears only black boxers, and his chest has ripples of muscles. His skin is tanned and rock solid, even his thighs are thick and rigid. He's like nothing I've ever seen before, a warrior of a man. My tongue darts out to lick my dry lips and I can't help to imagine licking over his abs, the firmness under my touch, worshipping him. A tingle between my thighs causes me to squeeze them together, a soft gasp leaving my mouth involuntarily.

Bren chuckles behind me as if sensing my thoughts. Heat travels up my neck and into my cheeks.

"You can't be embarrassed now, Sky. You've already seen me naked." I turn my head toward him, meeting his startling-blue eyes. A cocky smile encompasses his face, causing the wrinkles beside them to crease even more. "And you've seen me come." His eyes alight playfully and I almost sink into them, my breath hitching at how incredibly sexy he is. "Now, be a good girl and face the door so I can brush your hair for you."

I do as Bren tells me, and ever so gently, he untangles my hair and smooths it out with his palm. His thick fingers occasionally getting stuck in the knots, causing me to wince. "You're being a good girl, baby. Such beautiful hair." His sultry voice coos as he strokes his fingers through my long hair. Tingles build between my legs, wetness making me squirm ever so slightly.

When my hair is tangle-free, I feel a sharp tug, forcing my head back and my throat to elongate. My eyes latch onto Bren's from the awkward position, his are filled with desire. I lick my lips, desperate for him to touch me more, his eyes tracking the movement.

"Fuck. I'm not sure how I'm going to keep my hands off you," he voices lowly, almost to himself.

Bren clears his throat and releases my hair, making me

instantly feel the loss, and the need for him grows even more so.

He rises from the bed, his long and thick erection protruding from his boxers. He walks into a room opposite the bed, and I crane my neck to watch him. It's a closet, a huge walk-in closet. He begins rustling around and when he comes back out, he has a white t-shirt on, stretched tightly over his muscular form. His legs are now covered in jeans, but his feet are bare. He throws a bundle of clothes on the bed.

My eyes lock onto his hands trying to secure the zipper to his jeans, his erection clearly straining against his pants. "Need ya to put those clothes on, baby. My brothers will be here soon, and I don't want them to see you naked. You got me?" He stares at me pointedly.

I meet his eyes, his jaw tight, waiting for me to respond. I nod in agreement and his shoulders and jaw relax slightly.

"Good girl. Get dressed and I'll see you out there." He tilts his head back toward the door, and I can't help but wonder what their plan is? *What do they want from me?*

"Ya need me to carry you?" he queries with a raised eyebrow.

I realize I hadn't answered him, causing the prompt. I swallow away my nerves. "No, thank you. Okay, I'll get dressed and see you out there." I point toward the door.

Bren's eyes narrow before he stalks toward me. He gently lifts my chin, our eyes meeting. "Nobody here is going to hurt you, Sky. We just want to talk to you; we need some answers, baby." I scrutinize his expression, it's completely open. Living in the compound, I've become good at reading body language, and Bren is like an open book. I can already tell he isn't usually as gentle with others as he is with me, the thought warms me. This big brute of a man is usually in charge both physically and mentally. But I like the fact he's soft with me. I wonder if he's like this with all women?

Jealousy swells inside me, something I'm definitely not used to.

I want him to myself.

CHAPTER 11

Bren

I pull a beer out of the refrigerator and throw myself onto the couch, waiting for my brothers. My mind instantly goes to the girl in the room down the hall. My room, to be precise.

I bring no one back to my apartment, and I sure as shit wouldn't allow them to sleep in my bed at night, let alone multiple nights.

And bathe a girl? Brush her hair? *What the fuck is wrong with me? Who the hell am I?* I scrub a hand over my head, confused by myself.

Her body is to die for, and completely untouched? Fuck, she's like a wet dream.

That long, natural-blonde hair is not something I'm used to. The strippers in my clubs are cheap with nasty bottle-dyed shit, whereas the women in my social circle are pruned but just as fake, nonetheless, just on a more expensive scale.

Yet the girl down the hall? All natural and all innocent, my cock weeps in my already tight pants.

I brush a hand down my face just as my phone beeps beside me to let me know my brothers are in the elevator.

Moments later, the door to my apartment opens and my four brothers stroll in as if they own the fucking place. Finn and Con, the youngest two, they make their way over to the refrigerator without so much as a "hello," pulling out beers for us all. Con opens the cupboard and takes out the chips. Cheeky little fucker.

Cal sighs dramatically, like the stress-head that he is, before he slumps down on the couch opposite me. His eyes have dark circles around them, and his dark, wavy hair is tousled. Yeah, he's stressed the fuck out, as usual. Reece is a child prodigy, but with that comes all sorts of insane shit Cal has to contend with.

My eyes move over toward Oscar, our tech genius. He's already working like crazy on that tablet of his, his spine rigid with determination.

"How is she?" Finn asks while throwing himself down on the chair. His legs spread wide, carelessly. He dons his usual leather jacket and thick boots with laces open. The typical bad boy.

"She's fine."

Finn's eyes narrow on me skeptically. His mouth opens, but nothing comes out, the click of my bedroom door halts his words from forming.

We all fall deathly silent as we watch Sky walk into the room looking nervous as hell. Fidgeting with the bottom of my shirt. Her long blonde hair is down to her ass, now a little drier than before. She's petite and drowning in my clothes that she's attempted to tighten and bunch up; I chuckle when I realize she looks fucking cute in my shit.

Oscar side-eyes me, causing me to glare at him. His mouth quirks up at the side as if he has some hidden insight into my thoughts, weird prick. I take a pull of my beer.

Sky has stopped moving, rustling her hands together in nervousness. "Sky, come here, baby." She glances around each of my brothers, her face heating up.

Anger boils inside me. Does she like them? Find them attractive? My fists tighten. "Sky!" I bark in her direction.

She jumps at my tone before walking over to me. I hold out my hand for her and she takes it, letting me pull her onto my lap. One of her arms automatically bands around my neck, and she instantly starts to stroke my rough jawline, sending shivers down my spine. My heart beats faster and my cock twitches at her innocent touch. I nuzzle my nose into her hair, the scent of myself on her a comforting reminder she belongs to me.

A throat clears and my eyes shoot around the room. Each of my brothers gawk wide-eyed at us both. Con has a huge ass, cocky smile on his face. Finn smirks toward me. Cal's face is glowing with anger, and Oscar's eyes are darting between mine and Sky's, assessing.

"Sky, these are my brothers." I point to each of them in turn.

"So, I'm the oldest. Oscar is the serious one and the middle child. Finn, the bad boy. Con, the youngest and a cocky fucker, and Cal the stress-head, he's two years younger than me and my second in command." Sky nods silently, her fingers still trailing up and down my jaw rhythmically.

"Oscar has some questions for you. You can trust them,

do you understand me?" I tilt her chin toward me so she can see the truth in my eyes.

Her eyes soften at my touch. She swallows, answering without needing me to persuade her more. "I understand."

"Good girl."

I give Oscar a nod and he jolts, as if coming out of some sort of trance from watching us.

He sits straighter, if that's even possible. "What's your name?"

"Sky," her soft, breathy voice replies automatically.

Oscar's eyes meet mine accusingly and I glance away, not about to get into any shit with him right now. "Before Bren gave you that name, what was your name?" Oscar's accusing tone is blatant, making my muscles tighten in anger, he thinks I brainwashed her or some shit? Sky's soft fingers trail down my neck and her touch lingers on the bare skin above my shirt, soothing me. I instantly relax against her touch, her reassurance.

"My name was Red Seven." My brothers all sit forward at her words. She said the exact same thing to me in the car the day we found her. At the time, I thought she was delusional, in shock or some shit.

"Red Seven?" Oscar repeats.

Sky nods. "Red because of the compound I was in. Blue is the other."

"There's two compounds?" Oscar asks.

"The one over the fence is blue."

"How long had you been at the compound?" Cal asks.

Sky stays silent. I guide my fingers up and down her spine to coax her. Her voice is low and weak, a slight tremble to it. "I don't... I don't know."

BREN

My eyes narrow. How can she not know? Is she withholding information? Annoyance bubbles inside me.

"Weeks? Months? Years?" Oscar watches her closely.

She gulps. "Years."

We all sit straighter, my heart pounding at the fact she's been held in some compound for years. Oscar goes straight to the next question, not even picking up on how fucked up this is. "Do you know how old you were when you arrived there?"

"No. I was small." Like her voice, small.

"A child?" Oscar queries.

"Yes."

The room collectively gasps, and Finn jumps up from his chair, pushing a hand through his hair wildly. My chest heaves up and down as I struggle to rein in my own temper. Sky tilts her head toward me. "It's okay." She tries to reassure me. *What the fuck?*

"How old are you now, Sky?" Oscar asks. We all turn and wait with bated breath for her response.

She sits straighter and smiles. "Twenty-one. I just had my birthday. That's why I was going to my new owner." She sits taller, almost proud at the fact, while I sit dwelling on the fact that the innocent girl sitting on my knee is only twenty-one? *What the fuck?* I'm not all that far off being twice her age. *Jesus.* I push a hand over my cropped hair.

My jaw tight with anger, anger at myself.

Sky watches me closely, her face marred with confusion at my reaction.

"Do you know who your new owner was going to be?" My body jerks back at Oscar's words. Some fucker was buying her. My girl. I tighten my grip on her and she melts into me willingly. Oscar's eyes dart to my hands, not missing a damn thing.

"No. I was going to be a surprise for him, his father chose me when I was small. He said I looked angelic and innocent, that's why I had to stay in red."

I glance at my brothers, confusion coloring their faces.

"What's the difference between red and blue?" Oscar asks, his stare on Sky analyzing.

Sky sighs. "Red is where innocents go. Blue is for whores." Con chokes on his drink. My eyes catch on to Finn's. His body coiled tight and his knuckles white.

"So let me get this straight. You were brought to the compound as a child? Placed in red because you were a virgin? Chosen for someone to be sold at twenty-one. Am I right?" Oscar asks, his eyes not leaving Sky.

"Yes. Until Sebastian swapped the sticker on the crate."

We all sit forward at this information.

"Sticker?" Cal steps in.

Sky nods. "Blue for damaged goods." All our reactions change to the understanding behind the stickers on the crates. *Damaged fucking goods?* I'm seething inside.

"Sebastian?" Oscar queries, pulling me back to reality.

Sky nods, almost childlike. Expecting us to know who this fucking Sebastian guy is.

"He said I deserved better and was going to make sure I got it. So he swapped the stickers and changed the paperwork," she replies nonchalantly.

"Who's Sebastian?" I ask her gently.

"He's one of the foot soldiers. He used to sneak into my bed, and I'd look after him."

My body tenses at her words. *What the fuck did she just say?* I turn her head to face me, my temple pounding. "Shared your bed? How the fuck did you look after him?" I want to fucking kill him for laying his hands on my girl, the dirty little prick. Slaughter him and rid him of his skin.

Sky startles at my expression. A hand flies to her mouth. "Oh no. Not like that." She darts her eyes around the room, taking in my brothers' angry expressions. "He... he didn't. We didn't," she stutters.

"What the fuck was he doing in your bed?" I spit the words out.

"I was comforting him."

I scoff at her. "Comforting him? Comforting him how?" My chest heaves in fury.

"I played with his hair and stroked his back." She mimics her words with the action to me.

"Did he touch you? I want the truth, Sky. Did he touch you?" My eyes drill into hers, my voice rising.

Shock covers her face. "Of course not! We were little, he's younger than me. He was just a little boy and they hurt him, bad. Forced him to do things." Her chest starts to heave as if she's going to cry, her lower lip trembling. She's been through a lot of shit and only now while thinking of someone else is she getting emotional. Sky squeezes her eyes closed as if she's in pain. "He was in such a bad way one night. I had to wash his clothes because of the blood sticking to his pants."

The fucking bastards, hurting kids. My hands tighten, but I need to stay calm, to protect her.

I stroke her hair to calm both her and me. "Shh, baby, it's okay."

"He doesn't even like sex, and they make you do it in blue."

My heart sinks at the realization. The kid was being abused and she cared for him. "Jesus." Cal gasps.

"They have children in blue?" Oscar asks, completely ignoring both Finn and Cal, who are now pacing the room. Con's face is pale, his eyes locked on Sky.

"Yes, they have children in both."

Motherfuckers, my veins vibrate at my forehead.

Oscar continues on, "Do you know who was in charge of the compound?"

"Yes. Three men. The Don before he died. A Russian man before he went missing and the good-looking guy."

Oscar holds his hand up. "Go back, Sky. The Don?"

Sky nods.

"Who was the Don? Is that his real name?"

"That's what we called him. But he died." She shrugs.

"How?"

"Huh?"

"How. Did. The. Don. Die?" Oscar talks slower, emphasizing the importance behind the question.

"Some guys killed him. Someone at the compound said his family did it." Oscar darts his eyes down to his tablet before turning it around. "This him?" He points to the screen as my brothers step forward to look at it. Staring back at us in almost a taunting way is our Uncle Don. The one that brutally raped and trafficked Angel.

"Yes, that's him." I suck in a sharp breath. The room falls silent.

"What was he like?" Cal asks a little softer, raising his head from his hands. No doubt trying to understand how our uncle could lead such a double life. One so callous and evil, yet another so caring to his nephews who once adored him.

"He was tough. He liked punishing us." She swallows harshly. "He hurt Sebastian when they found him in my bed." She squeezes her eyes shut as if the memory pains her. "They hurt him bad. I didn't see him for such a long while after that. Blues aren't meant to mix with reds."

"Did they hurt you?" Con asks, concern etched on his usually playful face.

"Yes. They starved and whipped me. But the blues have worse punishments, I was lucky." She holds her head high, like the survivor she is. Pride fills me.

"Do you know where the compound is located?" Cal asks.

"No. I've no idea. I was in the crate for a long while."

"Did they ever take you out of the compound?" Finn asks, his entire demeanor screaming that he's desperate to release some aggression.

"No."

So she spent years in a fucking compound, never leaving.

"What did you do every day?" Cal asks, his eyes holding sympathy.

Sky sighs and sinks back into me. "We had lessons. Cleaned, cooked, looked after the children."

Oscar's interest is suddenly piqued. "Lessons in what?" His eyes narrow, as if Sky is suddenly a threat. I band my arm tighter around her.

Sky twirls her hair around her finger nonchalantly. "All kinds of subjects. We had a teacher who taught us math and English. Our new owners pay a lot for us, they need to know we're worth their money." She stares at Oscar pointedly, saying the words as if relaying what she's been told numerous times before. "We had lessons on how to please a man."

My muscles in my shoulders tense instantly. "What fucking lessons?"

Sky turns her head to face me. "We watched porn to understand how to please you." My mouth drops open at her blatant confession. "We watched people having sex so we could learn what to do. I learned a lot, so I can be good for you, Bren." Her eyes sparkling with lust, she licks those perky lips as if to both emphasize and torment the hell out of me and my cock.

Con chuckles, a disbelieving chuckle from his chair, causing my head to swing his way with a sneer on my lips.

Her words play over in my head as I slowly turn back toward her. *I learned so I can be good for you, Bren. Jesus fucking Christ*, I drag a hand over my cropped hair.

Sky brushes her fingers over the scruff on my jawline, the motion causing my heart rate to quicken. She shuffles her ass over my hardened cock, and I grip her thighs to still her movement. Moving close to her ear, I whisper the words gently to her, "Enough, baby." I close my eyes and breathe in her scent, the scent of me on my girl. Fucking edible, every inch of her untouched body. Edible.

My hands cling tighter to her thighs, causing her lips to fall open on a delicate moan. I'm so fucking screwed.

Oscar snaps me out of my thoughts. "You mentioned other men, Sky. The Russian, do you know his name?"

Sky appears deep in thought. "He had a strange one. We just shortened it to D."

Oscar sits forward. "Dimitriev?"

Sky's face lights up. "Yes!" She throws her hand out toward Oscar. "Him. He had a gold tooth and scarred face."

All our bodies tense in unison at the mention of the sick fuck's name. The same sick fuck that helped rape Angel. I just wish we could torture the cunt all over again. Him and Uncle Don.

"Tell me what you know about the other guy." Oscar's eyes drill into Sky's, causing her to sit back slightly, her breathing quickening a little more.

"He took over from his father. His father was the one in charge, him and the Don. They ran it but the good-looking guy started helping. Before that, I didn't see him much." I squeeze her sharply at her description of the good-looking guy? *Fucking prick.*

Sky feels my growing anger and placates me like a fucking child. Although, I can't help but relax into her and nuzzle her soft hair while she gently strokes her fingers up and down my face. I can smell my shower wash on her. She smells like she's mine. Knowing nobody else has cared for her or looked after her makes me all the prouder and more determined. No, she's not going anywhere, screw her being young. She's a fucking adult. She was made for me. I can feel it. The fact that I've never felt this way or reacted to a woman like this before is testament to that. I've never even kissed a woman for fuck's sake. I might have kissed their pussy but not their mouths, never seeing the point when you don't get anything out of it in return. But with Sky, I want to shove my tongue so far down her throat it comes out of her ass, and then I'll kiss her there too.

"The sticker on the crate…" Oscar turns his tablet toward us with the sticker evident. "Do you know what the letters stand for?" G.O.D stares back at us.

"They're the initials of the founders."

"The founders?" Oscar queries.

"Yes," Sky points to each letter innocently. "Garcia, O'Connell, and Dimitriev."

Cal gasps from beside the couch. He jumps to his feet and stands in front of us, his whole body vibrating with anger. He bends down with a face of fury. "Hold the fuck up. Did you say Garcia?" He points at the screen. My eyes dart around my brothers, all sitting with a wide-eyed expression at one another.

Sky swallows sharply, and I stroke her hair to soothe her. She stumbles over her words, pissing me off that Cal is unnerving her so much. "Yes. Mr. Garcia was the father that died, but I don't know the name of his son." Her eyes dart toward mine as if seeking my approval and to believe her words.

"It's okay, baby, Cal has history with the Garcias. You're doing great." She smiles innocently at my praise. Her smile lighting up her pale complexion. She shuffles her butt slightly and once again rubs against my aching cock, still struggling to soften. The little minx causes me to wince at the sensation of her tight little ass wiggling over me but not able to do anything about it. I grasp her thigh to stop the movement. Grinding my teeth together, I realize my action hasn't gone unnoticed when a chuckle escapes Con, and I side-eye him with a warning glare. The cocky shit wipes the smug-ass grin off his face in an instant.

"Sky, if I show you photos of Mr. Garcia, would you recognize him?" Oscar gently asks her.

"Yes." I stroke her hair, gently brushing my fingers through the velvety strands. Sensing eyes on me, I flit my own toward Finn. He's watching my interaction with Sky, his eyebrows furrowed together in confusion. I scowl at him, and he throws his head back on a silent chuckle.

Oscar shows the tablet to Sky. "No. I've never seen that man." She shakes her head.

"Are you sure?" Cal spits out. "You need to be absolutely positive, Sky." His face is contorted in rage.

"I'm sure. I swear it." She turns her head toward me again. "I swear, I've never seen that man, Bren."

Part of me wonders if Cal was hoping the guy on the screen, Nico Garcia, was one of the men in charge of the compound, then he would have the perfect excuse to kill him. He's been desperate to get rid of him since he found out Nico had stabbed his wife, Lily, causing her to miscarry. He then went on to kidnap both Lily and their son, Reece. I forbid him to go after the Garcias for revenge. Knowing how ruthless and what a large reach they have, I knew it was a war we'd be unable to win. Now I'm second guessing that decision, knowing we could have put a stop to this compound shit before now.

But then would someone else have taken over?

"How about this one? Do you recognize him?" Oscar prompts.

Sky nods. "Yes, that's him." The image is that of the oldest Garcia brother, Raul.

"But the other guy, you've never seen him? You're sure?" Cal goes on.

Sky's eyes catch on to mine and she nibbles her lip and shakes her head gently.

"Cal! E-fuckin-nough. Now!" I bark at him. He drops his head and takes a step back, realizing he's overstepped.

"So what do we do about this shit now, Bren?" Finn voices.

I sit forward, moving Sky slightly in the process. "Sky, baby. Go to your room." I ease her off my lap.

She nods and leaves the room.

The soft click of the door breaks the silence.

CHAPTER 12

Bren

As soon as the door clicks shut, Con throws his head back with a loud chuckle. I eye him quizzically. He points his beer bottle toward me. "You are so fucking screwed, man."

I don't confirm nor deny his analysis.

"She's trafficked." Cal eyes me with a quirk of his brow. Ever the fucking saint.

I shrug. "Not fucked her yet." I leave the comment open because I'll be damned if I'm explaining myself to my younger brothers. This is my fucking empire to run. If I want Sky, I'll fucking take her and answer to no one. My jaw hardens in annoyance.

"Just don't fuck her over, Bren. She's been through a lot, man." Finn exhales deeply, and I drag my eyes up toward my brother. His hair ruffled in aggravation, worry marring his face, no doubt thinking of the connection to Angel and the circumstances in which Sky has been living.

"She was certain Nico wasn't involved," Cal voices, almost to himself.

I nod to confirm his words. "Yeah." I trace my jawline with my fingers, absentmindedly tracing over Sky's touch.

"We can't go to war over this, Brother. It's bigger than us..." I glare at Cal and then cast my eyes around at my brothers, ensuring they all hear my words. "...All of us." They all nod or tip their heads in understanding. This thing. This compound, the reach it has. Mexicans, Russians, and, albeit reluctantly, the Irish combined are not something we can go up against. The thought alone makes me feel defeated. *How many innocent victims are involved and for how long has this been going on?* I exhale loudly.

"We approach Nico." Oscar's words snap me out of my thoughts and my eyes dart toward his. All my brothers in unison mirror my own shock with collective gasps.

"Absolutely. Fucking. Not!" Cal erupts. His eyes bugging out of his head, his face contorted in disgust.

I hold up my hand to quieten him, and just when I think he's going to disrespect me and continue with his tirade, his mouth clamps shut and his body coils tight with reluctance.

I nod toward Oscar for him to continue. He slowly licks his lips as if processing his words. "Nico isn't aware of the situation his family is in. We use him. Simple." My eyebrows furrow as my mind works over his thought process. *Use him.*

"Form an alliance?" I query with a raised brow.

"As such." Oscar shrugs.

Heat radiates from Cal, tension building as he stands stoically still above us. His fists clenched tightly by his side, a clear giveaway at his desperation to unleash his anger.

I run the tip of my finger over my lip and sit back, considering our options. I spread my legs, the jeans pulling tight across my hardened dick that shows no sign of abating.

"We're assuming he's blind to it?" Finn asks, stepping forward. Cal scoffs at his words, like a petulant child. I glare in his direction, a clear warning I can handle his insolence if need be. He turns his back to me and walks toward the kitchen, no doubt pouring himself another whiskey.

"Investigate. We need to be sure." My eyes drill into Oscar's and he dips his head in understanding.

"We'll need more evidence if he's going to be convinced," Con speaks up for the first time, leaning forward in his chair.

"Now we have names at least." Oscar shrugs.

I deepen my voice and lock gazes with Oscar. "Good. I want confirmation no one will come for Sky." Oscar scans my face, understanding the importance behind my words, almost like reading my mind, his lip quirks at the side in approval. If someone tried to take her from me, I'd go to war.

For her.

After arranging for Sky to meet with my brothers' wives tomorrow and seeing them out, I swallow the last of my whiskey and place the tumbler on the kitchen counter. Taking a deep breath, I push off the counter and make my way toward my bedroom.

I open the door as quietly as possible. Only since Sky

came into my life, have I become conscious of being quieter, desperate to make sure she's not scared. Her skittish behavior only appears around others, something that makes me smile. My baby feels secure with me.

The room is dark, but I instantly scan the bed—like I've done for almost two weeks now—ensuring her compact form is snuggled under the covers. My shoulders become stiff when I don't see the usual crinkled sheets. I tilt my head slightly to listen if she's in the bathroom.

Nothing.

A small gasp at the end of my bed sends my eyes darting toward it.

Sky is kneeling on the floor with her head down, her hair like a blanket covering her face and her hands placed flat on the floor in front of her. I take her in, her skin shimmers in the moonlight, telling me she's naked. Fucking naked and kneeling before me... *Jesus*. My heart hammers against my chest, my throat suddenly dry, desperate for a taste of her. I lick my lips, arousal releasing from the tip of my cock, so much my boxers feel drenched against me. Never in my fucking life have I felt like this. Sheer desperation, need for her, desire, consume every fiber in my body. My mind is tormented with conflicting thoughts. I want to fuck her so badly, so hard I mark that little body permanently, leaving my everlasting mark on her. But then I want to care for her, protect her, make her completely dependent on me, so she'll never leave and want nothing more than just me.

I swallow thickly, my ability to function is lost.

Sky lifts her head with uncertainty, and I want nothing more than to reach out and chase that uncertainty away. Her scared eyes quickly dip back down as if she shouldn't have raised them to begin with.

I step toward her, determined to protect my girl. Reaching out, I brush the silky strands of hair from her face and lift her chin. If I just widen my legs a little more, it's the perfect fucking height for me to ram my cock into those innocent lips. I banish away the thought as quickly as it came, I can't go there. Not with a trafficked girl, a twenty-one-year-old, no less.

I exhale loudly. "What are you doing on the floor, baby?"

Her lip trembles slightly, and I stroke my fingers gently over her cheek for encouragement. "I... I want to please you." Her soft blue eyes finally meet mine, a pink flush coats her cheeks, and I inwardly smile at her innocence.

Trailing my fingers over the heat of her cheeks, I can't help myself. "Please me how, baby?"

She visibly swallows. "I'm submitting to you, my owner." Her eyes don't leave mine. Her words should sicken me. The fact she said I'm her owner should repulse me. But fuck if I want nothing more than to be just that. Own her, every fucking delectable inch of her.

My head tells me to stop. That I'm old enough to be her father for Christ's sake. But my cock and body crave her, I know she's mine. I can fucking feel it deep within me.

I trace my fingers over her parted lips. The gasp that leaves her mouth causes me to close my eyes, allowing me to rein in the need to fuck her senseless.

I take a step back, feeling the disconnection instantly, the warmth of her lips still on the tips of my fingers. Her head ducks down in defeat and I want so desperately to give in, give her what she wants. What we both want.

"Is your pussy wet?" I ask her crudely, not giving a fuck.

Sky nods. "Use your words, Sky. Are you wet?"

"Y-yes." She raises her eyes slightly to watch me.

I tilt my head toward the bed. "Get on the bed and open your legs. Let me see."

She jumps to her feet, her golden locks falling over her tits like curtains. She looks fucking mesmerizing as she raises her head high and clambers onto the bed.

I take another step back, making sure she's not within reach of me, to keep me from throwing her down and fucking her into oblivion.

I tug my t-shirt over my head and unbutton my jeans, dropping them to the floor.

Then, when Sky is laid in the center of the bed, I finally take a step forward.

CHAPTER 13

Sky

I scan Bren's impeccable body. He has tight, solid muscles that don't seem to move. His skin is a natural olive tone, his boxers sit low on his waistline, a wolf tattoo on his left bicep stretches over his skin, and his chest is littered with symbols and tattoos. I use my tongue to wet my bottom lip as I imagine trailing it over the dip around his boxers, a prominent V evident. The man is gorgeous, a god, and I'm his. Excitement bubbles inside of me at the thought of him finally taking me, he'll own me then. I warm at the realization.

My eyes finally meet Bren's, his jaw clenched tight. If it wasn't for the heavy lust-filled look in his eyes, I would be worried with how angry he appears, but I think it has more to do with him struggling with his own needs right now. I squirm under his scrutiny.

Without breaking eye contact with me, he tucks his fingers in the waistband of his boxers and pushes them down before kicking them to the side.

My eyes take in his cock, it's thick and solid. It reaches his stomach and has a trail of sticky substance, I know to be pre-cum, oozing from it. I can feel Bren's gaze on me, watching for my reaction. I moan when his hand reaches for his cock and he begins pumping it in his fist, his lips part and his hooded eyes roam over my body. Wetness pools between my legs with his heat searing into me.

"Open those legs, baby. Let me see that wet pussy."

I do as he commands and spread my legs wide, keeping my feet flat on the bed.

"Fuck," he groans and tightens his fist, pumping harder. "Fuck, baby. I can see your juices pouring out of your little hole. Play with your tits, baby. Let me see you play." I do as he commands and squeeze my breasts between my palms, brushing my fingers carelessly over my nipple, a squeak evading my lips when the sensation tingles between my thighs. "You like that, baby? You like playing with your tits?"

"Mmm." I nod in response.

"Fuck. I've never been so turned-on in my life, baby. It's been motherfucking torture watching you," he spits the words out with anger, but they only warm me, knowing his need for me is consuming him.

"Pl-ay with your clit, ba-baby. Fuck, I'm close already. Play with it, darlin, let me see you come." His words come out stuttered and desperate. His chest rising faster with each pump of his hand.

I move my hand to between my legs and begin rubbing circles over the bundle of nerves. "Br-Bren, feels so good."

My mouth drops open on a whimper as I squeeze my nipple in one hand and rub my clit with the other.

His lips part in awe. "Baby, put your fingers inside your pussy."

I still. My body stopping immediately at his words. Bren's eyebrows narrow in confusion and his movements stop too. "What's wrong?" His tone comes out clipped, but I can see the concern etched on his face.

"I-I've never." I shake my head from side to side and dart my eyes to between my legs.

Bren's Adams apple bobs. "You've never had your fingers in your pussy?"

I shake my head again. "N-no, we weren't allowed."

Bren smirks slightly, and I'm unsure as to why. "Baby, you have to do as I say. Right?" I nod in agreement at his words, my training taking over. The submissive in me never wavering.

"I want you to push a finger inside your pussy, nice and gentle." He begins stroking himself again, slower this time. His eyes transfixed to the movement between my legs. "Not too far, baby," he chastises, and I nod in acknowledgment. "Another, open yourself up for me. Let me see inside." Oh, my god, his filthy words and mouth cause me to moan, the sensation of me gently pushing my fingers inside me, the feeling both foreign and welcoming. I use my other hand to stroke my clit while watching with satisfaction at Bren's body coiled with need.

"Fuck, that's it. Tight little pussy you have there, all desperate for my cock. Ain't that right, baby?"

"Yes, yes," I chant as my orgasm builds.

"Fuck, yes. That's it, baby, take what you need. Show me how much you need my cock in you. Fucking you."

The backward and forward of Bren's palm against his thick cock and the squelching sound of my slick pussy fill the room.

He tugs on my ankle and drags me roughly toward the edge of the bed.

"Gonna come all over this tight little pussy, baby."

My orgasm takes over, I throw my head back and stiffen beneath his words, my own need seeping from my lips, "Yes, please. Please cover me in your cum, Bren. Please." I all but beg as a flood of warm cum coats my fingers, my pussy, and my stomach.

I relish in the feeling of ownership. I'm his, he's marked me as his. I vigorously rub in his essence, ensuring it's not going to be wiped away.

Bren leans over me, his mouth parted in awe as he watches me. "Put some in your pussy too." I nod in response and push some of his cum inside me. His eyes track every movement and his cock twitches at the sight. "Good girl." The words drop from his lips, and I smile up at him, reveling in the feeling of accomplishment.

His eyes bore into mine before I notice a flicker of change, his face drops, and he pushes back from the bed. He leans over and picks up his t-shirt, throwing it in my direction. "Put the shirt on, Sky." His tone harsh, causing me to wince. Dread fills my veins. Did I do something wrong?

He storms toward the bathroom and slams the door closed.

Did I not do as I was told? Uncertainty swirls in my stomach. *Will he not want me?*

I swallow back the vulnerable feeling, but my eyes blur a little before I shake off the insecurities and do as Bren asked.

I pull the shirt over my head and climb into the bed, covering myself with the sheets.

CHAPTER 14

Bren

I fucked up. I stare at myself in the bathroom mirror, hating myself for losing control and using Sky for my own selfish needs. I needed a release and she was offering it to me on a silver platter. A trafficked girl that's been kept prisoner, for Christ's sake. I scrub a hand over my head in annoyance with myself. It was by far the hottest experience of my life, and I've had a lot of experience. Yet, nothing compares to the small little blonde woman laid out for me in my bed. Mine for the taking. *Fuck*.

I'm a sick bastard for even wanting to go there. But knowing how devoted she is to me already—dependent, submissive, and untouched—brings out the monster in me. I want her. I want to be her everything, because she sure as shit feels like she's mine.

I dry my hands and throw the towel in the sink, well and truly pissed off at how fucked up this whole thing is.

We need to sort out this traffic ring, and fast. There's no way we can let it carry on. Not when there's people like Sky being kept there, children even. I swallow the lump in my throat at the thought. Having young nieces and nephews makes it hit too close to home. It's not something we're going to stand by and allow to continue.

I open the bathroom door softly and walk into the bedroom. Sky is on her back with my white t-shirt riding up toward her stomach, her blonde locks splayed out over the pillow and a sweet, soft snoring sound coming from those pink lips. She's the epitome of beauty.

I walk around to my side of the bed, completely naked, and climb in. Pulling the sheet up, I roll Sky toward my chest and I rest her head on my heart—like I have done every night for the past two weeks. She automatically drapes her arm over my stomach, a soft content murmur leaves her mouth, and I smile back at my girl.

I've never felt so at ease with anyone in my life. And have never wanted to keep anything more than I do now either. I'd go to the depths of hell for her and come out burning in flames to do it all again. Stretching my neck, I kiss the top of her head and inhale her scent. Me, she smells of me. We're one, as we should be. I just need to get rid of these feelings of guilt somehow. Tuck them away and enjoy her, savor every little morsel before she realizes her heart doesn't belong to me.

The thought makes me grip her tightly, desperate to cling to any shred of her, determined never to let her go.

I just can't rid the feeling of dread inside, eating away at me. Something is going to take her from me.

I know, without a shadow of doubt, I'd start a war to keep her. I just hadn't realized until now that the war would be with myself.

SKY

I wake with a startle. Why hasn't the bell rang?

Jumping out of bed, my feet sink into the plush cream-colored carpet and my body instantly relaxes.

My mind has been so controlled by the ringing of the morning bell and my feet hitting the wood floor for so long now that I forgot where I was. *Bren's, I'm at Bren's.*

After using the bathroom, I decide to go in search of Bren. He held me all night in my sleep and spoke soft words of support in my ear when I was having my night terrors.

I walk into the kitchen and my eyes lock onto Bren's solid body. He's in a business suit, his jacket pulled tight over his shoulders. He pours milk into a glass and his eyes snap up to meet mine as his lips curve into a smile. "Morning baby, you sleep well?"

I fiddle with his t-shirt. "Yes."

"Good girl. I ordered some breakfast." He nods toward a brown paper bag on the counter. I walk over to it and open it up, inhaling the smell of freshly baked goods.

"What are you having?" I ask, placing the items on the counter.

He surrounds me from behind, placing his hands on the counter on either side of me, his knuckles whiten from the grip as if attempting to keep himself from touching me. Leaning over, his breath causing goosebumps to rise, and he whispers, "I'd love to have you for breakfast." He nips at my earlobe playfully, causing me to swallow sharply. "I gotta go to work, baby. My brothers' women will be here soon. Security will be on the door." He nods toward the door and pushes off the counter. *His brothers' women are coming here? Will they say something and try to take him away from me?* Panic fills me.

My eyes follow him as he goes over to the couch and picks up his phone. Glancing back up at me, he scans my face. As if sensing my worries, he comforts me by saying, "They're good people, Sky, they only want to be your friends, okay?" My shoulders relax as the truth seeps through his gaze. I nod in acknowledgment, and his normally stoic face breaks into a handsome smile that warms me.

CHAPTER 15

Sky

Bren left about half an hour ago, and I'd be lying if I said I wasn't nervous at meeting his family. I want them to like me enough to want to keep me around.

After eating my breakfast at the counter, I showered and put on a fresh shirt. I literally have nothing else to wear, but Bren doesn't seem to mind me wearing his clothes. On the contrary, I think he actually really likes it.

After showering, I clean up the rooms. Bren is really untidy and leaves his things everywhere. But I love looking after my man. I smile to myself as I wash the last of the dishes and turn to put away the milk he left out this morning. Opening the refrigerator door, I'm shocked to see it's almost empty. No wonder he ordered in breakfast. I frown, *what am I supposed to make him for dinner?*

I hear the door close behind me and spin around on my

heels, I'm shocked to see three women standing at the door with their hands full of bags. They're beautiful. I instantly take a step back, my ass hitting the kitchen counter.

"It's okay, Sky. I'm Lily. Do you remember me?" I scan her face, green eyes stare back, imploring me. Her brown hair is tied up in a messy bun and she wears jeans with a black t-shirt. An image of her face caring for me flashes in my mind and I relax with a nod of my head.

She scans my body up and down, no doubt taking in my lack of clothes. I move from foot to foot at her scrutiny.

Another dark-haired woman pushes toward Lily and virtually bumps her out of the way with a playful giggle. She's in cutoff jean shorts and a camisole top. She's dressed casually but she looks hot. Her boobs strain her top, causing me to glance down at my own. They're nowhere near as big as either of these women's.

"Hi, I'm Will. Nice to meet you, Sky." She waves at me; a huge smile engulfs her face when her gaze flicks over my shirt. I can feel heat creeping up my neck so I fidget with my hair.

Hesitantly, another woman steps forward. She's different from the other two. I can see it in her eyes. She approaches me with caution, and this time it's me that's scrutinizing. Wow, she's really pretty, her features delicate and her hair is almost white. She has tattoos trailing up her arms and numerous piercings in her ears. Her black jeans hold in a baby bump, and I smile at how cute it is. Her t-shirt covers it, but I can see it clearly. I work my way up to her face and her pink lips are tight, as though she's not sure about me or being here in general.

I glance around the room, wondering what could make her so uncomfortable. "I'm Angel. Nice to meet you." Her voice is raspy, as though she's struggling with her emotions.

"I'm Sky." I fidget on my feet and my hands play nervously together.

Angel breaks out into a huge smile. "I know."

"Yeah, yeah. So now that we have the introductions out of the way. Shall I show you what we brought you, Sky?" Will chuckles, lightening the awkward tension.

I nod and she points over toward the couch.

I sit with my knees drawn up as Will and Lily proceed to unpack bundles of clothes. I can feel Angel's scrutinizing gaze on me. Even when I flick my eyes toward her, she doesn't glance away like I thought she would. I chew my lip nervously.

"Sky. Sky." A hand waves in front of me. "Do you like the dress?" Lily asks with concern on her face.

I don't even glance at the dress. I chew the skin at the side of my nails and train my eyes onto my knees. "Yes, thank you."

Lily sighs heavily, then she turns her head toward Angel, then back at me. I catch Angel's eyes before lowering mine again.

"Jesus, Angel. You're making the poor girl uncomfortable. Can you stop?" Will snaps.

Angel startles as if she hadn't realized she was causing my nervousness. "I… I'm sorry, Sky." Her green eyes meet mine, brimming with tears that cause my heart to skip a beat. Something happened to this girl; I can feel it in the way she looks at me. She has that broken look about her, the one that's all too familiar.

"What happened to you?" My voice is barely above a whisper, but I can tell she heard me because her breathing escalates.

"Don," she replies. Just one word and it causes me to squeeze my eyes shut.

His evil eyes bore into mine as I kneel at his feet, my chin lifted high like I've been trained. My body's reaction is to duck away, hide. "It's a good thing you're worth more to me pure than you are tainted, little whore, because I would fuck you up so bad, you wouldn't be able to stand again." My body trembles, knowing what he's capable of. I've seen what he's done. "Get me the fucking whip. Let me teach this bitch a lesson," he barks at one of the girls from blue. He circles me like a predator before scooping my long hair from down my back and pushing it behind my ear. "Get on all fours, whore, and take your punishment." I Squeeze my eyes shut and do as I'm ordered. The sound of the whip fills the air, and I tense in agony at the first strike.

"Sky. Are you okay? Sky?" Lily's soft voice soothes me as she gently brings her hands up to mine. They're locked tightly around the sides of my ears, trying to lock out the sounds of the whip and my sobs.

I hadn't realized Angel had moved beside me. She gently pulls me toward her, and I instantly relax. Resting my head on her chest, she hugs me, our chests rising and falling together at the realization that one way or another, Don O'Connell hurt us. Bad. A connection we share.

I lift my head to face her, unshed tears blur the emerald color of her eyes, she lowers her head and kisses the top of mine. "You're safe now, Sky. Nobody is going to hurt you." She lifts my chin with her fingers. "Do you understand, sweetheart?" I nod at her gentle words.

———

We spend the rest of the morning going through various items they brought me, but in all honesty, I really don't care. I'd prefer Bren to choose what I wear, that way I know he likes them.

"Sky, are you not wearing any panties?" Angel asks with a cock of her brow. Her eyes trained on where my legs are tucked up, my shirt has risen, and my ass is on display.

"No." I shrug.

Both Lily and Will stare at one another dumbfounded before they break out into giggles.

"Do you own any panties at all?" Angel asks, biting her lip to stifle a laugh.

"No." I glance between all the women. *Are they hiding a joke from me?*

"Thankfully, we brought you some." Angel smirks.

"So, are you and Bren?" Lily rolls her hand in a forward motion, making my eyebrows furrow in confusion.

"She's trying to ask if you're fucking?" Angel clarifies, causing Lily to gasp and throw her the dead eye. Angel shrugs back at her. "What? That's what you wanted to know, right?"

"No need to be so blunt, Angel," Will grumbles while throwing herself on a chair opposite me.

"I'm not an innocent child. Jesus, I know what sex is," I snap at them, lifting my chin. "I've seen it a lot, and I've been trained on how to please a man." The girls look at one another, then back at me for an explanation.

"It's what I learned at the compound. After schooling, we learned how to please a man."

"Bu-but Con said you're a virgin?" Will queries.

"Oh, I am. But we watched porn and practiced on toys.

You know, how to take one into the back of our throats, stuff like that." Will and Lily's eyes bug out.

While Angel laughs. "So have you and Bren fucked?"

The girls watch me for a reaction. "Not yet, but I want to. Last night he came all over me."

Lily spits out her drink. "Wow, don't sugarcoat your words, Sky."

I shrug. "I won't."

"So, is Bren all growly in the bedroom too?" Angel asks, her face alight with glee.

I scan her face, unsure of what she means.

"Ignore her, Sky." Will throws a scrunched-up napkin at Angel.

"He's caring."

The girls glance at one another, and then back at me. "Caring?" Will queries.

"Hmmm, very." I smile softly to myself, remembering how he strokes my hair and cares for me.

"Caring?" Angel scrunches up her nose. "Bren?"

I nod in agreement.

CHAPTER 16

Bren

"So let me get this fucking straight. You want to use my wife to approach that scumbag? You do realize that the last time she saw him, he murdered her unborn child and attacked her, right?" Cal spits. The vein at the side of his neck pulsates.

I glance around my brothers as we sit in my office at the warehouse. Cal is a mess of a man, stressed the hell out. Finn has nonchalantly kicked his feet up onto the table. Con is sitting in a swivel chair, swinging around, staring at the ceiling while Oscar types manically on his tablet. All unfazed by Cal's outburst.

Oscar lifts his gaze from his tablet and glares at Cal over the frame of his glasses. "There's no other way. She's the only one able to get close to him."

"Great, so you're using my wife as bait!"

Oscar exhales with annoyance. "Essentially, yes," he replies, causing us all to sigh at his stupidity to even respond to Cal.

"You know what?" We all watch Cal unravel. "Fuck this shit. I'm outta here. Taking my fucking family and leaving this fucking town. Screw you all." He jumps to his feet and heads for the door.

Annoyance rumbles inside of me at his childish antics. He's meant to be a fucking Mafia man, my next in command. Finn is better suited to the position; I chance a look at Finn, and he dips his head in understanding. "Cal?" I bark. He stops with his hand on the door handle but makes a point of not turning around. "Don't forget dinner at Ma's Sunday."

His shoulders drop, and he nods solemnly before swinging open the door and leaving.

A silent agreement between us that he isn't going anywhere. He has obligations to fulfill, no matter how much he wants to hide. There's no running from our life.

I stare at Oscar, and without him lifting his head, he speaks the words I want to hear, "Leave Lily to me."

———

I've waited all fucking day to see my girl. I'm nearly bouncing on the balls of my feet when the elevator doesn't move quick enough.

The doors open and I practically push the damn things out of the way.

I scan my handprint and the door opens. Giggles fill the room, and before my eyes can search for her, she runs into my arms, her head barely making it to my shoulders. Her arms band around me and mine around her. "I missed you," she mumbles into my chest. Her words filling me with reassurance.

My hands roam up her back and into her hair as she nuzzles into me, causing my heart to constrict at the feel of her. I tug her hair back roughly, forcing her gaze to meet mine. "You good?" I question, my stare drilling into her.

Sky nibbles on her lip and nods gently. "Yes, thank you. The girls brought me clothes." She points over to the couches where the women all sit with smug expressions on their face. I narrow my eyes at them.

"Come see." Sky tugs on my arm and I allow her to. Like a fucking sap, I follow.

Neat piles of clothes are laid out on the couch, but my eyes instantly lock on to the lacy underwear. Anger bubbles inside me, my shoulders tense. *What. The. Ever. Living. Fuck. Is this?*

My jaw locks tight. They're trying to change my girl. I grab ahold of the lace panties, balling them up in my fist. Absolutely fucking not. I pick up a barely there lace bra and hold up the offending item by the straps with a quirk of my brow in Will's direction. She gulps before darting her eyes away.

"Do you like them?" Sky asks. I glance down at my innocent blue-eyed girl. She nibbles her lip waiting for my response.

Not wanting to disappoint her, I change the subject. "You got everything you need now?"

"Yes. I think so, thank you, Bren." I automatically lean forward and kiss her head.

"Good girl. Why don't you go and take some of these into your closet?" I wave my hand at a pile of clothes.

Sky picks up the pile. Will stands and begins to help

but I move to her ear so only she can hear me. "Sit the fuck down." She drops the pile and sits on the couch.

I wait for Sky to leave, watching my girl's cute little ass sway as she goes, before rounding up on the three women sitting on the couch like naughty schoolgirls. Will and Lily look a little concerned, but Angel looks like she's going to laugh at any given moment.

"What the fuck are they?" I point to the pile of scraps of lace.

Angel scoffs "Puh… lease. I'm pretty sure you're familiar with panties, Bren." She quirks a brow at me.

Aggravation bubbles inside me. "I mean, what the fuck are you doing bringing them here?"

"The poor girl doesn't even own a pair of panties, Bren, what do you think we were doing bringing them here? You said to kit her out. We kitted her out." She waves her hand at the underwear.

"Take them fucking back. I don't want her wearing that shit," I grunt out.

"Pretty sure you like them," she quips back with an annoying grin.

"Angel," I warn her, my fists clenching beside me at her defiance.

She rolls her eyes. How the fuck Finn copes with her insolence is beyond me. "Fine. Your loss." She gives me a sarcastic smile. But her words help relax me.

"She's innocent. She doesn't need any of that shit," I say almost to myself.

"Pretty sure she's not as innocent as you'd like to think." Angel can't help but laugh, making the other two girls glare at her like they have some sort of hidden secret. My eyes narrow. I don't like that one bit. She's my girl, and she doesn't get to keep secrets from me.

"Meaning?" I snipe the words out.

"Meaning we spent the afternoon discussing which sex toy fits down her throat the best."

I choke on fresh air. *What the fuck?* My mouth parts to tell her to shut the fuck up, but the words don't come out. A vision of my innocent girl sucking on a silicone dick fills my mind. My cock stirs at the thought.

"Yeah, figured I'd leave that one with you. Have a good night, big guy." Angel pats my chest with her hand as she picks up her handbag. Both Will and Lily make a quick exit too. All three of them shouting good night to me, but I'm glued to the fucking spot. Still imagining my girl with a dildo in her mouth.

My cock weeps in desperation.

I need to empty my balls, that's for sure. I turn on my heel and head toward the bedroom for a shower.

CHAPTER 17

Bren

After banging one out in the shower, I step out, wrap a towel around my waist, scrub my teeth, then open the door to the bedroom.

Stepping into our room, my feet stop on their own accord.

Kneeling naked on the floor with her head down is Sky. My jaw locks with annoyance. *How the fuck am I meant to keep rejecting this?* I scrub a hand over my head. There's only so much resilience a man can have until he reaches his fucking breaking point.

Sky's eyes draw up toward mine.

"Sky, baby. Come on, get in bed, I already told you, you don't have to do this shit." I step toward her and offer her my hand.

She swallows hard, my eyes locking on her throat.

Instantly my mind goes back to the conversation earlier today. *We spent the afternoon discussing which sex toy fits down her throat the best.* A groan escapes me, my cock thickening at the thought. I squeeze my eyes closed, praying for will power.

Her voice is confident. "I want to." My gaze snaps down to hers. She licks her lips, her eyes staring at the bulge behind the towel.

"I really want to." She glances up at me. "Please."

"Jesus." My throat suddenly dry as all coherent thoughts vanish.

I whip my towel off my hips. "Show me what you've got, baby."

Sky smiles and crawls toward me slightly. That motion alone makes my cock drip. I bend down and push her hair over her shoulders so I can view her beautiful face. Her hands find my hips, caressing them before she peers back up at me. "I want you to choke me."

I tilt my head, unsure if I heard her right. *Choke her?*

I use my fingers to draw her chin up. "Explain."

"I want you to love it so much that you make me choke on your cock." She holds me captive with her lust-filled eyes.

How the fuck I don't blow a load right here, right now, is beyond me.

I shuffle forward slightly. "Suck it, baby." I stand butt naked with my cock at full attention, waiting for the little vixen to suck me down like I'm one of her toys.

Instead, she nuzzles into my balls, taking me by surprise. She swirls her tongue around them, making me want to hiss out in impatience. Gently she begins nipping, licking, and sucking on my flesh as if marking my sack for herself. Loving the thought of her wanting to lay her claim on me, I grip her head roughly and all but shove her head into my groin. Her tongue moves lower, right underneath my sack, and I hiss out in both nervousness and appreciation. "Not much farther, baby." She attempts to nod. Her nails dig into my thighs, and I relish it.

Enjoying the sensation of getting the lower part of my sack licked, I lift my foot onto the bed to give her better access. I can feel the confidence oozing from her as she goes to town on my taint, shoving her nose right into my sack. The sensation is like nothing I've felt before. I grip her hair sharply, and she doesn't even wince. The thought should be worrying, but the only thing worrying me now is how the hell am I going to last long enough to feel her tongue around my cock? I begin rubbing her face up and down my groin, using it to give me some relief.

She mumbles and slurps, using that mouth like a pro.

She rises to her knees, and I watch in awe as she takes hold of my cock and feeds it into her mouth. Her lips stretch around me, my mouth drops open at the feeling of her throat embracing my cock. One of her hands tightens on my thigh and she watches my hooded gaze, as if silently telling me to fuck her face. I nod, gripping her hair and plunge my cock forward, loving the spluttering sounds she makes. I pull back, and without giving her chance to breathe, I push my hips forward again.

Fuck, she looks incredible on her knees, desperate for my cock. "So god damn desperate for a taste of it, aren't you, Sky?"

"Mmm."

I work my hips back and forth, ramming myself down her little throat. My balls tingle and my spine straightens.

"Fuck, yeah. You're a good girl, Sky. Taking all my cock, for the first time, baby." I pull back. "Such a good fucking girl." I plunge forward again. "Choke on my cock, baby." I thrust in and out, my hips working faster. "Fucking. Choke. On. It!" I roar, as my cum floods her mouth, spilling down her chin and onto her chest. My chest heaves up and down, and I gently pull my cock from her mouth. Never in my fucking life have I felt anything close to that.

As I come down from my orgasm, my chest still heaving, I watch in fascination as Sky gently laps around my cock. I make to put my foot on the floor, but Sky shakes her head. "I'm cleaning you up, Bren." Her eyes implore me, and my cock twitches once again. Like the greedy, selfish bastard I am, I nod at her to finish the job.

I caress her hair with affection as she licks my cock and balls clean. "You need to do that every time you suck my cock, understand?" I'm a bastard, but my lips quirk at the excitement in her eyes. Greedy girl.

I nod toward the bed. "Get on the bed, baby. I'm gonna make you feel good."

SKY

Jumping to my feet before Bren can change his mind, I crawl onto the bed, resting my head on the pillow and my hair splayed out. I watch with a pang of nervousness as Bren climbs on the bed. He ducks his head between my thighs and kisses them lovingly. Bren's palms spread out over them, caressing up and down.

His warm hands grip my thighs ever so slightly, as if desperation is trying to take over but he's forcing himself to go slow, to savor every second, every kiss and caress. His bristled jawline leaves a trail of goosebumps over my skin all the way to my nipples.

He slaps the side of my thigh. "Open." His voice is raspy. I do as I'm told in an instant, spreading wide for him as he maneuvers and settles in between my legs.

Bren drags his thick tongue up from the inside of my thigh to the crease of my groin before rubbing the scruff of his face into my pussy.

He blows on my clit, causing me to gasp, "Br-Bren."

"Shh, it's okay, baby. I'm going to make my girl feel good." His words leave my lips on a stuttered exhale.

Then he moves his mouth toward my pussy hole, his hands painfully gripping both sides of my legs, a sharp pinch of his grip adding to my heightened need for release.

He plunges his tongue forward, dragging it from my hole all the way up to my clit. My hand moves to his head, desperate to keep him in place and revel in the feelings he's bringing out of me.

He flicks his tongue over the needy bundle of nerves, making me dig my heels deeper into the mattress. He twists it, laps and sucks. Becoming frantic as I start to shamelessly ride his face, my hips rise off the bed, his grip tightening on my legs.

"You like me tongue fucking your little pussy?"

I throw my head back on his filthy words.

Bren slaps my thigh hard. "Answer me!" His breath hisses over my pussy.

"Y-yes. I love it, Bren," I pant.

"Mmm, my girl tastes so fucking good." He laps at my clit, pressing his face even farther into me, making me feel like he's inside me, eating away. The intense pressure builds, and I grip his head in place, bucking against him brazenly.

"Brennn, I'm…" I scream my orgasm out. Never having felt something so amazing, so intense in my entire life.

My chest heaves up and down, Bren lazily licks me as if savoring every mouthful of my essence. "Mmmm," he mumbles to himself.

My voice is as soft as a whisper, "Bren, I need your cock, now, please." His handsome face rises from between my thighs, his eyes lock with mine. Holding me in place.

He swallows harshly. "We do this"—he looks down

toward my pussy—"ain't no going back." I narrow my eyes in confusion. "You're mine," he clarifies.

My heart races wildly with a skip. It's everything I ever wanted. Everything I could ever dream of. A man.

A man like him.

My teeth catch between my bottom lip to stifle my jubilant smile. "Forever?"

He rises to his knees, his cock standing tall and proud, already oozing pre-cum. His voice is gruff. "Forever, baby."

"Yes, please," I respond quickly, before he changes his mind.

He chuckles slightly, then leans over me, resting his forearms on either side of my head. His blue eyes bore into mine before he plunges his tongue into my mouth. I move my hand to the scruff of his jaw, keeping him in place. Loving the feel of him.

I can feel his hand going between my legs and I open wider for him. He grasps his cock and rubs it up and down my pussy teasingly. A groan escapes him, and I revel in the knowledge of how I affect him.

Pulling my lips away from him, I beg, "More, please."

Bren pushes inside ever so slightly, his abs tightening in restraint. I wiggle in encouragement, and he pushes farther inside, making me wince slightly.

"Fuck, baby girl, so god damn small." He kisses my lips affectionately and I push my heels against his ass to thrust him deeper. He lifts his eyes to mine and quirks his brow.

"Please." I lick my lips.

"Fuck." He sounds annoyed, but he ravages my mouth with his and rams himself forward, causing me to moan at the sharp pain deep inside me. He releases my lips and his mouth drops open in silent awe, his eyes heavy with desire. "Fuckin, Jesus."

Bren holds still above me for a moment and then tilts his head to the side before swallowing forcefully. "So fuckin tight, baby, I need to cum inside you already."

"Oh god," I moan like an experienced whore. "Please. I want you to. I want to feel your cum in me."

"Jesus." He rubs a hand over his face and slowly sits back on his knees, pulling me with him to ensure we stay united. "I need to see my cock fucking your tight hole, baby."

He leans back on his heels for a better view of where we're connected, lazily running his hand down my stomach and over my clit. His eyes are fixed on my pussy being stretched by his cock as he slowly moves in and out. The feeling of being full consumes me completely. He flicks his gaze back to my eyes, then quickly diverts to where my hands are caressing my tits, rolling my budded nipples between my fingers, the heat of his stare eliciting a moan from my lips.

"Fuck," he mumbles with a growl. "Fuck." His movements become rushed, slamming into me. "Fuck, baby. You feel so damn good. This is my little pussy, understand me? Mine!" he growls the words out.

Slamming into me over and over. "Say." *Slam.* "It's." *Slam.* "Mine!" *Slam.*

"Ahh, it's yours, Bren, all yours," I repeat the words desperately.

He quickly drops to his forearms, his face hovering over mine, before he takes my lips in an all-consuming motion, his tongue sweeps in and I feel like he's going to swallow me whole. Bren pulls back slightly to repeat his words to me, "Mine." His eyes search mine for confirmation, and I give him a gentle nod of reassurance.

A rumble escapes him as he pushes inside me once again, harder this time, as if making a point, a statement of ownership. He grips my thigh tighter. "Fucking come, Sky." And like the good submissive I am, I detonate on command. A thousand tingles explode inside me, a gush of wetness floods my core as I arch my back and thrust into him, his cock hitting that perfect spot over and over, Bren completely knowing exactly what he's doing to me. My pussy tightens around him even more, until I feel him expand inside me and finally a burst, his movements stutter and a loud groan fills my ears, my body milking him. I reach forward and pull his mouth into a searing kiss, swallowing his moans.

Bren slows down until he completely stops, pulls his mouth away from mine, and our eyes lock. A mixture of awe and confusion, his eyes narrowing slightly before quickly disguising it. "Mine," he rumbles, his breath whispering over my lips.

"Forever?" I query, nibbling on my bottom lip.

His body tenses and my heart dips at the thought of him not wanting me. I look away from him solemnly. Bren takes my chin between his fingers, bringing my eyes back up to his. "Forever, Sky."

I nod at his words and smile coyly.

Slowly, he eases out of me, causing me to wince. Bren tilts his head down to look between us. A small, satisfied smirk spreads across his face. He rolls onto his back and tugs me with him. "Come 'ere, baby." I rest my head on his chest, already enjoying his thick fingers stroking delicately through my hair. Conscious of the wetness between my legs, I shuffle on his thigh slightly with a disgruntled moan. "Shh, baby. It's just my mark. Close your eyes and go to sleep like a good girl."

I trace my fingers over Bren's tattooed chest, my movements becoming slower as his fingers massage my head and my eyes become heavy.

Eventually, I begin to drift to sleep with Bren's comforting words echoing in my mind, *Forever*.

CHAPTER 18

Bren

I slept so fucking good last night. *Incredible.*

I stretch my arms over my head and glance down at my girl still laying on my chest. Pride fills me. She belongs to me. I own her tight little body, and mind too; I can feel it. Hell, I've never wanted any woman in my life, but I know with every fiber of my being that I want this one. When I told Sky forever, I meant every damn word.

My eyes lock on to the pink stain on my rock-hard cock, and I can't help but grin to myself. Definitely fucking mine.

I gently move Sky off my chest and decide to shower before making her breakfast. My eyes fixate onto the beautiful blonde in my bed, exactly where she needs to be. There's pink stains around her open legs and I revel in it. There's no denying she belongs to me.

I push my hand over my short, cropped hair as the water flows over me. Hearing the door to the shower push open, I peek over my shoulder, then glance down at my girl. She's smiling brightly and it's fucking infectious. I mirror her expression. "Morning, baby."

"Morning, Bren."

"You come in here to get clean, baby girl?" I flick my eyes down to her exposed pussy and move aside for her to get in, my broad shoulders filling the space.

She nibbles her bottom lip and nods. "You want me to clean you up?" I ask with a tilt of my brow.

"Yes, please, Bren." Her soft voice goes straight to my cock, causing it to jump.

"Good girl, lift your leg onto the seat, baby."

She does as I ask in an instant, giving me the perfect view of her swollen pussy lips coated in my essence and the evidence of her innocence. I lower myself to my knees without breaking eye contact with her. Taking hold of her hips, I use my tongue to clean her. She gasps and holds my head in place.

If my girl thought she could wash away our cum, she was wrong. You can't wash away the most intimate and passionate night of your life with soap as though it's something dirty to flush down the drain. Fuck that, my girl needs taking care of in a way that shows her I respect her and what happened between us. I show her with my tongue what she means to me, what she gave me.

The copper taste on my tongue doesn't dispel my need for her, it fuels it. Eager for more, I shove my face into her pussy and openly eat her out. Her fingernails grip my short hair and dig into my scalp, but I don't fucking flinch.

Her hips begin to move quicker as I flick my tongue over her little bundle of nerves and suck. I look up and watch my girl erupt around me. "Oh god, Bren."

I grin from ear to ear as she comes down from her orgasm. "I need…" Her chest rises and falls.

I kiss the inside of her legs, my palms caressing. "What do you need, baby?" I glare up at her, willing her to say the words.

"I need you," she pants out.

Before she has time to process what's happening, I'm up on my feet and lifting her by one of her ass cheeks, using my other hand to plunge my cock into that tight pussy of mine. Once seated fully inside her, I put my free hand on the wall for balance and go to fucking town on my girl. I'm fully aware of my orgasm fast approaching so I grind my pelvis into Sky and hit her in that sweet spot with my cock. Her pussy spasms around me, wetness coats my cock, and I roar my release into her. "Forever," I whisper in her ear as I place her gently on the tiled floor. "Forever," she whispers back, making me smile against her hair. I breathe her in, the scent yet another reminder of the fact that she's mine.

And nobody can take her from me.

Forever.

CHAPTER 19

Sky

After washing ourselves in the shower, Bren ordered us breakfast. I told him we needed actual food for me to cook and he grinned back at me, telling me he liked to look after me. Once I explained how much I enjoy cooking, his face softened and he told me to make a shopping list. Then said he would have the food delivered for me later today.

I stare out of the SUV window again as the buildings and vehicles become one. I've never been to a city before, and I'm buzzing with both nervousness and excitement. As if hearing my thoughts, Bren reaches across the center console and takes my hand in his. He brings my hand to his lips. "You're going to be fine, baby. You trust me, right?" His irises sparkle like sapphires, the corner of his eyes crinkle with his smirk as he waits for me to reply. "Baby?" he prompts again.

"Yes, I trust you."

Bren's shoulders relax, and I feel a pang of guilt that I hadn't noticed how on edge my nervousness makes him.

"I've just never seen anything like this…" I gesture toward the window. "I don't think I have anyway." My voice is soft.

"You remember something?" Bren quizzes.

I exhale in annoyance with myself. "No. I wish I did."

He kisses the tips of my fingers, and my heart warms at the contact between us.

Bren slowly parks and I peer up at the building from out of the window. "Club 11."

"That's right, baby. I've got a meeting, then we can do whatever you want today, okay?"

I smile up at Bren, in awe of the beautiful man beside me. "Come on, let's go."

He gets out of the SUV and rounds the front to open the door for me. Holding his hand out, I place my small one in his. His grip tightens on mine as he stands in front of me and nods at the guy securing the door.

BREN

The club is quiet, and that's why I chose to meet Marianne's father here. Out in the open, I can get the recorded evidence I need. Marcus Flemming, Chief of Police, meets with the Don of a Mafia syndicate on a regular basis—stupid, stupid man.

I exhale my cigar smoke and ignore the round, pompous prick as he approaches the table with a couple of his pigs trailing behind. Corrupt, the lot of them. I sneer in disgust. Stubbing out my cigar on the table, I scan up to the blacked-out window overlooking the club. Knowing my girl is up there watching me, I smirk to myself, loving her close to me, even in my place of business.

A throat clears, pulling me from my daze. "O'Connell." I look lazily across to the small, fat shit that is almost eye level with me. Only, I'm sitting in one of the booths and he shuffles, straightening his back to try and appear taller. I throw my head back on a patronizing laugh.

"Flemming," I spit his surname out with vitriol. Nodding toward the chair opposite, he pulls out the seat and sits. Both his pigs turn their backs, standing stoically still beside him but looking out at the club.

A handful of seedy men throw money at the dancers on the stage, but my eyes barely register them. Knowing my club is in perfect control, I relax my position with my arms lazily splayed out along the back of the booth.

"To what do I owe this pleasure?" I smirk sarcastically, causing him to shuffle with unease.

"Listen here, O'Connell. I've had enough of this bullshit of yours. You don't seem to understand the reach I have."

I roll my eyes at him mockingly, raising an eyebrow with a threat back, "The reach *you* have?"

His throat bobs, understanding his error before he continues, "You know as well as I do that I have shit on you." I swirl my glass nonchalantly to rile him. "You think I don't know your uncle disappeared? Just vanished off the face of the earth?"

I sit forward threateningly, drilling my eyes into his, causing him to fidget. "I suggest you leave it."

He smiles, knowing he's riled me. "And I suggest you start listening to me," he snipes back.

I scan his face, a smug expression I'm dying to cut to fucking shreds covers it.

"What exactly are you suggesting, pig?" I throw the slur out there for shits and giggles and to piss the old cunt off.

His eyes light up. Greedy, fat fucker. "A union. A partnership. You marry my daughter and we can own this city." He grins to himself manically.

I breathe out deeply, this old fucking chestnut. My temples pulsate with barely restrained rage. "I know a lot of shit about you all, O'Connell. You do this, we're tied.

Forever." His words cause me to jolt. *Forever.* He shouldn't be uttering those words. They belong in one place only and that's my baby girl's mouth... when I fuck her into oblivion.

My mind works over his words. *We're tied. Forever.* So, he keeps his mouth shut, knowing he'll take us all down. Makes good business sense, but not a hope in hell am I prepared to do what he wants. Not before meeting Sky and sure as hell not now.

"Marianne tells me you've been intimate." I wince at his choice of wording. Intimate my ass, my cock unloaded in a double-gloved condom multiple times, not exactly intimate. Nope, definitely not intimate when I fucked another woman in front of her to make a point of how not intimate we are.

"Marianne is intimate with half of New fucking Jersey. What's your point, old man?" This gets the old cunt pissed. His chest heaves and his fat fists ball. "Do not speak badly of my daughter, O'Connell. You won't like the consequences."

In the blink of an eye, I fly across the table and grip his fat neck with my hand, dragging him toward me, his stubby legs flailing behind him. His men turn around and immediately pull their guns on me. My men come from nowhere and pull their guns on them just as quick. They're surrounded, and I laugh menacingly at the old bastard who thought he could threaten me—a Mafia Don—and get away with it.

His face turns red and pulsates, struggling for air.

I speak low and deadly, "Listen here, old man, I don't give a fuck what you think you have on me. But I'm warning you, if you ever threaten me again, I'll bankrupt your precious daughter and your snooty bitch of a wife, but not before I slaughter you like the pig you are in front of their spoiled asses." I ease up on my hold, slowly releasing him. "Now, get the fuck out of my club. Do what I pay you to do and keep that fat mouth of yours shut before I stick your pigs' cocks down it." I glance to the left and right so they know exactly who I'm referring to.

He slumps back in his seat and adjusts his tie, trying to feign confidence.

I stare at him unabashedly, cocking my lip at the side in a taunting way. I dare him to disrespect me again. Like the good lap dog that he is, his eyes flick away from mine. *Coward.*

He stands with a wobble. "Remember this, Bren. I know things." He licks his lips and stands taller before turning and walking away. His words don't go with him though, and I can't help but feel a thread of doubt niggling at me, at just how much the bastard knows, his words causing me to exhale.

What I need is something to take my mind off this shit and that old bastard. My eyes catch on to the blacked-out windows once again.

CHAPTER 20

Sky

A tingling sensation skitters across my shoulders and I dart my eyes up from the floor below me, latching onto Bren's eyes reflecting through the window.

His hand strokes my shoulder and he lowers his head to place gentle kisses up and down my neck. I tilt my head to give him better access as he slides my hair out of the way, sniffing me in the process. My smile widens at the thought of how animalistic this man is. "Miss me, baby?"

"Uh huh," are the only words I can mutter. My breath catches in my throat when his delicate kisses turn to sharp nips of my flesh. Wetness pools between my legs and as if knowing it, Bren glides his hand down the soft fabric of my summer dress.

I grind my hips forward, pressing into his hand.

"Baby," he warns, and I can feel him smile against me. His large palm is splayed out over my stomach in ownership.

"Mmm, my baby tastes so fucking good." He nibbles on my neck.

With his free hand he unzips my dress, causing it to fall to the floor. I'm left standing in chunky sandals, a pale-blue bra, and no panties in sight.

Bren sucks in a breath behind me. "Fuck." He grinds his cock into my ass.

"Open your legs, baby girl."

"Br-Bren, can they see?" I point at the people below in the club.

Bren tugs on my neck with his teeth, causing a sharp sting before he licks away the pain and replaces it with a tender kiss. "No, baby, it's one-way glass. You think I'd let anyone see you?" His eyes lock on mine in the window's reflection, and I know, without a shadow of doubt, he'd never let anyone see me. I shake my head.

"Good girl. Now, let me fuck you." I lean forward and press my hands to the glass, my ass sticking out slightly.

Bren moans behind me while caressing my ass. The telltale sound of his zipper fills the room, and I struggle to keep my legs apart, a desperate need to rub my thighs together for even the slightest bit of relief.

I can feel Bren position the head of his cock at my entrance. He applies pressure to the back of my neck, causing me to bend over more. "I'm going to fuck you while they watch, baby."

My lips part at his dirty words before he rears back and slams into me, almost knocking me off my feet. Bren's grip tightens on my hips as he thrusts forcefully in and out of me.

"Fuck, yeah." He grunts, making me clench around him.

My pussy muscles pulling him in, and the sound of wetness fills the room. The smell of sex permeates the air.

Glancing down at the room below, I lick my lips at the thought of everyone watching us, my mouth drops open on a moan. I move one of my hands off the glass and begin to circle my clit.

"Fuck yeah, good girl. Play with that little clit, baby." My hand moves down to where we're connected, causing Bren to stutter in his thrusts. My eyes draw up to the glass, catching his reflection, and bask in his need for me, utter desire marring his face. His pupils are dilated, his muscles flexed, and his mouth fallen open.

"Play, baby. Show them what we've got."

I open my legs wider to give the guests below a full view. The bottom of my palm rubs my clit while my fingers stroke over our connecting bodies.

He practically spits, "Hit it. Hit that pussy." I do as he commands and smack my pussy. Bolts of pleasure course through me, a ripple effect taking place deep inside me.

"Ohhh, ahhh…" I scream out in ecstasy as Bren slams into me through my orgasm and until I feel him pulsate inside me. His release warms me and coats my fingers as I continue to rub at our linked bodies.

"Fuckkkk!" he roars. "Holy fuck."

Bren stumbles forward, slamming me into the glass. His heavy body leaning on my back, pressing me against the window.

"Fuck, you're incredible," he whispers against my ear.

"Forever?" I turn my head toward him. His fingers grasp my chin, and his lips meet mine in a gentle all-consuming kiss.

"Forever." He gives me a peck on the lips, and I smile at him, and he chooses this moment to pull out.

Cum drips down my leg, causing Bren to chuckle.

"Mmm, rub it in, baby." His reflected eyes glimmer in challenge and I smile back at him. Of course I bend down and rub it into my thighs and legs, making a show for him. I love the thought of this man covering me with everything he can give. Consuming me.

His eyes turn heavy as he watches me. But the shrill noise of his phone vibrating on his desk cuts through the air. "Get dressed." He turns, zipping his trousers up on his way over to his desk.

BREN

"What?" I bark into my phone, annoyed at the interruption, disturbing the moment I was having with my girl. I lean against my desk and watch Sky pull on her clothes.

"So sorry to disturb what must be a very important meeting with your girl, Bren. Excuse me for thinking you would be working and not fucking while I'm trying to do every fucking thing by myself here." Oscar's sarcastic tone doesn't rile me like it normally would. Before I give myself time to analyze the reason behind that, I push it aside, already knowing the answer is right before my eyes wearing an innocent yellow, modest sundress, walking toward me. I point at the chair beside my desk, and she sits in it without needing further instruction. God, I love her innocence and obedience, she was made for me. I want to ruin her in the best way possible, then care for her even more, show her she's my fucking world and nothing can touch us.

Sky clasps her palms together in a sweet gesture, resting them in her lap.

"Are you even fucking listening to me?" Oscar snaps.

"Yeah," I grunt, but find myself gazing into my girl's eyes, as if reading my thoughts of her innocence, she swallows deeply, making me want to fuck that pretty throat of hers. My cock twitches at the thought, as if it didn't just unload in her tight little cunt.

"Then what the fuck did I say?" He exhales loudly, totally pissed off.

"Say it again," I mumble back to him. I stand straighter and move behind Sky. I drape her hair over her shoulder and lean over to kiss down the side of her neck, causing her to break out in goosebumps. With my free hand, I graze up the column of her throat and she tips her head back so she's making eye contact with me. *Fuck, that's hot.* I take her neck gently in the palm of my hand and move up and down her throat as if I was jerking my cock.

"Just meet at the fucking warehouse at three. Leave your toy at home." He hangs up, not giving me a chance to react to him referring to my girl as a toy. *Little prick.*

"Is everything okay?" Sky's breathy voice breaks the silence.

"Yeah, baby. You wanna go home or stay with one of the girls? I got a meeting to go to."

"Can I go home? I want to make you dinner." My eyebrow quirks up at her comment. My girl enjoys playing homemaker, and fuck me, I like the thought too.

"What shall I make?" She watches me as I gather some paperwork from my desk.

I stop in my tracks thinking of my favorite meal. "Can you do lasagna?"

"Yes."

I break out in a grin. I'm so fucking lucky.

CHAPTER 21

Bren

"So we're good to go this Saturday?" I clarify.

"Yes, he'll be there. We don't want any trouble." Oscar glares over toward Cal, who looks like shit.

"Maybe you should stay home?" Finn suggests.

Cal's head snaps up, glaring venom at Finn. "Like fuck I will!"

Finn's lip curls up at the side, indicating he knew full fucking well Cal wouldn't be anywhere but beside Lily.

"I'll be with her at the bar," I inform him. He nods solemnly, knowing he doesn't have a choice. His entire demeanor is defeated, and I feel a small pang of guilt toward my brother before I quickly push it away. There's no room for those feelings in the Mafia. None, none whatsoever.

I shut down all thoughts and do what I've been taught to do.

Lead.

"Get Paul and the guys in here, lets discuss backup strategies."

Con stands and opens the door, leading Paul—one of our soldiers—and a few of our men inside, we spend the next hour going over where we want them located at the event, and if something should go wrong, what we expect of them.

Cal's phone vibrates on the table. He glances at it with a heavy sigh before turning his head and choosing to ignore it. We all know, without him even having to voice it, that the call can only be from Reece.

The phone buzzes again. Yeah, the kid is relentless, like a dog with a fucking bone.

Cal switches the phone to silent before slumping back in his chair. He needs to pull his sorry ass together before Saturday. We need it to run fucking smoothly and not become a shit show.

Oscar's phone rings beside him, and I throw my pen down on the floor plan in annoyance. Desperate to get this shit over with so I can get home to my girl. "It's Reece." He rolls his eyes in Cal's direction.

Oscar presses the accept button. "What can I do for you, Reece?" his voice drawls with boredom. He glares at Cal. "Your son wants to speak with you." He lays the phone on the table.

"Dad?" Cal sits forward at the sound of Reece's panicked voice.

"What's wrong? What's happened?" Cal's body tenses and we all lean into the table, eager to hear what Reece is about to drop on us.

"Where the fuck is your trimmer?"

Cal's eyebrows knit together in confusion. "Wh-what?" He glances around the table at us all, as if looking for help in deciphering Reece's shit.

"Your trimmer. Where the hell is it?"

"Trimmer?" Cal's voice is filled with confusion.

"Yeah, Jesus. Trimmer, you know, to trim your pubes. I need to do some manscaping and I need your trimmer to do it." Reece's tone is clipped and full of annoyance at the lack of understanding from his father. "Is it in your room? Which drawer?"

As if suddenly dawning on him what Reece is asking, Cal's face morphs into panic. "Do not go in my fucking drawer, Reece. Do you hear me? Reece?" The kid has gone radio silent. I glance around at my brothers. Con is wearing a shit-eating grin, Finn has his usual smug smirk plastered on his cocky-ass face, and even Oscar looks humored.

"Reece, redcars, do you hear me? Redcars!" Cal panics the word out. It's some sort of code word Lily came up with. Apparently, it's meant to stop Reece from doing something in an instant. In all honesty, I've yet to see it work.

"Oh, my fucking god. You use this shit on my mom?" Reece's voice fills the room, utter disgust oozing from it.

"Oh, fuck," Cal mumbles to himself.

"What's he use on your mom, Reece?" Finn asks in mockery.

Cal's eyes dart to his in venom, then he flies across the table to no doubt take all his built-up aggression out on his younger brother.

I decide to use this moment to shove my chair back, leaving the kids to play. "I'm out. Call me tomorrow."

Oscar's face falters, his head on a swivel, watching me gather my shit. "Wh-what? We've not finished. You never leave early!"

"I know. Nothing you guys can't sort. Now, I'm off to play with my toy." I wink sarcastically at my brother, and he narrows his eyes in a grimace, knowing full well I'm leaving him in the shit for that comment earlier

"Oh, and Oscar?"

He turns his head to face me.

"I'll cut off your cock if you ever refer to her as that again." I smile maniacally at him, and he gulps in understanding before giving me a firm nod.

CHAPTER 22

Sky

I spent the afternoon tidying the apartment and preparing the meal for Bren coming home from work. I love it. It's everything I ever wanted and more. I showered and pulled on one of Bren's used shirts, loving the scent of him on me. My thoughts ever consumed with Bren, his incredible body, his strength, and power.

The dominance behind him but also the caring side of him that he appears to only show me. He's everything every woman at the compound spoke about, and I never truly realized it existed until now.

Until him.

The door clicks open and my breath stills in my throat. My broad-shouldered, tower of a man is standing at the doorway, watching me with heavy eyes. My heart flutters when he licks his lips. His gaze travels slowly from the tips of my toes, to the hem of his shirt, and up to my face, causing heat to travel up my neck and into my cheeks. He fixates on me as much as I do him.

The oven timer buzzes, causing me to startle and Bren to chuckle at my reaction.

I turn on bare feet, making my way over to the oven. "I'll go shower, baby. Be out in five."

Watching Bren eat the lasagna I made feels like an accomplishment. He eats so fast and so much, I'm not sure how he doesn't have cramps. He even had second helpings and said it's as good as his ma's. I swelled with pride at that, knowing how much Bren's mother means to him.

After dinner, I give him a beer and tell him to go watch football on the couch while I clear the table. He eyes me skeptically before heaving himself out of his chair and falling on to the couch with a hand behind his head, choosing to watch both the game and me.

When I finish drying the last of the dishes, I make my way over to Bren. "Do you want anything else?" I ask standing in front of him with my hands clasped together.

Bren licks his lips slowly; the movement makes me squeeze my legs together at the memory of him filling me so well in his office today. The memory of all the dancers who perform for men, men like my Bren.

But he doesn't want them, he wants me.

An excitable tremor works through my body as Bren tugs on my shirt, pulling me closer.

"I want you to sit on my face, baby. Let me finish my

meal with the taste of your pussy on my tongue." His dirty words cause my nipples to pebble and excitement to fill me.

"Lose the shirt."

I pull the shirt over my head and stand before Bren completely naked. His eyes trail up and down my body. "I like you not wearing panties. Keep it that way." He smirks up at me, then tosses his own shirt off and positions himself before holding out a hand for me to take. I admire his broad, muscular chest covered in a variety of tattoos. My mouth waters to taste his skin.

His huge hand covers mine, the roughness of his against my smooth one is a perfect symbol of the contrast of the two of us. He's rough, strong, and dominant. I'm soft, small, and compliant.

He molds my body into a straddling position across his chest. "Gonna need ya to straddle my head and put your pussy in my mouth, baby."

My eyes lock onto his, and I stroke the crinkles beside his eyes. My fingers work down his face ever so slowly, exploring along his jawline. Bren swallows deeply, his eyes never leaving mine. "Baby." His voice is choked. "Gonna throw ya down and fuck ya if you don't climb on my face in a minute."

I nod in understanding and slowly rise onto my knees, unsure about what I'm doing. As if sensing my uncertainty, Bren pulls me into position, my pussy covering his mouth, then he explores me with his tongue.

I lean forward and grip the arm of the couch as I move backward and forward over Bren's face. The wet flick of his thick tongue causes me to clench my pussy. I can hear him fumbling with his jeans, and then I feel the swift movement of him jerking his cock with one hand while the other grips my ass, helping me ride his face.

Tingles begin to build inside me with each flick of his tongue. "More, Bren," I beg. He nuzzles his face from side to side, eating me like a man possessed.

The sloshing of wetness can be heard with each movement of my body. I revel in this man fucking my pussy with his tongue. I grind down on his face and throw my head back when I hear him mumble vibrations of approval.

I smother the "fuck" that falls from his tongue when my orgasm reaches its peak.

"Breeennnn," I scream, my throat raw.

My chest heaves up and down, my body falling lax above him. But Bren lifts me by my ass and slams me down on his cock without giving me a warning. He bucks up into me roughly, shamelessly, chasing his own orgasm. I squeeze his cock inside me as he continuously hits deeper and deeper with each thrust.

"Beg. Beg for my cum." He grits his teeth.

I tug at my breasts and squeeze them together. "Bren. Bren, please."

He sits forward and takes my nipple in his mouth, tugging at it before moving to the other one. I grip his head closer to me, forcing his mouth against my breast. From below, he rams into me faster and faster.

"Please, I want you to cum in me, Bren," I beg desperately.

He roars his release and the sensations of his cock pulsating inside me, sending me into my own orgasm. He pumps and pumps until he drops back on the couch, pulling me with him, cradling me to his chest. His cock is still inside me and his cum seeping between us.

Bren's chest heaves up and down, one large hand on my ass and the other gently stroking through my hair.

"Forever," I mumble against his chest.

"Forever, baby." He smiles at me.

CHAPTER 23

Sky

I can hear hushed voices coming from the living area, so I climb out of bed, finding comfort in the soft feel of the carpet.

Picking up one of Bren's shirts from off the floor, I make my way toward the door, but then I second guess myself when I hear Bren's brothers. Remembering that Bren doesn't like me around his brothers without clothes on, I decide to tug on some leggings to go with the shirt.

Opening the door, a rush of nostalgia hits me at the sound of a familiar voice.

My stomach somersaults and my mind rushes with emotions as I gaze from brother to brother before my eyes lock on to Samuel. "Sa-Samuel. What are you doing here?"

His head whips back as if he's been struck, his messy dark hair is longer than the standard soldier cut.

Before I can say another word, Bren and each of his brothers pull their weapons on Samuel. I gasp in shock. They think he's the enemy? *No. Please no.* I tug on my hair in frustration.

"Stop. Please stop." I rush toward Samuel but arms pull me back. Oscar, the only one without a weapon. I glance up at him with pleading eyes. "Please, stop them, Oscar."

They're shouting at him and swearing, but they're not letting him speak.

"Please, stop! He hasn't done anything wrong."

"You're one of them, aren't you?" Finn spits at Samuel's feet. Samuel's face morphs into panic.

"I'm going to fucking slaughter you, you fucking traitor," Bren seethes.

"No fucking way. He's mine." Finn stalks toward him with a knife gleaming in his hand. I don't even know where it came from.

I tremble against Oscar, and he pushes me away from him slightly, not liking me too close. I dart my gaze to his, pleading with my eyes. Oscar must see the panic in me because, although he doesn't let me go, his restraint on me loosens, giving me the confidence to say the only thing that might make them listen. Make them see sense.

My voice is loud and firm. "Hail. Call me your master, you're my servant. I will redeem you of your penance and sins, claiming your innocence once again. Heel, await my command."

At the familiar words, Samuel drops to his knees, bowing his head and holding out his hands, clasped together.

A wave of sickness washes over me. This was me. This was how I presented myself on a daily basis to my master.

Hoping and praying I didn't have sins that needed repenting. I squeeze my eyes closed, wishing away the images flashing before me.

"Jesus," Finn spits the words out like vitriol.

"What the fuck, man?" Con asks, his eyes darting from me to Bren, then once again to Samuel.

But I squeeze my eyes shut again. Not paying attention to them. Trying to block out the memories.

"Baby? Baby, open your eyes for me." Bren gently coos while rubbing his hand gently up and down my arm.

I react to him almost straight away, like a good submissive. My breathing begins to settle, and Bren finally asks, "How do you know Sam?"

"H-he's Sebastian's brother. He trained as a soldier at the compound."

Bren nods at my words. His jaw tenses a little, and without looking back at his brothers he tells them, "Take him to the basement." My eyes shoot open to Bren's concerned blues.

"Bren. You're not to hurt him." I grab his hand, begging. "Please, Bren, promise me you won't hurt him. He didn't do anything wrong, please."

Bren's face softens. "I promise I won't hurt him." I nod at him, and he gently guides me over toward the couch.

"Get one of the girls to sit with her," he tells Oscar, before turning away and walking out of the door, not sparing me another glance.

BREN

When I open the basement door, I find Finn kicking the shit out of Sam. He's crouched over on the floor, wheezing like a little pussy. I glance at Con, and he tugs Finn back knowingly. Pulling a chair into position, they both work in sync to strap a flaying Sam to the chair. "I haven't touched anyone, I swear," Sam pleads, snot and tears already running down his pathetic face.

I stand in front of him with my arms crossed over my chest, waiting for Oscar to join us.

Finn is bouncing maniacally from foot to foot. My younger brother has some serious issues and loves nothing more than to take his aggression out on others, preferably with a knife, giving him the Monika Finn-Finishing.

"P-please." He tries to plead again, but this time Finn snaps and lunges forward with a right hook I'm proud of. Sam's head snaps back with the force, then droops forward, lolling from side to side.

Behind me, I sense Oscar creeping into the room. The fact the dude can skulk around so quietly has always managed to piss me off. "Can he speak?" Oscar drawls, referring to Sam slumped forward in a semiconscious state.

"Probably not for a while," I quip back.

"Just wake him fucking up. I have shit to do."

"Like what?" Con asks, his face alight with a childish glee. "Is it Indulgence night?" he asks, wriggling his eyebrows up and down.

Oscar sneers at him, his face laced in disgust.

"Fine. I'll leave. I've better things to do anyway." He makes to move, and it snaps me out of my trance.

"Do. Not. Move. Another. Fucking. Step." I punctuate each word. Pissed he's trying to toy with me.

Oscar sighs and drops his shoulders. "Fine, we'll proceed then, shall we?"

"Wake him up," I spit toward Con.

He moves forward with the hose in hand, Cal turns on the tap and Con douses Sam with the ice-cold water. His body instantly jolts awake, his terrified eyes meet mine.

I take a menacing step forward, my knuckles white with tension. "Explain." My tone is baritone, firm, giving no room for untruths.

He swallows hard. "I-I was taken from my foster family. Me and my brother Sebastian. We were told we would be cared for, protected." He gulps in emotion and looks away with a shudder. "They lied."

His words lay heavy in the room.

"Who's they?" Oscar asks, his eyes as calculating as my own.

"O'Connell, Dimitriev, and Garcia, they run the compound."

"Nico Garcia?" Cal steps forward, desperation in his voice. The need for vengeance against the man that hurt his wife is clouding his judgment. He wants an excuse to go to war over it. That's not going to happen. He won't get the reply he so desperately wants.

"No, Nico is in the dark about it. His father thinks he's too soft," Sam pants.

Cal scoffs, then turns on his heel, tugging his hair.

"Did you know Angel? What they did to her?" Finn asks. He stands from the corner of the room, tilting his head from side to side, his eyes boring into Sam, making him swallow uncomfortably.

"No. No, I swear it." He shakes his head, blood streaming from his busted nose. "I swear, man. Please, I'm not like them. I'm not a fucking monster!" he screams at us, the veins on his neck protruding, his voice vibrates around the room, causing everyone to jolt, everyone except me. I don't so much as flinch.

I watch from the corner of my eye as Finn flips his knife over back and forth, back and forth. He's struggling to rein in his demons. Struggling not to tear apart someone that knew more than us. Someone that could have helped us put a stop to this shit before now. Someone we trusted around our families, around our kids, our women. Rage boils inside me, my muscles tighten at the thought.

"Why didn't you tell us when we disposed of Don?" Oscar asks. Sam flinches. He knows what we're capable of, what we've done.

Sam laughs to himself, a condescending chuckle before his face tightens. "I want my brother back. I want him alive! You think they'd let him live if I ratted them out?" He shakes his head solemnly, his split lip trembles. "Doesn't matter now." He stares down at the ground before drawing his eyes back up to meet mine. "He'll be dead for helping with Red Seven."

The realization hits me. His brother no doubt gave up

his own life, sacrificed himself to save my girl. Sam's broken eyes stay fixed on mine, for what, I'm not sure. Sympathy, maybe? He's looking at the wrong man. I turn to leave. "Get the location out of him." I nod at Finn; a smirk encompasses his face.

"You don't deserve her, you know. She deserves to be free," he shouts at me as I leave the room.

The door clicks shut, closing out the sound of his screams. But his words fill my mind, echoing on repeat. *You don't deserve her, you know. She deserves to be free.* I glance down at my phone. The photo of my beautiful, innocent girl splayed out on my bed with only a sheet draped over her delectable body. *Please, Bren, promise me you won't hurt him. He didn't do anything wrong, please.*

Guilt.

Guilt hits me.

The guy didn't do anything wrong, nothing I wouldn't have done myself to protect my brothers. My family. Loyalty is everything. I scrub a hand over my face.

"Fuck!"

I shoot a text off to Cal, telling him to refrain from killing Sam.

CHAPTER 24

Bren

I scan the ballroom again, my gaze zoning in on Nico Garcia and his muscle, he's barely ever left alone. How the fuck are we meant to talk to him when he's surrounded by all his heavies? Who knows if they can be trusted? In our circles, you trust no one, no one outside of your family anyway. I grimace at the thought of not even being able to trust our own uncle. I scrub a hand over my head in frustration.

Just when I'm about to give up all hope, I notice Nico breaks away from the crowd and only one guard follows him toward the bar. Now is our chance.

I whip my head toward Lily, and she nods in understanding. Before Cal can spout some shit to her, we make our way across the ballroom. Grumbles of Cal being held back by my brothers fill my ears, and I can't help but chuckle at how possessive he is of her.

We approach the bar, with me standing next to Nico and Lily on the other side of me, taking one of the stools as her seat.

Without turning his head in acknowledgment, Nico surprises me and begins talking, "Bren, Lily to what do I owe the honor?" I cast my eye aside and check over Lily. She's tensed by the sound of his voice alone and again that little shadow of guilt enters my mind.

Lily shakes off the tension and begins talking, fast, nervously so. "Nico. We have some information for you." Her chest rises and falls on a shaky breath.

He turns and I step in front of him, stopping him from being able to step toward her. His eyes narrow and he chuckles sarcastically. "Tell your guard dog to stand down, Lily." My fists tighten and my chest swells in anger. The piece of shit thinks he can dismiss me? I go toe to toe with him, but I'll give the smooth prick his due; he doesn't bat an eye. When neither of us looks like they're going to back down, he exhales and turns again toward the bar. He shakes his head slightly, and I clock about a dozen of his men take a noticeable step back at his action. I lick my lips at the realization we are well and truly outnumbered. I need to rein my temper in and keep control of Cal.

"What information?" he sighs the words out low and looks down at the bar counter as if bored. Presumably to make it appear like there's nothing happening around us. That he isn't discussing secret information with another Mafia family, his ex-fiancée. The enemies.

"It's about Raul, Nico." Nico tenses on the name of his older brother.

"What about him?" he snipes the words out on a

growl, giving away his obvious contempt toward his brother.

"Do you know anything about the compound near Fort Derne just outside of Mexico City?"

Nico's eyebrows knit together, deep in thought. "We don't own a compound near Fort Derne. What fucking compound are you talking about?" he clips the words out with irritation.

Lily's small hand pushes at my back, and I move aside for her to hand over the document.

She refuses to meet Nico's dark eyes, instead choosing to look down at her feet. "Here," she mumbles, handing over the brown envelope containing a map of the compound, photographic evidence of Nico's family's involvement, along with a memory card with all the information he could possibly need to take down his family's trafficking empire.

"What is this?" he asks, glaring at her, obviously pissed she won't even look at him.

She swallows hard, gets up from her stool, and turns to walk away from him.

"Abigail," he spits her name out like venom, the use of her real name stops her in her tracks.

She turns her head slightly to the side to answer him, "Human trafficking, Nico. It's a human trafficking compound."

Nico's face drains of color. He opens his mouth, no doubt to argue, but no words come out. It's at that moment I truly realize he knows nothing about his family's involvement in this. Sam was right, he is innocent.

Before he can say another word, a small blonde-haired woman walks up beside me. She's petite, pale-skinned, with a flurry of freckles over her nose, and big blue eyes.

She looks a complete contrast to Nico, who is olive-skinned with black hair brushed back, the epitome of Cartel. "Nicolas, I've been looking for you." Her soft voice fills the silence.

Lily's eyes dart to Nico, then down to the small woman, who doesn't look much older than Sky. Her eyes dilate briefly before she quickly darts her gaze away. She turns on her heels to leave, but Nico moves forward within reach of Lily. He touches her arm, but her stiffening body makes him drop his hold in an instant.

His desperate voice stops her in her tracks. "Pl-please, Abigail. Is Jacob okay?" His voice comes out slightly stuttered, and for a moment, I don't think Lily's going to give him an answer, but then I see her shoulders slacken and she responds softly over her shoulder, "Reece is fine, Nico. He's where he should be. Where he was always meant to be, with his family." Nico jolts at her words, and I watch Lily walk back to the table where Cal is being blockaded by our brothers. I watch him examine her like she's gone to fucking war. The dumb shit brushes hair from her eyes and strokes her face, causing me to internally roll my eyes at his performance.

I watch Nico's body language closely. I scan his body and notice a wedding ring on his finger, then dart my eyes over to the blonde who also has a ring on her finger. As if sensing me, Nico's body coils tight. "Get your eyes off my fucking wife." He takes a step toward me and once again we're toe to toe.

Once again, tension fills the air.

His wife senses it and swallows. "Nicolas, shall we go back to the table?" He seems to soften at the use of his full name.

But before Nico can turn on his heel, Cal comes rushing

over and literally throws himself onto him, sending them both flying into the bar. They scuffle, and I grab Cal under his arm pits, pulling him away.

Nico stumbles to an upright position. Wiping blood from his lips, he puts his hands up to stop his guards descending on us.

"Leave." His firm voice is aimed at me, and I nod in agreement, thankful he's going to let this go and we get to leave without issue.

Without a fucking war.

Cal's chest is heaving up and down in fury. "Stay the fuck away from my family, Nico. You hear me."

He wrestles against me. "Calm the fuck down before you get us all killed," I spit in his ear. "Think of Lily and the kids, Cal." He relaxes against me at the mention of Lily and the kids.

I loosen my hold on him, and he straightens his suit jacket before his eyes roam maniacally around the room before landing on the small blonde fussing over Nico. Cal laughs sarcastically while staring straight at them and in true fashion, Cal can't resist another fucking jab.

"Hope you're not pregnant with that monster's baby, sweetheart. He enjoys knocking pregnant woman around, don't you, Nico? Killing off unborn babies is your thing, isn't it?" he sneers.

Nico flies past the woman, coming straight for Cal. "I'll slaughter you all!" he yells in fury.

"Stop it. Right now, stop it, both of you," Lily screams, coming between Cal and Nico, who looks like he's barely restraining himself. "We're leaving now, Nico." His eyes meet hers on the use of his name, and for the first time tonight, she doesn't avert her eyes, lifting her chin higher as if making a point.

He stares at her for a moment before giving her a firm nod. Thank fuck for that. My body relaxes slightly as we back out of the room with Con and Finn walking behind a reluctant Cal.

Jesus, thank God that's over with. I exhale deeply.

The last thing I need is another fucking problem. I sure as shit have enough of my own brewing.

CHAPTER 25

Bren

I wake to a wet tongue lapping at my swollen cock, my balls being toyed with, and a soft, small palm gently stroking up and down my shaft.

I push my hand through her silky locks, loving the feel of her satin hair against my callous hands.

"Mmm, fuck, baby, that's good. You want my cum inside your little mouth?"

She moans in agreement around my cock, causing vibrations to travel down my shaft. "Fuck, yeah, baby. You're hungry for my cum, aren't you, naughty girl?"

"Mmm," she moans louder and positions herself over my thigh.

"Baby, are you going to fuck my leg while I pump my cum into your greedy mouth?"

My cock slips from her mouth with a pop, and I immediately miss the loss. "Fuck," I spit out in annoyance.

I grip her hair tightly and shove my cock back into her mouth. "Suck it hard, baby. Don't fucking stop again." My hips rise to meet her mouth, not giving her a chance to resist. I tug her head in a push-and-pull motion, the force dragging her sweet cunt back and forth over my leg. I fuck her face while she fucks my leg. My naughty little girl is desperate for a fuck. My balls tingle at the thought, and with Sky's moans around my cock, the sensations overwhelm me. I lift my ass off the bed and hold her head still as I shove my cock as far in that tight little throat as I can, choking my girl until I erupt at the same time her body tightens. Her mouth loosens around my cock with her orgasm hitting her hard. Cum flows from her mouth and runs down her chin. Her blue eyes latch on to mine, both seeping with admiration for one another.

Her body falls lax on top of me, and I chuckle, smoothing the hair from her pretty face.

"Baby, you made a mess." I cock a condescending brow at her. She raises her head from my stomach. "Clean it up." I nod toward my groin, and her mouth breaks into a pleased smile. So fucking submissive. She's incredible. I rest my arm behind my head as my girl goes to town to clean up our mess.

I'm so fucking lucky.

SKY

I fidget in my seat. We're on our way to a meal at Bren's family home, and I'm nervous as hell. I tug at the knee-length hem of my pale-blue summer dress; the one Bren chose for me to wear this morning.

He likes me to dress differently from the other women in the family, the other women outside of our home. Where they wear jeans or shorts, he likes me to wear dresses, more conservative clothes. I'm happy to wear anything he chooses; I just want to satisfy him like he does me.

My mind darts back to this morning, after cleaning him up, he carried me into the shower and washed my body with such care and affection that I felt treasured, special. The love seeped from his eyes as he tenderly washed me, telling me a thousand things all without uttering one single word from his rough lips. His hand trembled ever so slightly as he caressed my arms, stomach, legs, and finally he kneeled at my feet, lifting each foot onto his knee as he washed those too. His blue eyes never left mine, his throat bobbed with invisible emotion, an emotion that only we could see.

Love.

"You good?" His gruff voice fills the car as he side-eyes me. He gazes down at my fidgeting hands and takes one into his own hand, dwarfing mine. Acutely aware of the roughness of his skin, his warmth embraces me, already giving me the comfort I was seeking. He pulls my hand toward his mouth and peppers open kisses to it. I smile up at my handsome man. So strong, cold, and uncaring to the outside world, but here with me, he's everything I need him to be.

More even.

I watch the scenery slide by as we leave the city. The trees and fields remind me of the compound, only greener, more luscious. The road becomes rugged as we come to a standstill at a security gate. Armed men surround the car and scan underneath it. "We're here, baby." He kisses my hand again and his lips turn up at the sides, offering me a comforting smile.

Bren drives the car up the driveway. An expansive, well-kept garden is to my side, a patio area beyond it, leading to a beautiful stone-built house. Ivy creeps up the walls, giving it an old feel, but the house looks cared for and inviting, it looks like a home. A warmth settles in my stomach.

Bren parks the car behind a row of other equally impressive, blackened SUVs and gets out of the car. He walks around to my side and opens the door, unclips my seatbelt, and lifts me from underneath my arms. He slides me down his body between him and the vehicle. His strong, solid form scrubs against my softness. I can feel his erection pressed against my stomach, and I push into him slightly, enjoying his instant reaction toward me. A low groan escapes his lips and makes my tender bud pulsate. "Baby," he whispers against my hair, and goosebumps break out at his husky words. Bren trails his hand up the side of my dress and dips between my legs. He taps his shoe against my own sandals, hinting for me to open my legs wider, I oblige, giving him access to my wet pussy.

His words come out strangled, "Fuck. So wet." He spreads my folds and gentle strokes up and down. I bite down on my lip when he rocks his body into me, obviously trying to ease his own discomfort. "Bre-Bren. I want…"

His hooded eyes meet mine. "What do you want, baby?" He shuffles forward and lowers his mouth, nipping at my earlobe. His hot ragged breath flutters over my cheek.

"I want you to fill me." I tug open his belt and zipper, my fingers fumbling with eagerness. My eyes zone in on the tip of his erection, angry and weeping with desire. I lick my lips.

"Fuck, baby. We gotta be quick."

In a swift movement he has me hoisted up against the car, his cock deep inside me. Stretching and pulling, he rocks me against the window with vigor, and all I can do is hold on for the ride. I grip his back tightly, my nails digging into his shirt, my legs locked around his waist as he fucks me with a determined need. Lifting my hand, I tug on his neck, pulling his rough lips toward mine. They find mine in an instant. His tongue plunges inside my mouth, flicking and lapping. He groans when I mewl with satisfaction. His strokes against my body become labored, he bites at my lip, and I explode, causing him to release his own orgasm deep inside me, my contracting walls milk his cock. His feet stumble at the force and I become wedged tighter between him and the vehicle, his grip on my hips bordering painful.

"Bren, put the poor girl down!" a woman's voice bellows from across the lawn, and I still in embarrassment.

Bren chuckles in my ear at my reaction. "Come on, baby. Let's get you fed."

He eases my feet to the ground, tucking his spent cock away as he chuckles when I groan at the mess he leaves behind. I slap at him playfully; he grips my wrist and pulls me into a bruising kiss.

"Forever." He nods at me, his eyes searing deep into my soul as he waits for a reaction.

I give him the only answer I have. "Forever." We smile at one another and walk hand in hand across the lawn to the house.

CHAPTER 26

Bren

When I introduced my girl to my ma, she threw her arms around Sky and cooed over her as if she was a child. She stroked her long blonde—hair similar to how I do—and told her how beautiful she is. My girl's cheeks flushed bright red at the compliments, obviously not used to it. A pang of anger hits my chest hard at how she's been treated. She'll never be treated like that again.

Never.

As if sensing my change in mood, Sky bands her arms around my waist, clutching me tightly, then rests her cheek against my chest, giving me access to stroke the hair from her face. My heart skips against her forehead and anger dissipates quicker than when it struck me.

Sky calms me, softens me like nothing before. She's a drug, an addiction I crave with such intensity it threatens to bring me to my knees and splay me open, leaving me weak and vulnerable but without regret.

She's a danger to me, to our family, but I refuse to accept it.

———

My eyes never waver from Sky. Her long blonde hair rests on her ass as she kneels, playing with Cal's daughter, Chloe, on the floor, she's a natural around kids. My niece Charlie and nephew Keen adore her, both showing her their toys and around the property. I follow outside like a guard dog. Standing in the doorway to watch over them, they show her the treehouse that's recently been renovated. It was ours as kids, the one our uncle built us. I squeeze my eyes closed for just a few seconds to push away the memories of him.

His betrayal.

"She'll make a good mother." The voice behind me makes me tense, my da. I'm always on guard around him. He's a crafty fucker that thinks he's still in charge of this family and this business. As if he didn't hand over the reins to me when our brother Keenan was killed.

"Marry the lawyer and keep her on the side." He points his cigar out toward Sky. Pissing me off, and not only his words but his fat, stubby fingers pointing at my girl and talking about her as though she's a fucking dog for breeding.

"I ain't marrying the lawyer," I clip back at him without turning around. That'll piss him off.

His voice plays over in my mind from my childhood.

"Get your ass in here, boy." I scan the garden and swallow down my nerves, dropping the football at my feet. Cal's eyes

meet mine and quickly glance away. He knows what's coming, and he knows there's not a damn thing I can do about it. I might be a teenager, but it doesn't mean I get to act like one.

"Now!" he bellows louder, causing my heart to hammer. Shit.

I follow his voice to the garage located at the side of the house, only a stone's throw away from Ma's kitchen. Her cooking and comfort.

Our home.

I force my feet forward, dragging them with reluctance as I step into the garage. "Shut the feckin' door."

Uncle Don pushes me farther into the garage, and I almost trip at the force. I find my feet quickly, not wanting to show any signs of weakness. Hearing my father's words on repeat in my brain, "Mafia is a sign of strength, not weakness."

"You've been playing with the football again?" he spits the words out with disgust, his contempt at my passion for the sport clear at every turn. Where some fathers would be proud of their son's achievements in sports, mine hates it. He thinks it takes attention away from more important issues, such as the business, the Mafia.

There's no point in lying. My father can smell a rat a mile away. I hold my head high and look over his shoulder, not giving him eye contact. "I was showing the boys how to run with it."

"Look me in the eyes, ya little shite. A man always looks another in the feckin' eyes, even when he knows he's going to be punished. What are ya? A feckin' coward? A weirdo like your little brother?" Anger bubbles inside me, my fists clench. He can say and do what he wants to me, and he's right, I should look him in the eyes, but the moment he called my little brother a weirdo I lost all respect for him, I'd rather anger him into hurting me, let him think I'm a coward. One day, he'll realize I refuse to meet his eyes because it's my way of punishing him.

He hates it, and in turn, I hate him for bestowing this life upon me.

Upon us.

Da flicks his cigarette onto the floor. "You'll tell your ma you hurt yourself playing football. You understand?"

"Aye," I reply to him in his mother tongue, just how he likes. I can practically feel the pride beaming from him as he walks toward me, then he stops and grips my shoulder in what is meant to be reassurance. I fight the need to shake off his touch, watching his hand from the corner of my eye as though it's a trap, and I suppose it is, because I've just accepted my punishment.

He nods toward his men and the three of them move forward. My throat goes dry when my father shuts the door behind me. The first strike of the hammer against my leg brings vomit to my mouth and causes me to stumble.

The second, makes me choke on my breath with a sickening wheeze.

The third, I cannot stand any longer, crumbling to the floor.

The fourth, I almost lose consciousness with the pain.

But amongst the calculated kicks his men throw in after the hammer is discarded to the ground, I float away to somewhere I can be me.

Where I can play football, have a family of my choosing, and a life without expectations. A life with safety without constraints, a life of my own. To be free.

I know, without a shadow of a doubt, I'll never look my father in the eye. I'll never give him the respect he claims to deserve.

He'll never have that part of me.

"I'm feckin' talking to you."

"I hear ya, Da," I snipe back, turning my head slightly but not giving him my eye contact.

His voice weakens as if remembering his place. He's no longer the Don of this family. "Makes good business sense," he grunts.

I shake my head. He's wrong. On so many levels, he's wrong. "Marrying women isn't a business."

Da scoffs beside me. "Ya going soft, you sound like…"

I hold my hand up and straighten my spine in warning. "Don't. Even. Say. It." Oscar, he was going to say Oscar. He thinks Oscar is soft, weak, and vulnerable.

He's wrong.

So fucking wrong, it infuriates me. He refuses to see beyond the differences and recognize his son for what he is.

Oscar is clever, resilient, he's created a life around himself, his needs. His life is giving protection to this family. Yet my father is so pigheaded, so backward in his years, he refuses to see him as an asset. Unless his strength is in his fists, he refuses to accept him as such.

"He's your feckin' weakness, that boy."

My eyes meet Oscar's. He's sitting in the garden on his own, watching us, scrutinizing us. Analyzing.

"You're right. My family is my weakness. Shame they were never yours," I quip back.

"And just what the feck is that meant to mean?"

I shrug at the old bastard when he fidgets beside me, pissed at my words but not even understanding the reasoning behind them.

"Figure it out, old man." I walk away, leaving him to ponder on our conversation.

If we were his weakness, he wouldn't have been so hard on us.

So cruel and unjust. He could have made us Mafia but earned the respect while doing so, but instead, he and his brother treated us like soldiers instead of children. Punishing us for daring to dream. Knocking out any softness as a sign of weakness and treating us with contempt, as if we were disposable.

I often wonder how much influence my uncle had on my father; it's become evident how manipulative he actually was.

But when you love someone, you protect them at whatever cost, and I fully intend to honor that where Sky is concerned.

I nuzzle into her neck, and she giggles against me. The palm of my hand braces her waist. She turns her head up to meet my eyes. She trails her fingertips delicately along my jawline as if understanding before saying the words I long to hear. "Forever."

CHAPTER 27

S ky

I sit next to Bren at the family dinner table. "So, Sky. What's it like living with Bren?" Finn asks from two seats down. I feel Bren tense beside me, but I don't really understand why. I place my hand on his thick thigh and I feel the tension leave his body at my simple touch.

"Oh, wonderful thank you," I reply with truth.

Finn chokes on his beer as the words leave my lips. I glance around the table in confusion. Con starts chuckling, causing his fiancée to elbow him in the ribs. Oscar watches me closely, and if I didn't know better, I would think he didn't like me, but I know it's just his personality.

He clears his throat when he realizes I'm staring back at him like a puzzle I can't fix. "Reece, can I borrow the cat on Friday?" he asks out of nowhere.

Reece's fork stills before it reaches his mouth. He turns

to face him, scanning his face, as though looking for answers. He narrows his eyes. "Pussy?"

Oscar nods, casts his eyes around the table at us all, watching the interaction. "Yes, the cat." He waves his hand toward the fluffy cat that's sitting on the dining table next to Con's dog, Peppa.

"Pussy?" Reece repeats.

Oscar shuffles from side to side, his jaw now ticking and his temple pulsating in frustration. "Yes, the fucking cat, Reece."

"Say it." Reece leans back in his chair nonchalantly, a small smirk on his face he's struggling to mask.

"Say fucking what?"

"Say you want to borrow my Pussy." His eyes don't leave Oscar's as if taunting him into an argument, before adding. "Please." His sly lip curls up at the side.

"Reece," Bren clips out in warning across the table. His fist tightens around his fork. I stroke his leg to soothe him.

Oscar exhales loudly, acting disinterested in the scene. "Reece, may I please borrow Pussy on Friday?"

Reece's eyes narrow further. "What for?"

Oscar's jaw ticks once again. He glances down at the table and mumbles the words out, "She needs a checkup at the vets."

Reece scrutinizes Oscar's face before suddenly jolting with some sort of realization only he's aware of. Reece's mouth drops open. "Holy fuck, you're stalking the veterinary assistant, aren't you? You seedy motherfucker."

"Reece," Finn clips out and trains his eyes down on Charlie, giving him a warning about his language and conversation. I'm not sure why he does that, because they all swear around the children anyway.

I barely finish my trail of thought when I come to

realize what Finn was concerned about. He knows Reece is going to go further.

Reece sits back with his arms crossed over his chest. An enormous smug smile over his face, "So she's a whore at night and an innocent assistant during the day? Fuuucckkk, I gotta see this. Does she dress up for you and shit?"

Oscar looks like he's going to slaughter Reece. His eyes have darkened, the veins in his neck protrude tightly, and his chest is heaving.

"Reece, enough!" Cal snaps in annoyance.

Reece and Oscar are having a stare off, both unwilling to look away from one another, both glaring into one another's eyes as if they have secrets that neither one of them want to expose. I stroke Bren's leg again, feeling the heat radiating from him. "Cal," he warns in a gravelly tone that sounds both deadly and erotic, I squeeze my thighs together, the wetness from earlier a reminder of how my strong man can please with me. I glance up toward Bren but his eyes are trained on Cal as if staring at him will make him concede and force him to control his son. Something tells me it would take more than Cal to control Reece.

I tighten my hand on Bren's and he drops his own hand to under the table, stroking over my dress. His lip curls at the end and I know his thoughts are with me and not so much with what's happening at the table.

"Reece, enough now," Cal clips out again, frustration oozing from him.

"Reece, leave him alone," Lily begins to rise from her chair.

Reece exhales dramatically with a loud huff. "Fucking fine. You can borrow my Pussy, but I'm coming with you."

He raises an eyebrow at Oscar as if goading him to argue otherwise.

Oscar continues with his glare. "Fine." He pushes his chair away from the table and stands.

"Where the feck are you goin?" Brennan bellows across the table.

Oscar stands stoically still before slowly raising his head to stare his father down with calculating eyes. "I have work to do. If you want answers, I mean…" He waves his hand around the table, gesturing at us all.

Brennan goes to open his mouth, no doubt to argue, but Bren holds his hand up and stops him.

"Speak to you later." He nods at Oscar, then continues eating as if he hadn't just gone above his father's word. Oscar turns and leaves the room without speaking to anyone. Reece is mumbling to himself with his arms crossed over his chest like a petulant child, making me stifle a giggle at his reaction.

"Daddy, when I'm older, I want to be a whore vet nurse, too," Charlie says innocently, causing everyone's eyes to shoot up toward Finn's.

In a split second, he goes from calm and collected to all out savage when the words his daughter uttered register in his head. He lunges across the table toward Reece, literally diving over Pussy and Peppa, causing the poor animals to flee in terror. "You jack ass motherfucker," he screeches.

All hell breaks loose with the adults struggling to break up the scuffle and tidy the mess. While Bren keeps eating his dinner like nothing is happening.

His hand disappears under my dress and he roughly strokes over my folds. He mumbles a "Fuck" when he feels how wet I am. Putting another fork full of food in his mouth, he pushes one of his thick digits into my open pussy while stroking his thumb over my already sensitive clit. Bren moans when he exaggerates, eating as though the food is delicious, but he's clearly enjoying playing with me. I tighten my hand on his thick thigh when he begins pumping into me harder, his thumb circling my clit, and then he presses down hard on it and rubs me. My spine straightens and I struggle to maintain a nonchalant expression when my orgasm takes over. I cling to both the table and Bren's thigh for dear life, while Bren milks every drop of my orgasm from me, continuing to pump inside me.

My head drops forward behind a curtain of my hair, and when I finally come down from the high of my orgasm, the argument is still going on around the dinner table. I turn my head to look at Bren. His eyes have darkened and look heavy with arousal. He leans toward me, whispering into my ear, "Lick my finger clean, baby. Lick our cum off my finger." His eyes penetrate my own, causing me to shudder. I open my mouth and Bren pushes his glistening finger inside, pumping it in and out seductively. My breath hitches in response to his own obvious arousal. "Dirty girl," he mumbles on a chuckle and lick of his lips.

I cast my eyes around the room, and sure enough, chaos is still taking place. I smile at myself and our own dirty little secret that just happened, Bren's lips curve at the side too. *Forever*, I mouth to him.

He nods, moving to gently brush my long hair behind my ears. "Forever."

CHAPTER 28

Bren

Me pumping my woman at the dinner table was by far the best meal I've ever encountered. Her pussy wet with my cum had me hard as a fucking rock. My own cock was desperate for some friction, so much so I was grinding against the feel of my belt.

Having Sky around all my family today made me feel complete for the first time in my life. I was able to relax, if only for a short time, while my girl stroked my thigh. Her simple touch eases me in ways I never knew possible. I don't ever want to be in a situation without her again. Ever.

I walk toward the bedroom door, knowing about the parcel I had delivered earlier for her.

"Brennn," she screeches like a banshee, making a grin spread across my face at her cute reaction.

She's hovering over the bed but hasn't even opened the damn box yet. I lean against the doorframe.

"It's a present." She smiles childishly toward me.

"It is." I nod toward the box in response.

"What is it?" Sky waves her hand toward the box wrapped with a tight pink ribbon.

"Open it up and look for yourself, baby."

She nibbles on her lip adorably, and I make a note to buy her a shit ton of presents if this is the sweet reaction I get from her.

Her hands tremble as she pulls on the ribbon. Then she slowly lifts the lid as though something is going to fucking jump out at her.

There's two more boxes inside.

Sky takes the bigger one out and sits it in her lap, looking down at it as though I've given her the world. Thank Christ she went with that one first, at least if it goes down like a lead balloon, I've got the other to back me up.

She opens it and takes out the contents one by one. My heart hammers in my chest. I swallow thickly, my throat suddenly dry, worried at her reaction.

She nibbles her lip and then glances up toward me. All worry dies in my chest as I see the excitement in her eyes and the pink flush of her cheeks.

"You want to use these on me?" She waves toward the contents of the box now sitting in her lap.

My cock throbs against my pants and it takes everything in me not to stroke it; give it some attention.

"Only if you want to." I swallow, hoping to Christ she wants to. She moves the dildo, butt plug, and the silk tie onto the bed.

Her face lights up. "I do. Can we do it now?"

Holy fucking shit balls. I close my eyes to try and rein

in my eager reaction to her words. Opening them slowly, I hope to feel more composed. I fail.

My voice comes out husky as fuck. "Open the other one first, baby." I stalk toward her, taking my shirt off along the way. I throw it to the floor and sit behind my girl while she slowly opens the smaller box.

She gasps when she sees it. "Bre... Bren, it's beautiful." Her voice wavers, causing my heart to hammer.

"Turn it over." She turns the St. Christopher cross over and along it reads "Bren" and traveling down the cross is the word "Forever." Her hands shake as her fingers trail over the words.

"I've had it since I was little. All of us brothers had one, along with the wolf tattoo on my arm, it's a family tradition." Sky turns toward me, climbing into my lap as she glides her fingers over my wolf tattoo. I warm at her touch, my cock weeps at her small body sitting on my knee.

"Could you put it on for me, please?"

I nod, and she holds her silky hair in one hand above her to give me room to clasp the necklace around her delicate neck. The very same neck I intend on coating with my cum. I swallow thickly, staring into my girl's glistening eyes, the most beautiful woman I've ever seen in my life and she's all fucking mine. "Bre... Bren." Her lip trembles as my thick fingers struggle to clasp the delicate chain in place. With one final attempt, I lock it in place around her delicate neck. My fingers trail over her silky soft skin and I tenderly grip her chin in my hand. My love for her shines from my eyes into hers. I can fucking feel it, something so heavy and sincere, something so precious. We're to treasure every sacred moment.

"Are you going to be a good girl and do as you're told?" I nod toward the toys on the bed.

"Yes please, Bren." Her words go straight to my cock, making it leak against my tight boxers. "Get undressed for me, then get on the bed on all fours."

She practically leaps off my knee and begins to shrug off her summer dress. I follow suit, standing and opening my belt and dropping pants, kicking my boxers to the side of the bed.

I turn around to the most breathtaking sight my eyes have ever had the pleasure of seeing. My breath hitches in anticipation.

My girl on the bed, her tight little ass in the air, two perfect round globes desperate to be squeezed and marked, and I've every intention of doing both of those things.

I climb on the bed behind her. My cock already has cum leaking from it.

My words come out husky, deep, filled with lust. "Here's what's going to happen, baby. I'm going to get your tight little ass wet with my cum." I trail a finger down her spine. A moan escapes those perfect lips, a trail of goosebumps breaks out along her back all the way down to that perfect ass. "Then I'm going to push that plug inside of you. I'm going to fuck this tight little pussy —" I rub her pussy with my hand. She moans louder, my cock twitches at the sound. She bucks back into my hand, eager for more. "—with that plug deep inside you. All the while you're going to suck on that plastic cock imagining it's mine fucking your naughty mouth. Anything you're not good with you need to say, do you understand me?"

"Ah. Yes. Yes, I understand, Bren. I want it all." She struggles to pant out the words.

"Good girl. What do you say?" I slap one of her ass cheeks for effect and she moans into the mattress.

"Please. Please fuck me with your cock in my little pussy." I squeeze her ass cheek roughly at her words. "Please cum on me and use me to your pleasure." *Holy. Fucking. Shit. Balls.* My cock jumps in excitement, and I grit my teeth to stop myself from pouncing on her and just fucking her into the mattress.

"Please use me like I'm your little whore."

My mouth drops open at her words. This has to be a dream? She's every. Fucking. Thing.

I don't leave her time to think before I grab the plug and place it beside me and throw Sky the dildo. Her small hand reaches out and grips it.

"Put on a show for me, baby. Show me how well you can please me."

My balls draw up when she looks over her shoulder and darts her little tongue out, licking the tip of the toy. Fuck, I nearly lose my load then and there.

I punishingly grip my aching cock.

Squeezing the tip between my thick fingers, I rub the pre-cum over her puckered hole. The need to sink into her makes me clench my teeth.

I draw my gaze back up and see my sweet girl sucking on the cock like she's desperate to make it come. She moans and pushes back against me, causing me to push in ever so slightly. Fuck that feels good. I jerk my cock over the entrance of her tight hole. Her little pussy leaks every time she thrusts away from me.

I slap her ass cheek and she moans when I rub it with the palm of my hand. I do it again. "Ahh, Bren, please."

I smack it hard, causing her to jolt forward. "Be a good girl and suck that cock."

Sky practically shoves the damn thing down her throat. She's so eager to please me. "Fuck, yeah. Like that, baby."

I jerk my cock above her ass, tugging on the firm globes. I bend down and spit at the top of her crack, causing my saliva to trickle down, dripping onto her hole.

"Please, Bren. Please, fill me with your cum." I flick my eyes back up to her and her sweaty face, shoving the cock in and out of her mouth as she pushes back and forth against me. I slide my oozing cock to her pussy hole and push inside nice and slow, but she goes off like the Fourth of July. Her pussy convulses around me, so tight it's determined to milk my cock of its cum. I pump in and out faster, harder now, hitting those perfect ass cheeks with my pelvis. I stare down at her asshole, wet with my spit, throwing my head back at the overwhelming sensation as I push my thumb into her ass. "Fucking you in all your holes, baby." I breathe out through my flared nostrils, pounding into her.

"Daddy's little whore."

"Yesssss," she squeals, and I swear to Christ she's squirted. Liquid running down my legs, I come.

I come so fucking hard I almost black out.

CHAPTER 29

Sky

I don't know what just happened, but I came so hard my eyes rolled to the back of my head and I'm sure I stopped breathing for a minute. I'm panting into the mattress when I feel Bren pull out from behind me. A gush of wetness leaves me, but I'm too exhausted to care.

I think he's going to lie behind me, but I realize he's taken hold of his cock when he starts wiping it around my puckered hole. I moan at the sensation, completely foreign but not at all unwelcome. He then moves onto licking my thighs, lapping at the wetness that flowed from me. I bury my head into the sheets farther, hoping to hide my heated cheeks.

Bren slaps one of my ass cheeks, the sting in it biting. I lift my head and glance toward him.

"Did I say finish playing, baby?" He quirks a brow at me and tilts his head toward the toy.

"Swallow it down, baby." He lifts the butt plug, causing my eyes to widen. Bren spits on my ass. It feels both filthy and erotic. He uses his thumb to rub in his spittle over my puckered hole. The feeling makes my clit pulsate with need. He moves his thumb away and I feel the absence instantly. Bren places the plug at my ass. "Push back on the plug, lets open that little ass up."

"Oh my god," I moan around the toy, his filthy words making me swim in pleasure. Doing as he says, I push back against the plug, the tip slides in easily, then Bren has to guide me with a firm hand on my waist, pushing it all the way inside. It leaves a slight burning sensation and the feeling of being splayed wide open.

"Mmm, fuck, that's hot," Bren groans while trailing his hands over my ass and the plug.

He turns around and gets off the bed before adjusting an armchair in the corner of the room to face the windows.

His tall naked frame is incredibly hot, sweat glistens on his skin, and his thick erection stands proud.

He sits in the chair like a king. With his legs spread wide open, he takes his hand and grips his cock tightly, pumping a few times, causing him to hiss. My pussy flutters at the sound.

"Sky, come here." He holds his hand out for me and I climb off the bed. "Leave the toy, baby." His voice is deep and rugged. "Come, I want you to sit on my cock and face the window." I scan the scene in front of me, trying to understand what he's asking, as if sensing my thoughts as he tugs me between his thighs, turns me to face the window. "Up." He taps my leg and I lift myself onto his lap. "Lean forward, baby, I need to put my cock in you first." I lift myself up, my hands gripping his firm thighs. He rubs his cock over the plug. "Fuck."

Feeling the tip against my pussy, I lower myself down. Bren hisses as I do so.

"Oh, Bren," I whimper as he stretches me wide. It feels different in this position, thicker and harder to adjust to.

He grips me around the waist and pushes me down, not giving me any choice but to take it. "Take it. Fuck," he pants the words out. "Fucking take it all. All my fat cock, baby."

My lips part when he bottoms out. He pulls me back toward his chest. "Watch me fuck you in the window, Sky." Our eyes meet in the window, and I watch him lick up the side of my neck, stopping to tug and suck on the flesh there, determined to leave a mark.

I move up and down, up and down, in a slow, calculated motion. The friction of Bren's pelvis rubs against the plug, leaving a delicious feeling deep inside me.

Bren nips and sucks my flesh. One hand banded around my waist, the other moves from holding my throat and playing with my nipples, each touch and caress leaves a moan escaping my lips.

Bren grips me tighter, tweaking my nipples. My pussy clenches at the sensation. "Bren, I'm going to…" I can't finish my words. He tilts my head and pushes his thick tongue inside my mouth as he drives into me, again and again and again, until he erupts, his mouth gaping open when his cock pumps me full of his cum.

I finally droop against him, totally spent. My eyes catch on to the window. My legs on either side of Bren's muscular thighs. I'm stretched and swollen, with his cock still inside me. Tilting my head up to meet his gorgeous eyes, his finger trails down the side of my face in a loving gesture. "I need a shower." I nibble my lip, awaiting his response.

He chuckles beneath me. "No way, baby. I'm going to spend all night fucking you and marking you." His hand breezes over my pebbled nipple. "You good being tied to the bed?" He cocks a brow at me, asking for consent after how he found me. But this is Bren, and I know, without a shadow of doubt, he'd never hurt me.

"Of course," I answer him truthfully.

"Good girl." He taps my thigh, and I rise from him, leaving behind a trail of our essence. "You leave this plug in until I take it out, understand? And no panties." I nod in agreement. "Such a good girl," he coos at me, and I melt at his words, desperate to please him.

"Get on the bed, baby. I'm going to fuck you into unconsciousness." I giggle at his words. But I've no doubts they hold truth in them.

BREN

I fuck her through the night till the sun rises. I've had my girl gagged, bound, spread out.

We're a combination of sweat, cum, and saliva and the room reeks of it.

Sky is absolutely incredible; she took everything I gave her.

She lies on my chest, and I play with her blonde, satin hair, feeling like the luckiest son of a bitch alive. She wears my marks all over her body, and it's the most beautiful sight I've ever seen.

Her voice is a soft, tired whisper, "Bren, if you weren't in the Mafia. What would you be?"

I answer without a second thought, "A footballer, I was good at it too." Very fucking good at it. I fail to hide my disappointment in my words and decide to change the subject. "How about you? If you could be anything, what would you be?"

She lifts her head to look at me, completely fucking ignorant to her beauty. I trail a finger down her cheek. "A teacher." She lays her head back down and I continue to play with her hair. "I'd be a teacher in kindergarten, like you see on the television."

I squeeze my eyes shut at her words. She could be that; she could teach. It doesn't have to just be on television. I could tell her, give her the choice, let her know she has options and a future elsewhere if she wants it.

But I tighten my hold on her, being the selfish bastard that I am.

I refuse to give her a choice.

She's mine, and with that, there's no option of a normal life. There's no option of being a teacher.

There's no room for anything other than the Mafia.

Other than me.

CHAPTER 30

Bren

I'm sitting around the table at Con's house, or his fucking mega mansion, as he likes to call it. The guy has added more rooms to this place than Vegas added hotels. He only has one kid, for Christ's sake, and more than half the house is dedicated to him.

I'm feeling fucking wound up tight, because where we'd normally have a poker night at my apartment, we're having it here instead. Will decided on a fucking hen party at our nightclub, Club 11. So Will and the girls are getting ready at mine, and I'm stuck here sitting around the table with my four brothers, falling out over who has the best fucking pool for kids, like anyone really gives a shit. What makes it worse is Sky is going out with them, to a fucking nightclub… I scrub a hand frustratingly over my head.

"I think you're fucked." Finn points his toothpick at me gloatingly.

"I think you need to shut that fucking mouth before it needs wiring shut," I quip back at him, causing him to throw himself back into his chair laughing.

"I'm telling you, this wedding is going to be fucking epic!" Con's childlike smile spreads across his face.

"So we've heard a thousand fucking times. Now play your hand." Cal gestures toward the table.

"We just need to get Oscar a date." Con grins. Oscar straightens in his chair then glares at Con like he has some sort of disease. Con, completely oblivious to Oscar's death stare, continues, "you could get one of those Indulgence girls to come with you."

Oscar exhales loudly. "I might have a date. I just haven't decided whether to bring her." All our eyes shoot over toward Oscar, never in my life have I heard him openly mention a woman, let alone have a relationship with one. I mean, I know he uses escorts, but if it wasn't for Reece's snooping, I wouldn't even be aware of that. The guy is like a vault, locked up so tight.

"With a woman?" Cal asks, like the dumb fuck he is, making me want to instantly hurt him, but then Oscar does something we very, very rarely see. He breaks out into a smile. We all look at one another like our brother has gone bat shit crazy. *What the fuck has happened to him?* I glance at Finn, and he shrugs. Con has his mouth open like a fucking fish—dumb shit—and Cal is staring at Oscar like he's a puzzle he can't fix.

"Yes, with a woman, Cal." He stares at Cal head on.

Cal puckers his lips like a fucking woman. "What's her name?"

"What's it matter?" Oscar fires back quickly.

"I mean, it matters, so I can sort her invite and the place name thingy," Con says while scrubbing a hand through his hair. I grin at my little brother's shitty excuse.

Oscar shrugs. "I haven't decided yet if she's coming or not."

Cal throws a chip into his mouth. "You should probably ask her, not tell her."

"What, like you did with getting Lily pregnant? You asked her, did you?" he snipes back, still bitter at the way Cal got Lily pregnant without her knowledge.

Cal waves his hand toward Oscar as though he's an annoyance. "Change the fucking subject on that one. Back to this woman, you should ask her." He looks pointedly at Oscar, as if urging him not to make a mistake in telling the woman what to do.

Oscar sighs. "She's different." He stares down at the table as if it has all the answers.

"Different how?" Cal asks.

"She isn't completely submissive." Oscar raises his head and looks at Cal as though he's preparing for an argument. He's trying to tell us something about himself and his needs. He's sharing a piece of himself with us that he doesn't share with anyone.

"Will isn't submissive. I just don't give her a choice." Con shrugs.

"That sounds fucking creepy." Finn throws a chip in his direction.

"Please, I've heard Angel screaming as you fuck her, don't you dare. Fact being, some women like that shit." Con shrugs.

"Can you fuck her into coming to the wedding?" Con asks, as though the answer to everything is to screw the girl senseless.

"She's different," Oscar repeats while staring across the room blankly.

"You normally into the whole submissive thing, then?" Finn asks sitting forward with intrigue.

Oscar's spine straightens, his head snaps toward Finn, before he softens and gifts him with a firm nod.

It makes sense, perfect sense really. Oscar doesn't like to be touched. He has quirks, like his desire for control. Stands to fucking reason, if he's going to fuck a woman it needs to be on his terms, how he likes it.

"Angel is like a bitch in heat since getting knocked up. My dick is raw." Finn rubs his dick through his black jeans.

"You tap Sky's ass yet, Bren?"

My hand tightens on my beer bottle and my jaw clenches tight at the thought of them discussing or even thinking of my woman. But then I remind myself they're my brothers, I trust them, and they all have women, women that are crazy about them, in fact.

I nod my head. "Yeah."

Con starts bouncing in his chair and laughing like a kid in a candy shop. "Fucking knew it. Pretty sure there was some finger bashing going on under the dinner table on Sunday. Am I right?" He wiggles his eyebrows in jest. My chair slams to the ground and I fly across the table at the cocky little shit. All the while, he sits there grinning at me.

"You cocky, jackass motherfucker," I bellow as the beers and chips go flying.

Finn pulls Con away from me, but not before I land a punch to his jaw, causing his head to swing to the side.

I'm so fucking wound up, my shirt feels like it's going to rip against my shoulders. How dare he disrespect my woman like that?

"Take it she's yours then? 'Mr. I only pump and dump?'" He has a smug smile on his face, acting like a little bitch. He groans when he works his jaw from side to side. I should have broken the damn thing.

Slowly, I move back to my seat. My chest heaves and my face is hot with fury. I'm normally wound up tight and this little prick insists on making matters worse.

"She's mine," I mumble the words under by breath, but they hear. They hear as though I was loud and clear. All of them drop silent.

I sit back, legs open wide, in my chair, feigning indifference, acting like the scene never happened, while inside I feel like a coiled snake ready to attack. My teeth ache from gritting them.

"You think the women will behave tonight?" Cal asks, breaking the tension. "Lily is desperate to let her hair down. I'm pretty intrigued to see how she acts." He smirks at himself.

My girl hasn't so much as touched alcohol in her life and the thought of her drinking pisses me off. The thought of her going out dressed up makes me feel murderous. The fact she's going to be dancing and men are going to be there. Yeah, I could torture some cunt and fuck her in their blood to make a point.

Tonight is going to be a shit show. I can feel it.

CHAPTER 31

S ky

Getting ready with the girls has been so much fun. They decided to come over to Bren's apartment, and we've all been pampered and preened. Lily brought me a silver sparkly dress. Angel has done my makeup, and Will has styled my hair into big curls. I feel like a movie star. I turn again, looking in the mirror.

"Your ass looks incredible in that dress, Sky." I smile back at Angel; she's lying on my bed, watching me with a smile on her face. She absentmindedly strokes a hand over her bulging stomach, her black sheer dress clings to her bump.

"Thank you. You look beautiful too." I nibble down on my bright-red lip as I trail my hand over my stomach. I look like a completely different person. Once again, I turn, checking myself out in the mirror at how long my legs look in heels.

"You're happy, right? Here, I mean." Angel glances down at the bed, picking at a nonexistent thread.

I face her, my own face marred with confusion. "Of course." I hope she can hear the sincerity in my voice.

"It's just. You have other options, you know." She stares at me, her words laced with concern.

"Wh-what do you mean by other options?" My heart races in my chest with uncertainty.

"If you didn't want to stay here. If you weren't happy. We can help you, Sky. We can help you find somewhere else to live."

My heart plummets at her words. Panic crawls up into my throat.

"I..." My lip trembles. "I want to be here. I want to be with Bren." My words stumble out.

Angel sits up and moves toward me, brushing my hair from my face in a sweet gesture. "Shh, I'm sorry, Sky. It's okay, I just... I care about you. We want to know you're happy, that's all. I want you to be everything you can be."

I don't understand what she's trying to say. What she means. I'm everything I want to be. I'm Bren's.

"I'm happy. I'm everything I want to be," I mumble the words out.

But Angel doesn't seem convinced because she sighs and takes a step back from me. I can feel the disappointment radiating off her, and I'm not sure why, but I can't help but feel guilty.

We're interrupted by a knock at the door. Lily pokes her head in. "The guys are here." She clears her throat. "Bren insisted on taking you, Sky." She looks at me pointedly, then glances over at Angel as though having some sort of private conversation. Angel shakes her head and Lily nods in understanding.

I don't like not knowing what they're doing, especially when I know it's about me.

I can feel it.

BREN

I walk into the apartment completely and utterly on edge. Lily and Will are in the kitchen area helping themselves to my drinks, all sorts of shit laid out on the counter. I sigh in annoyance, scrubbing a hand through my hair.

Angel leaves my bedroom and again, I'm pissed. My jaw grinds in irritation.

Nobody should be in that room other than me and Sky.

"Bren." I'm snapped out of my thoughts with Angel hovering around me as if she wants to say something. I narrow my eyes on her. "I was thinking…" I notice she's fidgeting with her hands clasped in front of her, my senses now on high alert. She's going to say something to piss me off, I can feel it. "Sky could leave if she wanted to, right?" My body jolts at her words, my heart dips. *Does she want to leave? Leave me?*

Absolutely fucking not. We said forever. I don't say that shit to anybody.

She's mine.

I raise my head and glare at her, my eyes no doubt appearing deadly because she takes a step back. One I should feel guilty about, but I don't, not when she's implying taking the only person from me that I care about. The only person I want. "No." My voice is deep and firm, leaving no room for argument.

Angel chokes, as though in shock. Really, she shouldn't be surprised. Finn never had any intention of letting her leave. She never had a choice in the matter, either. Nor Will, nor Lily. When we decide we want something, we make it happen and fuck the consequences.

"Leave," I practically bark at all three of them, my hands opening and closing into fists as if I'm ready to battle but I've no intention of battling with women. I might be a monster but I'm no coward.

Angel hasn't moved from where she stands, as though she's frozen to the spot, staring at me with wide eyes and mouth agape. Lily comes over and speaks in her ear before they all leave the apartment.

As soon as the door clicks shut, I storm toward our bedroom to have it out with Sky. *Just what the fuck have they been talking about?* I swing the door open so hard it hits the wall.

My step falters when I see her, my breath clogs in my throat. She's absolutely gorgeous and she's mine. With that thought, I storm toward her, grasping her chin in my fingers as my eyes roam over her body. She looks sensational, but I'm pissed she's dressed up like this for something that has nothing to do with me. Her blue eyes soften as if understanding my thoughts. "Forever," she whispers, her breath lingering on my fingers. I relax against her and give her a nod, the tension in my body giving way.

Whatever they discussed, my girl wants me. I can see it in her eyes and feel it in her actions. She's choosing me. My shoulders relax and I crash my lips down on hers.

Sweeping my tongue into her mouth, I use my hand to hold her head in place.

She practically climbs me, so I pick her ass up and walk her over to the wall, propping her up with her legs wrapped securely around me. I frantically unbuckle my belt, desperate to fuck her. Remind her who she belongs to by filling her with my cum. I shove my cock inside her without preparation. Her tight pussy molds against me, and I'm forced to close my eyes at the sensation. Grinding my hips back and forth to hit her spot, I fuck her hard. "Oh, oh god, Bren." I tug her head back roughly with one hand and bite into the side of her neck while driving into her hard and fast. She convulses around my cock, almost making me lose my load. "Ah, Bren. Oh god," she screeches so fucking loud my ears vibrate.

As soon as her pussy finishes contracting, I pull out and push her to the floor, where she opens her mouth like a good submissive. I survey her while fucking my hand, her hair a tangled mess now. Sweat coats her like a second skin, her neck marked, ravished by me. But she still looks so goddamn fucking beautiful in her skimpy little dress, she's going to get attention, that's for sure. I hate it. I fuck my fist harder until I feel the telltale signs of my orgasm.

I decide to mark her again, make sure they can smell me on her, she's mine. I roar my release down her neck and over her face. My lips part in awe as ropes of my thick, warm cum spray across her. My girl doesn't falter, she kneels there and takes it. Absolutely fucking incredible. Then she does as trained, she moves forward and takes my cock into her mouth to lick me clean, trailing her tongue down my shaft and over my balls. *Fuck, that's incredible.* I tangle my hand in her hair and force her face into my groin, rubbing up and down over her face, mixing my cum with her makeup. "Ah fuck, baby, so good. Keep licking, be a good girl, and keep licking." Jesus, I'm an animal but I can't help it, not around her. I have a primal need to consume her like she consumes me. I rest my fist on the wall while I begin fucking Sky's face, knowing my girl would rather be here sucking on me than being out with the others is all the reassurance I need.

Sky's mine, and I'm hers.

Forever.

CHAPTER 32

Sky

Bren hasn't said a word to me since we left the apartment.

After he came in my mouth, I cleaned up in the bathroom and re-applied my makeup just how Angel showed me to. When I came back out, Bren was sitting on the bed, staring solemnly at the floor. I stood between his legs, and he nuzzled into my stomach while my fingers played in his short-cropped hair. I asked him if he wanted me to stay home and his sad eyes met mine and he asked me if I wanted to go to the club. I nodded, biting my lip, causing him to sigh, he then pushed off the bed to stand, kissing my forehead.

I clear my throat. "Bren, are you mad at me?" He's sitting in the seat farthest from me in the limo, gazing out of the window, almost in a trance.

He snaps his eyes to mine, his voice gruff. "No." Then he goes back to staring out the window.

Nerves gather inside me, a desperation to hold him, get him to tell me what's wrong. I want to know how I've disappointed him. I unclip my seatbelt, crawl over the seat, and climb into Bren's lap. His arm automatically bands around me, the strength and warmth of his weight encompassing me, it's protective and loving. I follow his jawline with my fingertips, and he gazes into my eyes.

"You're worried about something." It's not a question, it's an observation.

He nods. "Yeah."

"What is it?"

He swallows hard. "You."

I try to move back slightly, stunned at his words, but his arm holds me in place with fierce determination.

"Why?" I can't hide the shock in my words.

"Don't want you around other men. Wanting other men." He looks at me pointedly before swallowing heavily. Delicately, he tucks a curl behind my ear. "Wanting someone other than me."

My heart aches for him. This big brute of a man sits here all vulnerable and exposed, worried I'm not going to want him. I gently take hold of his chin between my forefingers, replicating how he usually holds mine; I draw my lips to his and, with a ghost of a whisper, I tell him, "I love you, Bren. I don't want or need anyone but you." He fills the gap, crashing his lips to mine, his body relaxing into me. Our tongues tangle at a sensual pace but stop the second the limo halts and our driver announces we've arrived.

Bren draws away from me. The feel of his lips lingers on mine and I touch them, willing the sensation to never leave. He smirks down at me as if reading my mind, before his hand travels over the column of my neck, landing on the bright-red mark he's left on me, his touch a reminder of his ownership.

A reminder of forever.

His voice is deep, almost threatening. If I didn't know Bren any better, his tone would scare me into submission, as it so happens, he has that already. "Be a good girl, Sky. I'll be watching." His eyes darken and I swallow, giving him a nod and small reassuring smile.

———

I've never seen anything like this in my entire life, not even on a television. The floor vibrates beneath me. The colorful flashing lights make my dress sparkle like a disco ball. I take another sip of the fruity cocktail Lily poured me.

The nightclub has three floors and one basement. Bren told me I wasn't allowed to go down there, so I assume it has many things going on. Probably where you go to have sex with strangers.

"Sky, how do you like the club?" Angel sits back in a huge throne-like chair that Finn had brought over for her. She strokes a hand over her enormous stomach.

"I love it!" I bounce in my seat with excitement, the plug in my ass gives adds to the promise of a night I'm going to remember.

"Lily, are you drunk already?" Will asks a very flushed Lily. She's swaying from side to side with the music, but her eyes are a little heavy. I giggle at her pouting face.

Lily sits forward. "Maybe a little." She scrunches up her eyes as she talks, then leans forward for another drink.

Lily doesn't pour the cocktail into her glass. She's put lots of straws together from the jug to make it extend toward her mouth.

Will throws her head back laughing. "Cal is so screwed tonight. He's going to be stressed out of his head."

Lily chuckles, then hiccups. "He is. You're soooo right. He has to take Chloe to ballet tomorrow, then she has toddler piano and a baby Spanish lesson." She ticks the activities off her hand using her finger but misses her hand each time.

"And he'll get very sloppy head, if that's what he wants tonight." We all break out in laughter at her words. Her tone goes all serious as we hang on her every word. "It's true, I can barely see straight. He needs to make sure he puts it in my mouth properly and uses me." She holds her finger up at our giggling. "Wait, wait. He needs to make sure I don't think he's a breadstick, because then I might chomp down and…" She makes a breaking motion with her hands, and we all burst out laughing.

"A breadstick? Seriously, Lily, you're comparing your husband's dick to a breadstick?" Will splutters on her drink, causing it to come through her nostrils.

My eyes stream with tears, and my cheeks hurt from laughing at their antics.

"Oh, I only say breadstick because when he ate me out earlier, I was munching on a breadstick."

"I'm sorry, back the fuck up! You ate a breadstick while he ate you?" Angel asks with her eyebrows raised.

Lily nods dramatically. Taking another big suck of the straw. "Hmm, mmm, I was eating a breadstick at the kitchen counter. Chloe had just gone down for a nap…" She waves her hands around at the unnecessary part of the story. "Anyway, I was munching on a breadstick and Cal came up behind me and said"—she makes her voice deep and contorts her face, trying to mimic Cal—"'I'm hungry too, but hungry for this pussy.' Then he pushed me against the counter, parted my legs, and dropped to the floor, and I dropped the breadstick on the counter. He goes to town on me. He was very hungry." She nods to herself, and we all burst out laughing, no longer able to contain ourselves from listening to her voice change and watching her facial expressions. She moves forward for another drink, and I take note of the jug being almost empty. "So, after he finished, I picked the breadstick back up and carried on eating."

Will snorts out a laugh. "You didn't finish the poor guy off?"

"Nope. He stood there with his hands on his hips as though he wanted something in return. I told him"—she points at us as though she's pointing at Cal—"'Behave tonight and you can have my mouth.' Then I turned around and started making a sandwich." She shrugs, but it causes her head to loll slightly.

"So, what you're saying is you chose a breadstick over your man?" Angel asks, quirking a brow.

"I chose food over cum. Sue me." Her eyes roll for longer than necessary. I've never met anyone so funny in my entire life. We all break out in laughter while Lily throws her hand up in the air to order another round of drinks.

BREN

Cal paces back and forth in front of the balcony like a tiger in a cage.

I knock another whiskey back, enjoying the entertainment of him stressed out of his fucking mind because his wife is getting wasted.

"Dude, we're gonna have to replace the carpet, chill the fuck out." Finn grins over toward Cal.

"She's absolutely fucking wasted," he spits out in disgust, glaring down at the table.

From our elevated height on this floor, we can see directly onto the girls' table. They can't see us due to the smoke machines and strobe lights between us, but we have the perfect view to make sure they're behaving. According to Cal, Lily is certainly not behaving. I smirk once again into my whiskey, the tension I felt earlier almost completely gone.

He gasps. "Jesus, she's ordering another round."

"Cal, seriously, man. Sit the fuck down, have a fucking drink, and unwind." Con smiles broadly in Cal's direction. I'm not even sure he realizes his smile is patronizing.

Cal sighs and throws himself onto the chair like a goddamn toddler but can't help himself to look over at them again. He looks like a creeper peeking his head over the balcony rail, his eyes not missing a trick.

Con sits forward in his seat, clasping his hands together as though he has some inside information for us. "So, you'll never guess what I managed to get for the wedding." He's like a kid in a chocolate factory, his eyes alight and his ass edging off the chair with excitement. I stifle a grin behind my glass at my brother's childish glee.

"What?" Cal asks with disinterest, glancing over his shoulder again at the table below.

"A tiger."

Finn chokes, really fucking chokes, and when I turn my head to him, he's picking one of those damn toothpicks out of his mouth with a disgruntled looking face.

"A tiger?" That's got Cal's, interest.

"Yep, a motherfucking tiger." Con sits back in his chair with a grin as wide as the Cheshire cat. He tucks his hands behind his head as though he's some sort of king.

Cal's eyes widen in confusion and disbelief. "What kind of tiger?"

Con makes a laughing noise that sounds like a choke. "Fuck if I know. I know a dude, that knows a dude, so I got Keen a tiger." His smug smile encompasses his face.

"Might be a cat. They call some cats tiger cats," Finn suggests with a shrug. "You probably ordered a cat, man. Ya know, like Pussy." He grins back at Con and winks at him just to fucking piss him off.

I scrub a hand over my head at their banter, knowing very well how this is going to play out. I'll probably be pulling them off one another in a minute.

Con's head whips toward Finn. "It's a fucking tiger,

here." He pulls his phone from his pocket, swipes a few buttons and sure as fuck a tiger sits on his screen. "A tiger." He smiles to himself smugly.

Cal glances back at the table again. "You've got to be fucking kidding me!" He rises from his chair, his face morphed into sheer horror.

We all shoot from our seats to go over to the balcony, sure as shit Lily is dancing on the table, with Will and Angel clapping and cheering her on. I scan the area for Sky but don't see her with the girls. Not until the lights shine on a shimmering silver dress do I see her on the dance floor, my heart rate settles slightly, that is until some douche touches my girl's waist and pulls her toward him.

I'm going to fucking kill him.

I analyze the drop and decide I'd shatter my fucking kneecaps if I try jumping it, so instead, I have to rush down the fucking stairs and plow through a bunch of assholes on the dance floor. I finally get to the guy, who doesn't seem to understand my woman is brushing his hands off of her. Hell fucking no!

I grab the dude with my hand, squeezing tightly at the back of his neck. I drag him to the nearest table and smash his face against it, over and over again.

Before I know what's happening, soft hands glide over my heart, stilling me in an instant. "Bren, enough, let's go home." She nuzzles her head into my chest, and I hold her against me with one hand on her head. I bend down and kiss her hair.

Finn stands beside me. "Throw him out back." He nods knowingly.

I bend down and scoop up my girl, carrying her over my shoulder, her small fists hammering against my back.

"Bren, Bren, put me down. Bren, I can walk."

Like fuck she can walk. Stepping outside into the fresh air does nothing to alleviate my anger. My blood pumps through my veins rapidly, causing my temples to throb and my muscles to ache. I open the limo door and practically throw her onto the seat. "Stay," I bark and slam the door shut.

Now to alleviate some of this tension on the prick that thought he could put his hands on my girl. Think again, motherfucker.

I stand in the alleyway outside of our club, seething, absolutely fucking seething. I spit on the piece of shit that clearly doesn't know when to keep his hands to himself.

"You thought it was okay to touch my girl?"

He tries to stand, but I use my foot and push him back onto the ground. He falls backward, his face now on display under the security light.

Finn shoves another toothpick in his mouth and watches on with his arms crossed over his chest.

"Asked you a fucking question." I take a step closer, and the shit bag tries to get back up and escape, it's fucking comical.

There is no escaping.

"I didn't know she was with you." His voices quivers like the pussy he is.

I raise a questionable brow at his words. "She shrugged you off and you still put your filthy hands on her." My fists tighten beside me in anger, the knuckles painful.

"Hurry the fuck up and end him so I can get home to my woman." Finn sighs.

I pull my gun from behind my back.

"Oh shit, man, I'm sorry. I swear I didn't know she belonged to you. Please, I swear, please." I aim the gun at his dick and fire, hitting my target. A loud wail escapes the piece of shit's mouth, his legs flaying frantically. I tuck my gun back into my pants.

"Fuck his hands up. Make sure he never touches another woman again." I turn on my heel.

"Should I just chop them off?" Finn shouts after me.

I don't even turn round to reply. Done with this shit already. I've got a girl to get home and punish. "Whatever." I throw over my shoulder as I walk away.

And punish her little ass, I will.

CHAPTER 33

Bren

I throw Sky down on the bed, still absolutely seething from tonight.

The whole build-up to the night had me feeling out of control, not something I'm used to, nor something I intend on getting used to.

My jaw ticks when her small body bounces on the mattress, looking so goddamn beautiful it hurts.

"Are you going to punish me?" She sits up on her elbows, her bright-blue eyes penetrate mine, making my heart thump with an unsteady rhythm. She nibbles on her bottom lip, bright-red lip to be precise. I groan, tilt my head toward the ceiling, and squeeze my eyes closed, trying to rein in my temper and the control I need over her body. I attempt some stupid breathing technique that Oscar has tried to teach me.

"I think you should punish me."

I open my eyes and lower my gaze, my eyes clashing with hers. They're full of lust, heavy and sultry.

Yeah, she needs punishing; she needs her ass tanned.

I grab her ankle roughly and drag her down the bed. Her blonde hair spreads out like a fucking halo. My eyes roam down her body, all the way to her tight little pussy. My spine straightens. "You're not wearing any panties?" I snipe the words out accusingly, my eyes locking on to her bare, glistening pussy. My shoulders bunch and tighten to the point of pain. *She went out to a motherfucking nightclub without panties?*

Sky raises her head slightly from the bed. "You said not to wear panties." My jaw clenches, pissed at myself as much as her.

I did say that. But I meant around me, not around dirty, perverted, sick fucks who can easily touch my girl when I'm not there to protect her.

I grip her legs and throw her onto her stomach. Now her bare ass is on display with the shiny butt plug still firmly in place. My cock leaks in appreciation, and I waste no time unbuckling my belt and unzipping my pants. I tug down my boxers and my cock springs upward before I stroke my length roughly while kicking my clothes to the side.

I tighten my hand around my cock and hiss. It feels so fucking good, I bite the inside of my mouth and groan, imagining how her tight little ass is going to feel around my cock.

I stand at the end of the bed with the belt in my free hand.

Sky glances over her shoulder, her pupils dilate slightly when she sees the belt in my hand. She pushes her ass up in the air, and I can practically smell her pussy juice from here. Fuck me, she's hot. I want nothing more than to shove my tongue as far up that little pussy as I can. But my girl needs punishing.

"Gonna whip your ass, Sky." My voice comes out husky, filled with need.

"Oh god," she pants, gripping onto the sheets.

"You're going to apologize after each lash," I state firmly.

"Yes."

I stroke my hand over her smooth globe. Take a small step back and raise the belt, lowering it on her ass, loving the sound of it slapping against her skin and the flinch it causes. The bright-red welt makes me want to kiss and lick it better.

"I'm sorry," she pants out into the sheets.

I raise the belt again. "For fucking what?" *Smack!*

"F-for being a whore."

Jesus. I drag a hand over my face and have no choice but to pump my cock in my fist a few more times, forcing it to release a bit of pre-cum. I grip it tight while raising the belt and smacking it against her ass again.

The clench of her butt cheeks against the plug makes my cock ooze more cum.

"I'm sorry, I'm your whore. Nobody else's, Bren."

Fuck. Hottest damn thing I've ever heard in my entire life. Her pussy leaks onto the sheets and it takes everything in me not to sink into her.

"Please. I need you." She moans into the mattress.

"Fucking wait," I sneer and raise the belt again.

"Ah, oh god. I'm sorry."

"You want my cock, whore?" I snipe the words out. Never in my life have I called a woman a whore in the bedroom, but with me and Sky? I feel like anything goes and we're both good with that.

"Please. Please." She nods against the sheets, and I can't take it anymore. I pull out the butt plug with no pretense, tug her thighs wider, and grip her small hip with one hand while positioning the tip of my cock at her puckered hole with the other hand. Her hole is still open a little from the butt plug. I fill my mouth with my saliva and spit it onto her ass, watching it flow down her asshole makes my jaw lock in anticipation, *hot as hell*. I use my thick fingers to rub it around. Sky clenches her cheeks and moans into the sheets. *Dirty girl.* I waste no time pushing the tip of my cock inside, her muscles clench around me, causing me to grit my teeth together. She moans into the mattress as I push inside, inch by inch, ignoring her whimpers. I give one final thrust and I'm all the way inside. Sky's body is coiled tight, her ass choking my cock, and I fucking revel in it.

I pull out and slam back in. "Oh, Jesus, Bren."

"You like that?" I slap an ass cheek and do the same again. This time I pick up speed, quickly thrusting in and out her tiny hole.

"Oh shit, baby. Feels so fucking good," I pant while trying to stave off my already impending orgasm.

"Yes. Yes, please."

"My little whore to fuck." I bite my lip and groan at the sensation, already wanting to come deep inside her as far as I can fucking get. I shove in harder, determined to make a point.

"Yes," she screeches and tightens around me even more. *How is that possible?* I grind my teeth so hard I'm surprised they don't shatter.

"Fuccckkk." My balls tingle and I throw my head back,

squeezing my eyes shut. But it's no good. "Fuck. I'm coming. Pumping this little ass with my cum." My hand tightens on Sky's hip as I pummel into her harder and harder. I come with such force I fall on top of her, and she collapses to the bed, taking me with her.

Our breathing is heavy, our bodies sweaty and panting. I roll onto my back and pull Sky with me so she's laying on my chest with my cock still seated in her ass. I chuckle at the thought, causing goosebumps to spread out over her skin.

I nuzzle into her hair and kiss her neck tenderly.

"Mine." I nip at the flesh, adding another mark to her perfect skin.

She sighs contently against me. "Forever."

"Damn, fucking right forever." I kiss her head and hold her tighter, vowing to always be there for her.

CHAPTER 34

Sky

I wiggle in my seat, a little sore from last night. Bren went hard on me, like a wild animal. Primal and fierce, determined and strong. I can still feel the imprints of his fingertips digging into my hips while he fucked me from behind. The roar from his release still echoes in my ears. He was like a man possessed and I reveled in it.

"You good?" he queries, glancing at me before focusing back on the road.

I wiggle again and his lips curl up at the edges into a knowing smirk.

"I'm good," I confirm with a reassuring smile.

"Good girl." His praise goes straight there, straight between my legs, making my clit throb once again.

"Are we nearly there?"

"Yeah, baby." He points ahead, and I crane my neck forward to see better.

Bright lights and a coastline come into view. Excitement bubbles inside me as if I'm a child. I bite into my lip to stop myself from giggling goofily.

Bren turns his head to watch me, his grin taking over his handsome face, causing his eyes to crinkle in the corners.

I sit forward some more but find the seatbelt restricting me. "Bre-Bren. Is that an amusement park?" My eyes bug out.

"Yeah, baby, it's an amusement park."

"And a boardwalk?"

Bren chuckles to himself. "Yeah, and a boardwalk."

I peer out of the window again. "And the ocean?"

Bren nods. "And the ocean."

"Oh my god, this is incredible. Thank you." I lean over the center console and kiss his cheek. He makes a low grumbling noise in the back of his throat that leads me to believe he wishes he wasn't driving. I bite on my lip at the thought.

The car comes to a standstill, and I practically bounce with excitement.

BREN

My girl definitely deserved a night out and I could guran-fucking-tee she hadn't seen anything like the Jersey Shore coastline and boardwalk before.

Giving the valet my keys, Sky hops out of the truck, gripping my hand tightly. She's both nervous and excited. My chest swells with pride that she's all fucking mine and I'm the one that gets to experience this with her. Another first.

My gaze roams up and down her body. She wears a tight, strapless, summer dress and is the epitome of hotness. Her neck displays my marks, but just to be safe, I brush my fingers through her hair and tuck the strands behind her ears so every fucker can see she's taken. She needs some sort of permanent mark on her, just to make it known. I gaze down on her, trying to figure this shit out. I've never wanted to keep a woman before, so I'm not quite sure what to do about it. I don't want her skin permanently marked, but that might be the only option I have.

The concern in her voice shakes me out of my

thoughts. "Bren, is everything okay? Your lip is bleeding a little." I drag my hand across my mouth and glare at the blood.

"You were biting your lip. I do that when I'm nervous too."

I choke because I almost want to chuckle at her innocence. The concerned expression on her has me leaning in and giving her a quick peck before my cock gets any other ideas.

"Where do you wanna go first?"

"Can we go on the Ferris wheel?" She nibbles on her lip and my cock instantly swells, causing me to blatantly adjust my jeans. She notices the movement and smiles back at me happily.

"We can go anywhere you want, baby."

She turns on a nod to take in the park, her eyes widen in glee, and I know without a shadow of a doubt that I'm a goner, an absolute fucking goner.

"Are you enjoying the hot dog?"

After half a dozen fucking rides—I never intended to go on in my life, let alone twice—she's still fucking buzzing, showing no signs of slowing down.

"It's really nice, thank you."

Shit, she had to tack on the thank you. I scrub a hand down my face. Now my cock is at full mast because watching Sky eat a fucking hot dog is now something close to porn.

I pick up the burger and stuff it in my mouth in annoyance.

BREN

"Bren. You ate that in one go!" She giggles and throws a napkin in my direction. "You literally shoved it all in."

I chuckle with my mouth full, then I finish swallowing and lean over the table. "Gonna shove all my cock in your mouth, baby, and see if you can eat it like a good girl."

I watch her cheeks blush and her eyes dart around to see if anyone can hear me. I smirk at her reaction. So damn cute.

I draw back and stand up straight, leaning back slightly to loosen the crick in my coiled muscles. When I stare down at Sky, her innocent eyes are widened at my obvious bulge. "You gonna sort that out later?" I crook a brow in her direction.

"Yes, please."

My lips turn up at the sides. "Good girl." My girl fidgets in her seat. *Fuck, I need her.*

I clear my throat. "You want me to win you one of those stuffed toys on the stall?" I nod toward where the shooting stall is located. *Fucking perfect*, I grin internally.

Sky jumps to her feet. "Yes, please." And then we head over to the stall.

"Which soft toy, baby?"

Sky doesn't need any time to think about it. "The elephant." She points to the large plush toy with enormous ears.

"I'll take the big guy." I point to the biggest of the toys.

The spotty-faced, cocky, little shit sighs and talks to me slow like I'm some sort of moron, pointing at the guns, then the targets. "You need to shoot first, old man. Then you can choose a toy."

Oh no he fucking didn't.

I clench my jaw in annoyance, my shoulders tighten.

Sky feels the change in my demeanor because she instantly glides her hand over my midsection.

But all that does is make my dick harder. I wince at the fucker trying to sneak out over the top of my jeans.

In a swift movement, the little reject doesn't see coming, I withdraw my weapon from behind my back, double check the clip, and without even having to check the targets, I let off six rounds, hitting the bullseye in each.

The kid's mouth falls open and I lower the weapon slowly, aiming it at his dick. "Not bad for an old man, right?" I quirk a brow at him. The sappy shit looks close to pissing his pants. "She wants the baby elephant too." I nod toward the smaller ones.

Reject startles with a deep breath of air, stumbles over to the toys, and unhooks them both. All the while Sky has the biggest fucking smile on her face, making all the tension fall away. *Fucking perfect.*

SKY

I glance around at everyone dancing. Bren has brought us to a country bar just off the boardwalk and let me have some sort of fruity cocktail. He watches me closely even though his security detail has followed us around all night, his eyes never waver from me for more than a minute.

His stare penetrates me, a comforting blanket of both protectiveness and need.

"Can we dance?" I ask, full of hope.

Bren sighs and winces, he runs a hand over his head, and then scrubs his palm down his face dramatically, his eyes oozing sympathy. "Baby, I don't dance."

I fake pout, and he throws his head back on a belly laugh. "Fucking Jesus, get your ass up, let's go."

I jump to my feet with excitement. My sandals click against the wooden floor as we take a position on the dance floor. I'm a little unsure of what to do. My nervousness suddenly takes over and, as if realizing my awkwardness, Bren tugs me toward him, wrapping an arm around my waist and cupping my chin with his free hand. "You good?" He scans my face.

I relax into him. Always there.

Always the protector.

"I'm good."

He nods at me, then starts to drift and I follow his lead. I'm pretty sure the rubbing of his rock-hard cock against me and his roaming hands on my ass aren't part of any dance, but I relish in it.

The song finishes, but Bren holds me close, not wanting to leave the dance floor. I stare into his eyes, feeling an overwhelming amount of love. Warmth spreads through my chest and tingles break out over my body at his intense gaze. His Adam's apple bobs, and I know he's feeling the same connection.

I rest my head against his chest and his heart pounds against my cheek, my head tilted to stare into his eyes, not breaking the connection.

Our connection.

"It's you (I've been looking for) – Lewis Brice" Playing.

Listening to the song play, Bren moves us side to side across the dance floor, like it's only us here. The lyrics seem to be playing just for us, and Bren mouths the words to me, causing my heart to hammer at the meaning behind them. It's perfect, absolutely perfect. I never knew a happiness like this existed. A love like this, so utterly consuming that it hurt your heart just to feel it.

Bren's hand occasionally glides over my hair, smoothing it out as though he needs reminding of its feel. My heart flutters with every touch, causing air to catch in my throat. He moves his face toward me, lightly touching his lips to mine, and my body sinks into his. I moan lowly and Bren pulls back to look at me.

Staring into one another's eyes like no one else exists.
Nobody but him and me.
Forever.

CHAPTER 35

Bren

The shrill ringing of my phone wakes me. The ringtone belonging to Oscar, I know, without a shadow of a doubt, it's important. I mean the guy never calls for anything other than duty. He's not like my other brothers that would call on a whim. Cal will call to complain about Reece, Con to talk kid or puppy shit, and Finn to discuss how someone whined like a bitch when he cut them up. But Oscar? Purely fucking business.

I roll over and curse out a groan; I forget I'm fucking thirty-eight now but feel like I'm closer to fifty. The years have not been good to me, not when I've been shot, stabbed, tortured. Not when my father would take out his frustrations on me. Nope, I'm fucking aching like a hundred-year-old bitch.

I scrub a hand down my face and press the phone to my ear. "What?"

Sterner than his usual tone, he snipes the words out, "Meeting at the warehouse. Now." He cuts the call before I have a chance to ask any questions, and I stare at the phone, cussing at my brother's shitty attitude.

I stare at the clock beside the bed, 5:30. Great. Throwing my feet off the side of the bed, I glance back over my shoulder at my beautiful girl, sleeping peacefully like a fucking angel with her halo of light-blonde hair nestled around that perfect face. My heart thumps deep inside.

I never imagined caring for someone, let alone loving them.

Not me.

But there's no mistaking what I feel for Sky, this insatiable need I have for her. An obsession, really, a beautiful, all-consuming obsession.

I can't resist turning and stroking my calloused fingers down her delicate cheek.

Mine.

"Forever," I whisper the words.

A promise.

―――

I throw open the door to my office to find Finn, Cal, and Oscar awaiting my arrival. All in their usual seats.

No sign of Con—the guy always has to make an entrance. I sigh and make my way over to my seat at the head of the table.

As head of the family.

Cal pushes a whiskey into my palm, and I stare at him

with a crook of my brow in question. He nods toward the drink, and I tip it back. A sinking feeling rising in my stomach.

What the hell has Oscar discovered?

The door swings open and in walks Con, with the rat-bastard dog he says is some Chinese-crested thing, tucked firmly under his arm. "He whines for me if I leave him alone." He winces at his own dumb excuse for bringing the bold thing with him, before taking a seat and patting the mangey-looking thing on the head with a childlike grin on his face, happy the damn dog needs him.

Jesus, my family is screwed up.

I stroke a hand over the scruff of my chin and turn to Oscar. "Hit me with it." Because let's fucking face it, whatever he dragged us all out of bed for—and shoved a drink in my hand—has got to be something serious.

"It's not good." I eye my brother at his response; it's rare Oscar shows any emotion at all. But there was a hint of sympathy in his tone, and I don't like it. Not one fucking bit.

I nod at him to continue and the guy almost winces.

I side-eye Cal to see if he's aware of what Oscar has discovered, but my brother's eyes are narrowed, trained on Oscar, confirming he appears just as in the dark about this impromptu meeting as me.

Oscar retrieves something from a manila file before sliding it over the table toward me. My brothers lean in to see the document, a photo, to be precise.

A photo of two small children, little girls with dresses, one a toddler and the other a small child, maybe aged around four?

I scan the image, the picture not giving much away, apart from those eyes. They glare back at me and sear deep into my heart, causing my breath to stutter with the force. My chest tightens and so does my grip on the image. "Sky?" I question with a tick in my jaw. Why the hell I'm frustrated at his findings is beyond me, but I am. She's mine.

I don't want her to have anything but me. Call me a selfish, arrogant, self-centered prick. I'm all of those things and more. But I want to be her everything, like she's mine.

My eyes lock on to Oscar's, and again I see a glimmer of the unwanted sympathy. I squeeze my eyes shut and ball my fists together.

My eyes fly open at his words. "Jenny Olska, aged four years and eight months was reported missing from her foster family after the local Sunday School alerted authorities they were concerned she and her sister, Anastasia, had not been seen for five weeks." Oscar talks in a monotone voice as though he's reciting a newspaper report.

I nod at his words before repeating them over in my mind. *She has a sister.*

"She has a sister?"

Oscar nods. "Apparently so. Although, there's been no sign of her either. The foster father was taken in for questioning and later disappeared, turned up floating in a lake a few weeks later. No doubt to keep him silent."

"The guy was probably trafficking kids. They shut him up, before he had a chance to snitch," Finn snipes the words out, his temple pulsating and his leg bouncing with the need to release some aggression. I get that. My own need to hurt something is only hindered by the innocent face staring up at me from the table.

"Does she know she has a sister?" Cal asks, his voice soft.

"No." I shake my head.

"She was young. She won't remember shit. Keen can't remember half the shit before I came along." Con grins smugly, like it's a good thing. He's probably right, it probably is a good thing.

"Should we try to find the sister?" Cal asks.

"No," I clip the words out. "Oscar has enough shit to deal with. And I don't want Sky upset. What she doesn't know won't hurt her. This—" I stab my finger on the table, at the photo "—this will hurt her."

They all nod in understanding. God only knows what happened to her sister. I glance down at the photo of the sweet little girls holding hands, but a look of panic and uncertainty on Sky's face makes me turn the photo over. I swallow hard, my throat suddenly dry. Thank Christ she doesn't remember.

I take a deep breath and pull my shoulders back. Chancing a look at Oscar, I watch him fidget nervously with the file.

"What else?" My eyes seer into him.

He closes his eyes and does that breathing thing he tried teaching me to do before opening them with a new determination. At least it works for one of us, I guess.

He clears his throat. "Their parents died in a car accident." He stops speaking.

I furrow my eyebrows, because although it's bad, it's not what he wants to say, there's definitely more to it. Something I'm really not going to like, I can feel it.

Fed up with all this pussyfooting around bullshit, I slam my fist on the table. "Fucking say what you got to say, Oscar!" I bellow, sounding just like my father. The thought makes me wince.

He swallows nervously. "Sky just turned eighteen."

The wind is taken from my lungs, stolen, sucked out, and drained of air. I blink. *What the fuck did he just say?*

"Are you sure?" I hear Cal ask, but I don't register his words.

"Certain."

My brothers fidget uncomfortably but I can't move, I can't fucking breathe.

I stare at Oscar, dumbfounded.

"Eighteen?" I question.

I can feel my body pale.

He nods again, his concerned eyes never leaving mine.

"Age of consent is sixteen or seventeen in New Jersey, man." I dart my eyes over to Finn, who waves his hand around nonchalantly, his words stabbing into me. "Age of consent."

"I slept with a teenager?" I grimace.

I don't even have to look at Cal to feel him tense behind me. He has a son only a year younger. I blanch. A fucking teenager, a kid. I'm a grown ass man.

Panic starts to build inside me. The things I've done. I took her virginity, for Christ's sake, and reveled in it. Enjoyed breaking her in, calling her my little girl. I fucking loved it. I push back on my chair and turn to stare at the wall, a wave of sickness trying to expel the contents of my stomach.

"She said she was twenty-one." Con's voice is low, but I hear him.

"She was wrong. She recently turned eighteen, not twenty-one," Oscar states, loud. For me to hear. For me to know I took a teenager, a trafficked teenager, and fucked her hard.

My hands find the table we use as a bar and overturn it with ease. I crash my fists into the wall over and over.

But I feel nothing, nothing but a deep sickening feeling.

Before I know what's happening, I'm heaving my guts into the trash can, emptying it of its contents.

Eighteen.

A teenager.

A little girl.

I'm a monster.

CHAPTER 36

Bren

Lily hands me ice wrapped in a towel for my fists.

Cal paces back and forth in his living room.

I stare up toward the mantelpiece, an array of photos staring back at me. Family photos. Mom, dad, baby, and their teenager all staring back at me with smiles on their faces.

This is what Sky needs, wants, craves, and deserves. She's just never been given the opportunity to allow it, to feel it, to have freedom.

Until now.

"You're sure?" Lily asks me again, and I nod in response, unable to say the words out loud.

Lily's face is coated in worry as she stares back at Cal. He nods back at her and her shoulders slacken in defeat.

"She's going to need support, Bren." She looks at me pleadingly.

"She'll get it." I glare up at her, hoping she can see the truth behind my words. She'll get whatever the hell she wants. Whatever the hell she needs.

Just not me.

A flurry of activity breaks our stare when a screeching Angel comes barreling through the door. I grimace, take it Finn has told her.

"What the hell, Bren?" She stands before me with her hands on her hips. "You're doing this?"

I nod.

"You coward. You utter fucking coward." She points at me accusingly. I don't have the fight in me to warn her, to threaten she doesn't get to speak to me like that. I don't care. Everything I want, everything I crave, has been taken from me. What the fuck does it all matter anyway?

I stand and take a deep breath, steeling myself for what I have to do.

"Why?" she asks, her lip trembling. "It's going to break her, Bren."

I shake my head at her words. "I'm doing this for her." I meet her eyes. "For her."

She shakes her head as tears stream down her face. Finn bands his arm around her and tugs her toward him.

I turn and push my hand on the door handle. "I won't forgive you, Bren. And neither will she," she shouts from behind me as I make to leave the room.

"And I won't forgive myself," I tell her over my shoulder.

"Forever," I whisper the words for only me to hear, squeezing my eyes closed at the way my heart constricts.

"Forever," I mumble again, lifting my chin with a renewed sense of determination.

It's late when I return to my apartment. I spent the whole day coming up with a plan for my girl. I wince at the thought. She's not my girl. She's not anyone's. Least of all, mine.

I head toward the refrigerator, desperate to take away the dryness in my throat. I pull out a bottle of water and almost empty the damn thing in one swallow.

"Bren." Her sweet voice makes my muscles coil up tight. "I was waiting for you. I was worried about you." She covers my back with her small body, barely able to wrap her arms around me. They stop on my chest, one covering my beating heart. *Can she hear it thumping crazily for her, breaking with every pulse?*

"What's wrong?" Her voice is low and full of concern, no doubt feeling me tense under her touch. I lower my head, unable to voice everything I'm wanting to say.

I want you. I know it's wrong, but I want to keep you, anyway. Like I promised. I want forever. Our forever.

But you deserve better. And I'm giving you that. I'm setting you free.

"Nothing's wrong, baby." My voice is husky with a crumbling edge to it. Even I can hear the lie. She can too. I feel her arms tighten, and she tucks her head against my back, kissing me over top of my shirt, but I feel it all the way under my skin. Burning into me. I close my eyes and bring her hand to my lips, smelling her scent, my scent on her. I kiss her fingers tenderly and her body responds by going lax, sagging into me.

I need this.

I need her.

One last time.

One time to last me a lifetime.

Although I know it's a lie, one more time will never be enough. But, if this is the last time I can have her, I'm taking it. I'm taking her and I'm going to treasure every single second of it.

Abruptly, I spin on my heel, causing Sky to gasp. Roughly I pull her along to the bedroom and throw the door open. I don't look at her as I start undressing. I can't. I can't see the love in her eyes. I can't. "Strip," I snipe the words out like vitriol, causing her to jump into action.

"Do you want my ass?" she asks, tilting her head to the side.

I wince at her words. I even took the girl's ass… *Jesus*. I sigh up at the ceiling. She knows I like to be rough when fucking her ass. I like the thought of a bite of pain with the pleasure, and she knows right now I'm teetering on the edge of something, and the girl is offering her ass up as a form of release for me.

Annoyance bubbles through my veins at how she's learned to read me, know me, and fuck, even love me. I grind my teeth. I did this, I let her in, made her depend on me. A fucking teenager.

"Bren?"

I glance down at her soft voice and my breath stutters. She's laid out on the bed completely naked, bare. Toying with her glistening pussy.

My cock throbs, and I realize I have a tight grip on it. The pre-cum pools from the tip.

I climb onto the bed and settle between her open thighs while she continues to play with her clit, her breathing escalates into a pant, and she rises, her hips bucking for relief against my body.

Bending down, I drown out the voice telling me to stop. Telling me that what I am doing is wrong. Telling me I'm a monster.

I flick her little nipple with my tongue and revel in the moan escaping her pouty lips. Her nipple peaks and she grips my head to hold me in place when I suck the tip into my mouth. "Bren, please." She bucks beneath me. "Please, Bren. Fill me with your cock."

Jesus. I don't even think, I act on instinct of her words, giving her what she wants. Always what she wants.

I use my free hand to position my cock. Her warm, wet heat encompassing the tip and causing my temples to pulsate with the need to drive into her.

My hand shakes as I push myself inside her, achingly slowly, determined to make it last.

"Ahhh. Bren." Small gasps and moans leave her lips, and I watch every one of them, searing them all to my memory.

To keep.

Forever.

I position myself so I have my arms on either side of her head, staring down into those bright-blue eyes, the color of the sky on a clear day. *The most beautiful girl I ever laid eyes on.* "Thank you." She smiles up at me and I realize I said the words out loud.

Painstakingly slowly, I push in and out of her slick, wet heat. Her lips part on each thrust and her legs tighten around my waist. I dip my head and her lips meet mine. A flutter of butterflies in my stomach makes me slam into her harder, to grit away the pain inside me.

I slam harder again.

I pull back from her lips and watch them part as I slam into her, making her body move up the bed.

I slow my pace, determined to savor every second of this. Of us.

I grind my hips into her pelvis and her pussy flutters, clenching around my cock. I draw back out and repeat it. Slowly, ever so slowly. Wrapping my fingers through her hair, cradling her skull in my hand, her eyes shine with tears as though she knows I'm making love to her. Her fingers find my jaw, causing me to break out in goosebumps. She strokes it gently while we stare into one another's eyes.

I have to tell her. I have to say the words. Make her understand why.

I touch my forehead to hers. "I love you, Sky." Her face breaks out into a content smile, one that breaks my heart.

"I love you too," she replies with a tear tracking down her face and the bastard in me even wants that, every part of her. I lick the tear away. Mine.

"I'd do anything for you," I whisper against her ear as I pick up my pace.

"Oh god." She clenches around me again as I fuck her pussy harder.

"Any. Fucking. Thing," I gripe the words out, pounding into her, harder and harder.

Sky's body tightens, and she throws her head back on a squeal. Her lips part, and just like that, I come deep inside her. My hips keep moving, determined to coat every inch of her. Determined to keep this connection for as long as I can have it.

Forever.

I'm laid on my back with Sky on my chest, stroking her soft, satin hair between my fingers. I try not to think about what tomorrow will bring. Or the next day. Or the one after that.

"You know what I'd like?"

She raises her head from my chest and looks me in the eye. I cock a brow for her to continue. She nestles her head back down but watches me closely. "I'd like to go to the beach. To see it for real, I mean. The sand between my toes." She smiles, a picture of innocence.

I stroke her cheek tenderly, conscious of how my hands are rough on her smooth skin. "You can have that, baby." She nibbles her lip and smiles.

The pool of dread swishes around in my stomach at the unsaid words. She can have that, sure, but not with me.

I lay my head back and stare at the ceiling.

Her voice a soft whisper, "Forever?"

The lie curdles on my tongue as I repeat her word, "forever."

She snuggles into me. Her warmth should reassure me of her presence, when in reality, all I feel is the familiar coldness settling over me once again.

Forever.

CHAPTER 37

Sky

I wake with a start to an empty bed. I feel around on the sheets but they're cold, a clear sign Bren hasn't been in them for a while. Sighing back against my pillow, I remember how he made love to me last night. Because that's what he did, made love to me.

Listening carefully, I can hear muffled voices. That's strange. *Is Bren still here? Did something happen?*

I leap out of bed and head toward the door, then quickly remember Bren doesn't like me naked in front of anyone but him; I dart back to the chair and grab the robe, covering myself and tying it in the middle. I head out to the living area.

Cal, Lily, and Will are all here, all with looks of concern on their faces as they stare at me. Panic fills me. *Did something happen to him?* I dart my eyes around the room to be sure he's not here. Then my eyes land on a bag and two suitcases by the doorway. "Sky, honey, why don't you come over here and sit down?" Lily says while walking toward me, slowly, like I'm a wounded animal. I stare at the cases and keep my feet plastered to the tiled floor.

"Sky?" Her hand brushes up and down my arm in a soothing motion, then I look into her eyes, concern pools in them, and I let her tug me along to the couch. I sit down with unease curdling inside me.

I fidget with the gown's rope in between my fingers. "What happened?" I glance up at Will.

She shakes her head from side to side. "Bren? He's fine." Her words come out choked, full of emotion. *Why do I feel like she's lying to me?* She can barely look at me.

Lily kneels in front of me. "Sky, honey. You remember when you said you wanted to become a teacher?" I nod at her words. *How does she know this? Did I tell her? Did Bren?* I scan her face, trying to figure out where she's going with this.

"Yesterday, honey, Bren found out some information about you."

I freeze. *What information?* I glance at Cal, whose eyes are trained on me. "What?" I snap in annoyance. *Why are they treating me like a child, trying to soothe me like a child?*

"What? Tell me!" I shove Lily's hands away from me and raise my chin in defiance. My heart pounds against my chest.

Lily sighs. "He found out your age. Your real age, Sky." She stares at me pointedly as though trying to emphasize something.

"And?" I snipe.

"You're not twenty-one, honey." She shakes her head from side to side.

I gasp. *How can I be wrong? How can I not know how old I am?* My lip wobbles at the realizations. I have no idea who I am and how old I am. *No, no, that's not true, I'm Bren's.*

"You're eighteen." Her words make my heart skip a beat. *Eighteen? I'm a teenager.*

I jump up.

My lip trembling so much I struggle to get the words out. "Where's Bren?" I need him to tell me. To tell me everything's going to be okay. To tell me they're wrong and I'm right, that I know my own age.

"I want Bren," I demand, struggling to see Lily now that tears are pooling in my eyes. I snap my eyes over toward the door, the cases. "Whose are those?" I point over toward the offending items.

"They're yours, honey."

I shake my head, unsure what's happening. Panic claws into my throat, making me choke on nothing.

Lily moves toward me, trying to embrace me, but I shove her hands away. "Sky, calm down."

"Sky. Listen to me!" Cal snaps firmly, causing me to spin and face him. "Listen carefully." His voice is demanding, leaving no room for me to argue. Like the good submissive I am, I listen and hang on his every word.

"Bren decided yesterday that he wants you to live your life like every eighteen-year-old girl should. He wants you to be you, he's set you free. Do you understand, sweetheart?" His eyes are full of concern as he watches my face closely.

"We've gotten you into a good school, Sky. They have everything there for you. You have a good allowance, your own place. You can do anything you want, honey." Will walks toward me, her voice sounding coaxing.

I turn back to Cal. "I don't want to be set free. He said

forever," I grit the latter out. He said it. He said it just last night when he made love to me. Emotions clog in my throat. "He said forever." I glare around at them all, searing them with my look. *Do they not understand?*

I squeeze my eyes closed at their faces marred with sympathy. My breathing escalates and I crumble to the floor in a heap, repeating the words over and over again in anguish. "He said forever. He said forever. He said forever."

Lily brushes the hair from my face and cradles me like a child. I guess I am, only a couple of months ago I was a child. The sob gets stuck in my throat, and I choke painfully. "Please. I want Bren."

I stare into her eyes, begging and pleading with her, but she shakes her head at me.

I hear her loud and clear, they're loyal to him.

Not me.

I ball my fists and push away from her, pushing to stand.

I walk toward our bedroom.

His bedroom.

Slamming the door shut before I slump to the floor. Looking around the room, I get stuck staring at the rumpled sheets where he told me he loved me.

My heart crashes and I scream out a wail, "You promised me forever!"

CHAPTER 38

F inn

I stride toward the living room door and push it open. Bren is holed up here at Cal's—like a bitch—while we have to deal with the fallout this drama is causing. Why the fuck Oscar just couldn't keep this shit to himself. I don't know.

What the fuck does it matter as long as the girl is legal?

If it was Angel, nothing and no one would keep me from her. It's clear my brother loves her, and she's absolutely in awe of him and quite literally dotes on the emotionless prick.

Bren raises his head from his hands. Okay, so he's not as emotionless as I thought. He has dark circles under his eyes and they're red. If I didn't know better, I'd say he's been crying.

"Why the fuck didn't you just keep her?" I snipe out at him, my temper wearing thin as usual.

He stares at me as though I'm an idiot, but hey, I'm the brother with a ring on his woman's finger and a kid growing in her belly, I know how to keep a woman.

"It wasn't right." His voice is distant, as though unsure of himself.

I scoff at his words, since when does anything we do have to be right?

"You love her?" I quiz with a raised eyebrow, but I don't need him to reply. I already know. But he doesn't reply anyway. He glares at me as though I'm a piece of shit.

"You're a fucking dick!" I spit at him. "You're going to lose her man. Believe me, I've fucking been there and it's hell. You might not be so lucky to get her back again. Don't regret it, Bren."

"How is she?" He stands and walks over toward Cal, who, unbeknownst to me, followed me in.

Cal lowers his head. "Not good man." His voice solemn. "She wants you." He lifts his eyes to meet Bren's, as if giving him the opportunity to change his mind. The stubborn ass dick shakes his head and turns toward Oscar.

"Tell me again what's happening."

Oscar sighs, as though he's already been through what he's about to say a thousand times.

"She'll be living on campus, she has a credit card, all clothes and meals are included in the college experience. She'll want for nothing, Bren." He meets Bren's eyes as though trying to reassure him.

I scoff. "Apart from you."

Bren throws me a warning glare.

Oscar continues on, "She'll have a cell phone, but with

only Lily's number in it. Just until she gets settled, then I'll delete that too." Bren nods but I don't miss his shoulders tighten at the realization the plan is to long term cut her off completely, for her own safety she can't have any ties with us if she's going to live a normal life, as Bren so eloquently put it.

The slamming of the front door makes us all turn our heads in that direction and my gorgeous woman, Angel, comes barreling into the room like the little spitfire she is, my grin widens on seeing her and her fucking bump carrying my baby.

But when I glance back up at her reddened face with tear tracks, I'm about ready for slicing a motherfucker up.

"You son of a bitch, Bren!" she spits the words at my brother, who stands stoically still and takes the verbal assault, completely unheard of from him. Disrespect is not something that goes unpunished in the Mafia.

"You bastard. You made her fall in love with you and now you're throwing her away?"

Bren jolts at her words, his voice a roar through the room. "I'm giving her a fucking life, Angel, she deserves that. She's just a fucking kid..." His words hang in the air.

Angel laughs mockingly. "Bullshit, she wasn't a kid when you were fucking her."

Bren's temple pulsates, and I move to stand in front of my woman. His eyes clock the move, and he takes a step back.

"I'm doing this *for* her," he repeats lowly.

Angel shakes her head. "You're wrong. She's one of us." She points at herself and her lip trembles, causing my heart to drop. She means like her, trafficked. My woman's legs give way, but I catch her before she hits the floor. She curls her fist into my shirt while sobbing uncontrollably into me.

I zone in on Bren's eyes, guilt clearly visible in them, before looking back to Angel.

"She needs us, Finn." Her eyes plead with mine to do something, but when I glance back up at Bren, he shakes his head in response, tearing my insides apart. Do I stand by my brother, the Mafia, my family?

Or do I stand with my woman, the mother of my babies? The girl who's always had my heart and been through hell and back brought on by this family. My arms tighten around her.

"Finn!" Bren snipes out in warning, and I meet his eyes, as if reading my thoughts, he says, "Don't." The warning is loud and clear.

Don't go against him.

I duck my head in understanding, knowing what I have to do.

Hating it all the same.

CHAPTER 39

Bren

It's been three months and two days since I made the decision to give Sky a fresh start, a life... without me.

I'm sitting in my SUV waiting for the campus bell to go off so I can catch a glimpse of the girl that not only opened my heart but stole it too, leaving behind a gaping hole that grows with each day that passes.

The cell rings over the car's speakers, and I press answer with a heavy sigh when I realize it's Oscar again. Every fucking week.

I grind my teeth, "What?"

He sighs dramatically, as though I'm the irritant. "The whole point of her moving nearly two hours away was for her to be far enough away from you that you can both live your own lives."

The clock hits fourteen hundred hours and I zone out,

staring out of the window as groups of young adults push through the double doors with excitement. My eyes dart around, searching the crowd, desperate to find her. Just for a glimpse. Like the sad, desperate bastard I am, I'm happy for any connection, no matter how small.

And like a fucking magnet, my eyes hone in on her.

My heart skips a beat at her natural beauty. Her long blonde hair shines and glimmers in the sun, all the way down to her perfect round ass encased snuggly in a pair of torn jeans. I rub my fingertips together, trying to remember the soft satin feel of her hair. My throat goes dry as I work my eyes slowly up her body. She's filled out, healthy, so her hips are slightly bigger, making her clothes hug her tighter. What I'd fucking give to hold her right now. My dick starts to throb when I notice her tits looking perkier. A flush creeps up her chest as if sensing she's being watched. Her tongue darts out to wet her lips, and I squeeze my eyes shut at the memories assaulting me. My obedient girl on her knees, always prepared to take anything I was willing to give her.

Her head darts around as though someone has called her, and my eyes narrow on the guy running across the college manicured lawns toward her. I sit forward to watch the exchange, my fists tighten when her face lights up like fireworks on the Fourth of July, causing my heart to plummet. The pompous-looking, little prick throws his arm over her shoulder, and she beams up at him as though he's a fucking hero. Like she did to me. A wave of sickness washes over me and I struggle to swallow.

He bends his head. He better fucking not.

His lips touch her hair. Rage boils through me, desperate to escape somehow on someone. My face must be manic because that's how I feel, like a caged animal. I grab the door handle to burst open the door, but without warning, the doors automatically lock. My body stills in confusion. *What the actual fuck?*

"Do. Not. Even. Think. About. It." Oscar's firm voice echoes through the vehicle.

"You locked the doors?" I choke in disbelief. *Is there anything he can't do?*

"Yes."

"What the fuck, Oscar?"

Oscar exhales loudly. "Tell me, Bren, does she look happy to you?"

His question throws me off guard, stilling me in my fit of jealous rage. My chest heaves as I contemplate an answer to his question. My eyes lock on to the girl across the street, the couple to be precise, because it's clear now with the way they look at one another that that's exactly what they are.

"Yeah," I grunt out in response.

"Come home, Bren. You need to finally do what needs to be done." His words were ominous and hanging in the air like both a threat and a certainty.

Dread fills me at his words, and nausea pools in my throat. *"You need to finally do what needs to be done."*

I nod, swallow harshly, clip in my seatbelt, start the engine, squeeze my eyes closed, then open them to say goodbye to her.

But she's already gone.

Forever.

CHAPTER 40

Seven weeks later...
Bren

"You should start coming to dinner again on Sunday. Your ma misses you." Lily looks at me pointedly as she hands me another beer from her refrigerator.

Things have been fucked up since I let Sky go.

I can't even bear to attend a family meal. The thought of Sky not being there with me. Her playing with the kids and me fondling her under the table.

I swipe a hand over my head, wishing I could switch off the craziness that consumes my mind where she's concerned.

Jesus, Oscar even resulted in drugging me one night. The little prick said it was necessary to stop me from going in and kneecapping the little bastard who had his arms around my girl.

I also don't like to be alone in my apartment. I hardly

stay there anymore. It feels emptier than ever before. I wouldn't even allow the housekeeper to change the sheets, desperate to keep any part of her with me.

I shake my head at Lily, and she sighs.

I gave up asking if she's heard from Sky weeks ago. She said she hadn't, but I'm not convinced. I think she's scared of saying she hears from her in case we put a stop to it like we threatened. The women feel the loss too, Angel is still struggling to speak to me and hardly ever makes eye contact, even after she gave birth to her and Finn's son, Prince. It still hasn't softened her toward me.

A buzzing noise breaks through the room and Lily picks up her phone from the glass table and she looks to me, and I know straight away she's been hearing from Sky, she darts her eyes away and starts to walk out of the room.

I can't help myself; I grab her wrist as she goes to walk past and snipe the words out, "Answer it." Nodding at the phone in her hand.

She searches my eyes, and I nod once again, narrowing my eyes. Cal must realize something is wrong because he slides open the patio door and steps inside, analyzing the scene before him.

He exhales loudly in annoyance, giving away the fact he was aware of some exchange between them. I should be pissed. But I'm not, if anything, I'm relieved Sky hasn't severed all ties, that she still has some support, that she still needs us.

Lily lifts the phone to her ear. "Hi." Her voice squeaks in response to the caller.

Her eyes widen and her face pales, causing my spine to straighten, my defense mechanisms kicking in.

"What?" Lily sounds panicked and that panic ricochets to me. *What the fuck is happening?*

BREN

"Put it on fucking speaker!" I demand, pissed I'm even having to tell her this.

Lily's hand trembles as she fumbles with the keys, Cal stands beside her, his face full of concern. I stand up, ready to rip the phone from out of her clumsy hands.

"I… I need… help, Lily," Sky's terrified voice fills the room.

Blood rushes to my head, making me feel lightheaded, *she needs help?*

"Go slow this time. What happened, honey?" Lily's voice is calm and collected. She looks anything but.

I stand stoically still, my legs feeling like heavy weights from the mere sound of her voice alone.

"There's blood." Her voice rises. "It's everywhere!" She's clearly panicking.

"Did someone hurt you?" Lily's panicked eyes find mine, her own bugging out.

"I was working… please help."

Working? Why the fuck is she working? Where the fuck is she working? My fingers hurt from being curled into fists.

"Okay, honey. Breathe for me, did you ring 9-1-1?"

She sobs, and it breaks my heart. "Yes."

"Good. Good. Get them to take you to Jameson Memorial. Will is there today for Keen's annual checkup, she can meet you there and we'll follow, okay?"

Sky's voice wavers, "Yes. Thank you." My heart dips at her words. My innocent, well-mannered girl.

"Okay, we'll see you there, honey. Please try not to worry."

"O-okay." Her breathing hitches and her voice falters, "Tell… tell Bren I love him."

Jesus, I bite my lip and scrub a hand over my head, pacing the room. Hearing those words sends me into turmoil, I want to scream, "I love you back. I did this for you. It was the right thing to do." But instead, I bite my lip to the point of making it bleed.

"Bren?"

A hand hits my shoulder roughly, causing me to spin on my heel. "Bren, are you coming?" I stare at my brother like he has ten heads. *Is he for fucking real?*

Of course I'm coming.

Where else would I be?

CHAPTER 41

Bren

We burst through the doors of Jameson Memorial Hospital like a stampede. It took us way longer than I anticipated to get here.

En route Cal called Oscar, who gave us the floor number she's been registered on. He let Will know she needed to be there for Sky, and he sorted other shit out that needed to be dealt with today. Shit I'm stuffing in the back of my mind while I deal with whatever the hell is wrong with my girl.

My jaw feels like it's locking, I'm clenching it at the thought of someone touching her, hurting her. She said there was blood and lots of it. I want to know who the fuck I'm killing, slowly. I'm snapped out of my thoughts when someone who looks like a doctor strides in our direction. "Mr. O'Connell? Mr. Brennan O'Connell?"

I push past Cal to greet the doctor, but I'm not given the chance to tell him it's me before he clips out, "Follow me." The dude quick walks toward a room, leaving Lily and Cal behind. Dread fills my stomach and I have to clear my throat to speak, my words coming out gruffly. "What happened?"

He turns his head to look at me with sympathy before pushing open the door. He doesn't get a chance to explain because the sight before me almost brings me to my knees. Nothing in the world exists apart from her.

The distressed look on her blotchy, tear-streaked face, but it's her eyes that make my heart hammer with despair. They're terrified and pleading, pleading for me.

I storm across the room without thinking, making a beeline for my girl. She's sitting up in the hospital bed and I swoop down to bring her face to my own. I kiss her cheek and she throws her arms around me, squeezing me hard around the neck. Her sobs are muffled against my neck, but I hear them, feel them, every single one of them stabbing into my core.

My ass finds the chair behind me without even realizing but I don't let go of her. *How can I ever let go of her again?*

"Bren!" My eyes snap up to an irritated-looking Will.

My own eyes glisten as I reluctantly release my girl and take in the room.

A team of people in gowns are talking in hushed voices. I glance back at Will for answers. Her own body covered in scrubs. *Just what the hell happened?*

I take in Sky's shocked, pale face. Her lip trembling, her body in a gown and her legs in stirrups? *What the fuck?*

"What the fuck's happening?" I snap, irritated I don't have answers already.

BREN

Will swallows, her face pale. Sky's words come out on a panicked stutter, "Th-they said. They said it's a baby. They're lying…" Her pupils are blown, and her voice rises on each word. "They're lying, right, Bren?"

Of course they're fucking lying.

"I'm not pregnant." She shakes her head from side to side, becoming hysterical. "I'm not."

I attempt to soothe her, running my hand over her silky hair. My own hammering heart starts to settle.

Sky sniffles and raises her head. "I have the thing in my arm." She points to her contraceptive implant. "You said, Bren." I nod my head in agreement. *She's right, she can't be pregnant.*

She whimpers in pain and that about does it, I've had enough. I push back from my chair and stand my full six-foot-four, staring down one of the doctors, he nods in acknowledgment and approaches me nervously, no doubt knowing who the fuck I am and feeling the tension radiating from my broad shoulders.

"Sky, we need to get the baby out soon for any chance of it to survive." My eyebrows rise at his words. *A baby?* My mouth drops open.

I scan her body, sure she's fuller, but there's no fucking baby bump, leading me to wonder how far along she actually is. *And who the fuck put one in there?*

Anger boils inside me, that sleazy little motherfucker, knocking up my girl and leaving her in this state. My fists pulsate and my shoulders tighten. The vein at my temple feels like it's going to implode.

"Bren." I spin again to face Will's voice. "She needs you." Her eyes flick to a horrified Sky, sheer terror marring her delicate features. "Maybe. Maybe we should contact the father?" Will suggests on barely a whisper, as though scared to even suggest it.

Sky whimpers and grips my shirt in her fist and squeezes as though in pain. I watch the action, and then look down her body, toward her legs, toward the team assessing and talking at the foot of the bed. I sit back down beside her, needing to be as close as possible, for both our sakes.

I nod my head at Will in agreement. The prick needs to be here. Then I'll deal with him once all this is over; he'll never walk a-fucking-gain after what he's done.

"Sky." Her eyes snap to mine on the command of her name, and I close my eyes to stop the assault of emotions her submissiveness brings me. "The dude at the college, the one who did this..." I wave my hand in the direction of her pussy. "What the fuck's his name?"

Her face is laced with confusion and her mouth opens to speak, but nothing comes out but a whimper and a squeeze of her fist on my shirt.

"You know his fucking name, right?" I scrub a hand over my face. Someone should have been watching her better. Protecting her.

I open my eyes to see her gawking face. "The dude's name you hang out with at college," I repeat, firmer this time, irritations bubbling inside, reaching the fucking boiling point.

I clench my jaw, waiting for an answer. Her fingertips trace my jawline and a thousand tingles break out along my body at the warmth and softness of her fingertips.

Her voice is low and unhurried, but with uncertainty behind it. "Martin. My friend at college, his name is Martin."

I snap my eyes up to Will. "Contact Oscar, get this Martin prick in here." She nods in response.

"I don't understand," Sky whimpers and shuffles uncomfortably, making me glare toward the doctors. *Why the fuck aren't they doing something?*

"I don't want Martin here." Her eyes plead into my own, causing the hairs on the back of my neck to rise. *Did he hurt her? Did the fucker touch her against her will?*

"I don't want him seeing me down there." She nods toward the end of the bed.

"Sky, honey, I'm pretty sure Martin has seen it all before." Will laughs nervously, trying to soothe her.

But Sky glares at her, openmouthed. "He hasn't seen mine!"

I'm getting pissed, especially when her ass lifts off the bed and her face contorts in pain. "Sky, what the fuck are you talking about?" My eyes drill into hers for answers.

Her voice becomes low, as though she doesn't want the room to hear. I have to swoop down to hear her. "Martin doesn't like women." Her eyes bug out as if trying to silently tell me something.

The college dude is gay?

I draw my gaze up to Will's, whose eyes widen.

Just what the fuck is going on?

Sky's words tremble on her quivering lip. "You… you promised forever." I nod at her words, but I'm still unsure what she's telling me.

"Excuse me, can you tell us what's happening? The baby, how old is the baby?" Wills words cut into my thoughts when I see she's holding onto the arm of a nurse who's holding a clipboard and clearly checking Sky's readings.

I stare at the nurse, desperate for answers.

"The pregnancy appears to be a cryptic pregnancy." She gazes down at Sky with sympathy in her eyes. "It means the pregnancy was hidden, sometimes showing no signs of pregnancy at all. Sky also has a placental abruption, meaning the placenta has become detached, hence why we need to deliver," she says the words, but they don't register.

"How old's the baby?" I snap.

"We're estimating around six months, maybe a little more. It's really important that you push when the doctor tells you to Sky, we're going to deliver the baby soon." She nods at Sky, conscious of the fact Sky hasn't accepted she's expecting a baby.

The air is sucked from my lungs, my heart plummets, then soars at the realization the baby is mine. I choke, unable to say another word. I'm going to be a daddy. The baby is fucking mine, and I'm going to be a dad. My eyes glisten.

"Bren, I'm not…" I snap my eyes open to a completely bewildered and in-denial Sky, her head shaking side to side. "I'm not…" Her lip quivers, her eyes full of tears.

I keep my voice low as not to startle her more, but firm and determined. "Baby, listen to me. You're having a fucking baby…" I point down toward her feet. "You're going to do as you're told, and everything is going to be okay." I glare into her terrified eyes.

"I… I'm." She shakes her head.

"Sky," I warn, my words sharp, making her jolt.

I soften my tone. "You got this." I tug her head toward mine, resting our foreheads together. "Forever."

She repeats the words in a gentle whisper, "Forever."

CHAPTER 42

Bren

Sky withers in pain and I can't control my temper anymore. "Fuckin' get it out!" I scream at the team of doctors.

Will strokes Sky's sweaty hair away from her face. Her face is red from pushing, and she's gripping my hand.

"One more big push, Sky," a doctor coaxes.

She sits up more and pushes hard into her ass. "Ahhhhh," she roars with a scream, and I can feel her body give way to something as she drops back against the bed, completely and utterly exhausted.

I kiss away her tears and stroke her hair lovingly. *Such a brave girl.*

I feel her body still below me, and I draw my head back to stare into her terror-filled eyes. Tears begin to blur her vision. "Why is the baby not crying?"

I stare toward the doctors who are working away in a hospital crib with a small bundle almost hidden amongst them. Panic fills me. *Did the baby die? Is our baby dead before we even get to meet him or her?* My body begins to shake.

"Why the fuck isn't the baby crying?" I stand and bellow in their direction, making their heads snap up. "Make it fucking cry." I point at them accusingly.

"Sir, the baby is receiving oxygen. We're going to take him to neonatal care. If you'd like to join us?" the same nurse as before explains in a soft tone.

A boy. We have a boy. My eyes flick back to Sky's, to see if she heard it all. Tears stream down her face. "Please. Please go with him, Bren." I stare back at my girl. There's no fucking way I'm leaving her. Not again.

I shake my head.

"Bren, I'll stay with Sky. You go. Be with your son, Bren," Will tries to coax me, but I stand firm, glancing desperately back and forth between Sky and the baby. If something should happen to either one of them, I need to be there. I need to protect them both.

Forever.

"Please, Bren. I don't want him to be alone. I want him to be with his mommy or daddy, please," Sky whimpers, her eyes pleading with me.

I nod solemnly, going over to my woman, I kiss her lips softly. "I love you," I tell her with all my heart.

"I love you too. Forever."

"Forever," I repeat.

———

BREN

The loud beeping of the machines would normally irritate the hell out of me, but this time? This time it brings me comfort, because that beeping noise means my son is alive.

My eyes don't leave the tiny baby in the incubator, small tubes coming out of him from all directions, both turn my stomach and reassure me at the same time. *How is that possible?*

He's tiny, only as big as my palm, with an ever so light dusting of hair, when I squint my eyes, I'm sure it shines blond like Sky's.

He's so small, I can't make out his fingernails, not without scrutinizing him anyway. No wonder Sky wasn't aware he was there. Sure, she's filled out but not enough to look pregnant and with the extra weight she's put on, she undoubtedly put it down to becoming healthier, eating more since her rescue.

"Bren, Lily messaged to say they removed what we thought was the implant in her arm." I turn my head toward Cal's voice but keep my son in my periphery. How the fuck I'm ever going to let him leave my line of sight is beyond me.

"Thought?" I query with a confused tone.

Cal nods. "Thought. Apparently, it's a tracking device." My spine straightens. *What the fuck? Someone's tracking her?* Cal shakes his head as if reading my thoughts. "It was broken. The image was sent to Oscar, and he's convinced it was done before they inserted it."

That would make no sense, unless… "It seems the boy that helped her…" He leaves the words hanging there. He saved her, well and truly saved her. I nod my head in understanding.

"Lily says Sky's being patched up and they'll bring her up soon, to see the little one." He waves in the baby's direction and my heart skips a beat at the thought of Sky being here too.

The door clicks open softly and Con walks in, deathly pale, his eyes flick to the crib holding my son. Con licks his lips, his hands shake uncontrollably. He looks on the verge of having some sort of breakdown and the thought alone irritates the fuck out of me.

"Do you think Keen looked like that?" His voice wobbles and he clamps his mouth down on his fist, his eyes transfixed on my son, lying helplessly in the crib. "Jesus, he must have." His voice wavers.

Con's son was born prematurely, but he wasn't around when that happened. No, the dumb fuck pushed Will so far away she had to go through hell and create a secret identity.

"Con, pull yourself together, it's not about you," Cal snipes the words out in a tone he doesn't share often.

Con's eyes flick to mine and they ooze sympathy. They move to my palm that is splayed across the incubator, desperate to be as close to the little man as possible.

His little chest rises and falls, and I feel like mine is mirroring his. If I breathe, then he will too. Keep breathing, little man.

"Go get a drink or something." My eyes dart up to Con's and he nods, turning around in agreement. "Jesus, he's a fucking nightmare." Cal groans. I grunt in response, unable to formulate words right now and determined not to take my eyes off the little man in the crib to acknowledge him.

It feels like forever before the doors open and Sky is wheeled in by Lily pushing the chair. I stumble to stand up, desperate to greet her, hold her.

Sky's eyes are transfixed by the crib. She looks exhausted, wounded, and terrified all rolled into one.

I want to fix it, fix her and our little man. I stride over to her and, without warning, gently scoop her up bridal style. Walking her back over to the chair so we can sit and watch him together. Her head rests on my chest and her hand tangles in my shirt as she quietly sobs. My arms tighten around her, breathing in her scent. My nostrils flare when I realize she doesn't smell of me. I grip her tighter. Never again.

Never again will I be without her.

Without my son.

They're mine.

Forever.

"How's he doing?" Lily's voice cuts through the silence in the room.

I clear my throat, feeling the overwhelming emotion clogged there. "They said he's strong. Gotta make sure he can breathe okay on his own. Doc came in and did some tests, said he's coming back later to talk about feeding him." I scrub a hand over my head, the tension inside me pounding. My hand automatically goes to Sky's hair, silky, smooth, soothing.

"We'll leave you guys to it," Cal says, but I don't raise my head in his direction. I nuzzle into my woman's hair, determined to put my scent back on her, reassuring me she's where she belongs.

"Bren. She's going to need some things, Sky and the baby." Lily's soft voice floats through the room.

I glance up at the sound of her voice. "The baby's going to need things: a crib, clothes, diapers."

I exhale loudly, *shit*. We don't have a thing for him. Nothing.

Sky stares ahead at the little man, seemingly completely unaware of our conversation.

My voice comes out choked up. "Can you sort it?" I plead at her, my throat becoming dry at the weight that's just landed on me.

"Sure." She squeezes my shoulder in reassurance before bending down to face Sky. "Honey, I'm going to go and get you and the baby some things, okay?" Sky turns her head in Lily's direction, panic filling her eyes. "Shh, it's okay," Lily soothes her with a stroke of her arm. "I'll be back soon. Why don't you and Bren choose a name for the little guy while I'm gone?" she talks to Sky like a wounded animal, and I watch my woman, she looks seconds away from crumbling.

I nod a thanks in Lily's direction, and as soon as the door clicks closed, Sky breaks down and cries.

"Shh baby, it's going to be okay. I've got you. I ain't ever letting you go again." I tilt her head and grip her chin in my fingers. "You understand me?"

Her blue eyes shimmer and she dips her head. "Yes, thank you." My heart stutters at her words.

"What shall we call him?"

Her fingers tremble when she touches the incubator. "Sebastian. I want to call him Sebastian." I nod my head in understanding. She wants to call him after the kid she cared for, the one that saved her.

"Sebastian," I repeat, staring at my little man.

CHAPTER 43

Sky

It's been two months since I gave birth to our baby boy that I knew nothing about, and today we finally get to take him home. I've stayed with Sebastian in the hospital, so has Bren, barely leaving our side. He's been completely and utterly devoted to us both.

When I was scared about holding him for the first time, he was the one that took off his shirt to do skin-to-skin contact first to show me what to do. His large palm held all of Sebastian, and the grin that encompassed Bren's face will be forever engrained in my mind. He held Sebastian against me when I was worried I'd drop him.

When I was struggling to breastfeed him, it was Bren that coaxed and reassured me that I was doing my best, and eventually, Sebastian latched on, helping me finally feel important.

Bren even changed my bloody pads in the days after Sebastian's birth, when my energy and mood were at an all-time low and the doctors were worried I'd lost too much blood.

On the day the nurses showed us how to change Sebastian's diaper, it was Bren who did the wiping while I did the holding of his tiny legs, both of us smiling over at one another that we were hitting another milestone together.

Bren was the one that held Sebastian when he needed tests done. He rocked him and soothed him with a stroke of his light hair when I was too mentally weak to do it. Then he'd climb into the bed with me and scoop me up, holding me until I fell asleep.

"Are you sure you have everything?" his words cut into my memories as he scans over the hospital room again.

"I think so." I bite my lip in nervousness.

"Baby, everything's going to be fine. We got this. I mean, look at him." He points down at Seb, all snug in his baby carrier. He looks so much different from when I brought him into the world, so much stronger. "I got the nurse coming over every day until you don't want her anymore." He looks at me pointedly.

Bren took it upon himself to employ a nurse to come over daily to check on me and Sebastian after I had a meltdown in the hospital when they told us Sebastian was being discharged. The fear of doing it alone without medical assistance terrifies me. I know Bren and the family will be there, but still, what if something goes wrong?

"Baby, we're going to be fine." He kisses the top of my head and tugs me toward him. I really don't know how I would have managed this without him.

"The cars are ready," Cal cuts in, poking his head

around the door before stepping into the room. His smile widens when he sees Seb all tucked up with a little knitted hat on that Cyn, Bren's ma, made him.

"Sky, could you come and sign your discharge forms, sweetie?" The nurse hesitates at the open door with a clipboard in her hand.

BREN

As soon as Sky leaves the room, Cal's smile slips. "What the hell are you doing, Bren?"

My spine straightens, my tone darkens, "Taking my family home. What the fuck does it look like?"

Cal scrubs a hand through his already messy hair. He has dark circles under his eyes. Clearly, the weight and stress of the business has been taking its toll on him. "You know full well what I mean. Have you told her yet?"

I gawk at him. *Is he a fucking idiot?* We're leaving the hospital to start a new life together. What could possibly lead him to believe I've told her? Because when she finds out…

When she finds out…

Fuck.

She can't find out. Panic bubbles in my chest.

No, there's no way I can let that happen. I've managed this long. "She's not gonna find out," I snipe the words out. Even to my own ears, it sounds deadly as I stare him down in warning.

He scoffs in my direction. "Seriously? You think you can keep this from her?"

"I do." I raise my chin.

I have to.

"I'll sort it before she even questions anything."

Cal sighs dramatically, like the pansy ass he is. "Bren. Secrets… lies. They have a way of coming out…" He shakes his head from side to side. "Trust me this will not end well." His eyes implore mine.

"You're right, Brother, it isn't going to end at all." I glare at him with a confidence I don't quite feel.

Sky enters the room, and her eyes flit between the two of us as if sensing tension. "Is everything okay?"

I plaster on a smile. "Everything's fine, baby. Shall we get Seb home?"

She smiles back at me in earnest. "Yes." Her eyes light up and I'm pretty damn sure it's something to do with the thousand I slipped the nurse to give Sky a pep talk about what an excellent mother she is. No matter how many times I tell my girl, I knew she'd react differently if it came from a medical professional. "I'm ready."

"Good girl." I press a soft kiss to her head and draw back to see her eyes flared and her pupils dilated. Fuck me, her responses get me every damn time. I adjust my cock blatantly and she grins at me, as if proud of herself.

Cal clears his throat from the door. "Ready?" he sneers out with a distasteful glare in my direction, making me chuckle.

CHAPTER 44

Sky

As soon as we walk into the apartment, I feel a comforting familiarity, a warmth. Home.

The dining table is full of welcome-home balloons, a hamper of fruit, and gift bags full of things for Sebastian. My heart warms at the amount of effort made by Bren's family.

"Are you tired?" Bren scans me up and down.

"I just want to settle Sebastian down and have a bath." I sigh, suddenly full of exhaustion, weeks and weeks' worth of worry and stress.

Bren nods toward the bedroom and I follow behind him. He carries Seb's carrier as though it's nothing, whereas I struggle to lift the damn thing.

As soon as the door opens, Bren's scent encompasses

me, clinging to my body like a second skin. Our bed is made, which is rare for Bren. Clearly, he's had someone in to tidy up while I've been gone.

"Got a surprise for you." His face lights up with excitement, the corners of his eyes crinkling with mirth, his smile smothered by his teeth tugging on his bottom lip almost nervously. He bends down and unclips Seb, lifting him out of his carrier with ease. His little butt is all scrunched up with how sleepy he is. Bren kisses his cheek gently and lays Seb's head on his shoulder and uses his arm to secure him, his palm holding his head in place. He takes my hand and leads us to the walk-in closet.

When he pushes open the door, I soon realize it's no longer a closet, it's now a beautiful nursery. My vision blurs with happy tears and my heart stutters with overwhelming emotion. Walking farther into the room, I trail my fingertips over the rolltop crib; I open the double door closet and take in the heaps and heaps of clothes in every shade of blue I could imagine.

Bren says he likes Seb in blue because it brings out my eyes when I hold him. He's also convinced our boy is going to have my hair color and shade of eyes. I turn and see the changing station with an array of products, blankets, and diapers. Blue elephants are painted onto the wall, causing my heart to skip a beat at the sentiment behind it. A crystal chandelier lights the once-bachelor closet, giving it an expensive and elegant feel.

"Bren, it's…" I'm at a loss for words. "…incredible." I meet his eyes and he grins, his shoulders relax in relief.

"Lily said if you need anything else to let her know."

I glance around the room again, taking in the toys and playmats. "I… I don't think we'll need anything else."

"Here, take little man. I'll go run you a bath."

He hands me Seb, who is still completely down for the count. His warm body against mine makes my heart flutter. He's so adorable with his little pursed lips and button nose. His hands open out in a stretch, and I'm convinced he's going to be as big as Bren because his hands aren't in proportion to his tiny self.

I lay him down gently in the crib. A soft toy elephant makes me smile and marvel at how far he's come, we've come. We're finally home where we belong, and I couldn't be happier.

———

I stretch out on the bed, my hair splayed over the pillows. I awoke in the night to Bren encouraging me to feed Seb but other than that, I slept through.

Not soon after I had taken a bath, I was in bed and fast asleep, all while Bren had been changing Seb and ordering food I never got around to eating.

A light cooing noise makes me turn my head, and I'm greeted with a smiling Bren propped up on his elbow with a very awake Seb staring up at him. "He's getting ready for a feed, baby. Little man's getting restless, aren't ya?" He talks in a low voice to Seb, one reserved just for him.

"Pull your top up and feed him, baby."

I do as he tells me straight away, lifting my top and unclipping the nursing bra to release my breast. I gently scoot Seb against me, and he latches on instinct. His little sounds make me smile as I smooth down his light dusting of fair hair while he feeds.

I glance up at Bren and watch his Adam's apple work,

his eyes transfixed on my bulging breast. I stifle a laugh, biting my bottom lip, then roam my eyes over his body, reveling in the ripple of his corded muscled six pack. His body now adorning new tattoos, one with Sebastian written along the bottom of his neck and the other has the words, "Sky Forever" trailing up the side of his neck all the way up to his ear. A sense of ownership and protection toward us makes me clench my legs together.

"Gonna put Sebbie down for a nap?" Bren quizzes with a knowing quirk of his brow.

I nod and chew my lip with excitement. "Doc says you're good?" His eyes meet mine, already knowing the answer but still wanting the confirmation all the same.

"Yes." My words come out breathy.

"Give him here. You can top him up later." Bren scoops his hand underneath Seb's butt and holds his head with the other, detaching him from my breast and taking him over to the crib in his nursery.

I lift my top and unclip my bra, dropping them to beside the bed just as Bren strides back into the room, his eyes now hooded at the sight before him. I've kicked the sheets off and spread my legs to give him a full-frontal view of me naked and waiting, needy and aroused.

His footsteps falter ever so slightly, and he uses the opportunity to push down his boxers and kick them to the side.

His cock stands proud, pointing in the air, and I lick my lips at the thought of tasting the saltiness shimmering from the tip. Bren pumps his hand up and down his thick cock, once, twice, before climbing onto the bed and nestling between my legs.

My pussy now has a light dusting of hair that I need to

wax but haven't had the time to do so. Bren trails a finger lightly through it. "I need to wax," my words come out breathy as tingles race up my spine from his gentle touch.

He shakes his head. "I like it. Keep it short, so I can eat your pussy good, then let my cum drip into your hair. Fuck, that'd be hot." I'm sure he's not talking about my short pubic hair, but I nod in agreement anyway, willing to do whatever he wants.

"I missed you so fucking much." He breathes in my pussy, and I can't help but try to squeeze my legs around him, but he holds them firmly open, his fingers digging into my thighs with force. A slow, soft flick of his thick tongue makes me arch my back in approval. "Mmm, fuck, you taste good." He drives his face forward as a groan leaves his lips, a swirl of his tongue, lapping and teasing, pushing against me, eating and nibbling at my opening. I buck into his face, screeching and moaning.

He works me into a frenzy, relentlessly fucking my pussy with his tongue.

"Can I come? Can I please come?"

I feel his face nod against me and a muffled mumble before I throw my head back and scream out, "Oh my god, yes. Yes. Yes."

Bren doesn't stop. He licks me through my orgasm, then gently laps away the moisture. He raises his head and crawls up my body, trailing his tongue slowly over my stomach and chest along the way. Bracing his elbows on either side of my head, he comes to a stop, staring straight into my eyes, his lips a whisper over mine, "I love you so fucking much." He scrunches his face up as though it pains him to admit it before swallowing harshly. "I can't lose you again." He clasps his fingers around my chin and pulls my mouth toward his, his tongue sweeping in and flicking against mine, giving me a taste of my own arousal. His chest hammers against mine. I scrape my nails down his spine, not quite able to reach his ass but desperate to mark him, remind him I'm here, I'm his, and he's mine. Forever.

Bren moves his hand from my face and uses it to position his cock at my entrance. He releases my mouth from his grasp, his eyes wander down my body, filling with lust and an unmistakable look of awe. "Fuck baby, I want to fill you with my cum so bad."

"Oh god," I moan when he rubs the end of his cock against my clit, up and down along my slit, the moisture a combination of the both of us. We both pant in unison.

Bren rises slightly, sitting back on his heels to watch as he plays with my pussy, tormenting us both. He swallows thickly and his eyes grow heavy, before they slowly work their way up my body, landing on my breasts. He trails his eyes down to my stomach before leaning forward and pressing a palm over it. Closing his eyes, he breathes heavily, as though deep in thought. His eyes shoot open wide and snap up to mine as if on a realization. "I'm going to fuck a baby into you."

Before I get the chance to respond, he surges forward, slamming me up the bed from the force. "Gonna fuck you good, baby." *Slam.* "Gonna fill you with my cum." *Slam.* "Gonna fuck another baby into you." *Slam.* He grits his teeth. "Fuck yeah, I am."

The bed pounds against the wall with each of Bren's forceful thrusts. *Slam.* "Fuck, yeah." *Slam.* "Jesus, I missed you so damn much." *Slam.*

I can only hold on as he continuously slams into me, the familiar sensations of an orgasm stir inside me, I tilt my head back and relish in it, in him, the forceful, domineering, powerhouse of a man filling me with everything that he has, everything that he owns. "Holy…" Bren's words hang in the air when his cock swells and he releases his warmth deep inside me, he tilts his head toward the ceiling and squeezes his eyes closed, his mouth dropping open in ecstasy when my pussy clamps down around him, bringing us both to orgasm.

Bren drops down beside me, and I turn on my side to face him. His chest heaves up and down. Bren laughs to himself. "Fuck, you've no idea how much I missed you." He turns on his side, propping his head up on his elbow. His eyes roam down my body, as if he's making sure I'm still here, working their way back up slowly before stopping on my breasts. They feel heavy under his scrutiny, and I can feel the moisture of my nipples leaking. Bren licks his lips. "Fuck, baby."

My mouth opens to say something, but before I can respond he's tugged me toward him and dipped his head. The scruff of his jaw is rough against my breast, but his gentle tongue flicks over the peak, licking the milk away, making me gasp out loud at the sensation and taboo surrounding his action. He pulls back with a knowing smirk. "Everything about you tastes so fucking sweet, baby girl. So damn perfect."

I lift my leg over his, opening myself up to him.

"Mmm." His voice is gravelly and full, ready for more.

"Oh, Bren. I need you again. Please."

Bren pulls his mouth up to mine, tenderly kissing my lips. He shifts his hips forward and pushes inside, closing his eyes at the overwhelming sensation. No doubt feeling his cum still inside me, still warm. I cling to his hair and move back and forth with him.

"Yes, Bren. Yes."

Before long, I'm throwing my head back on another orgasm and Bren is clamping his teeth down on my neck, the sting sending another wave of sensations through me.

We both drop to our backs, sweaty with heaving chests, our bodies spent.

CHAPTER 45

Bren

The past few weeks has been nothing short of bliss. With Sky and Seb in my life, I feel a sense of ease and completeness I never knew could exist. They're it for me. I'll never want for anything more.

Forever.

But there's a tinge of dread hovering in the pit of my stomach. It lingers in the air amongst my family as the weight of my secret sits heavily upon us all.

"I just don't get how the fuck you've not told her yet?" Finn snaps out. "Angel is blowing her motherfucking stack at how you're treating Sky."

My spine straightens at the insinuation that Sky is being ill-treated. As if I would ever do anything to intentionally hurt her. My jaw clenches tight, threatening to fucking break with the pressure, every muscle in my body tense and eager to release some of the aggression coiled up inside. I sneer toward him from across the table in my office.

"Look, it's fucking happened." Cal sighs. "Now we need to deal with it. Any suggestions, Oscar?"

All our eyes flick toward Oscar, pleading with him to have the answers to all our problems. Past, present, and fucking future.

"Leave it with me. I have a few ideas." He sits taller. "We have other issues to deal with." He stares at me pointedly. I'm not sure whether it's accusingly or not because I can never work him out. Never.

"Jesus, spit it out. I have a fucking wedding to plan, and I swear to Christ I'm not pushing it back again." Con glares in my direction.

After Sky went to college, and I hit an all-time low, Will refused to get married without her being there. Throw in the fact that Sky has now had Seb, Con is obviously chomping at the bit to actually marry his woman. Not that I can blame him. If I could marry Sky right now, I would. I just need to deal with this shit first.

We all groan in unison at the number of potential issues we may have to deal with.

"What issues exactly?" I blow out a breath in frustration. I mean, take your fucking pick with the issues: human trafficking, family fucking psychopaths, bunny boiler women, and apparently pansy-ass weddings are an issue now too.

"Teddy."

Oscar's words bring us all to a standstill, all eyes on him.

"He's dead." His words come out cold and unfeeling. A lot like him.

I mean I admit, I'm not a compassionate person, not until my Sky came into my life, but fucking Jesus, he sounds like he's just ordered a coffee at a store. Unfeeling prick.

"Dead?" I repeat, just to be sure.

"Yep." He pops the p nonchalantly.

Cal sags back into his chair. "Oh, shit." His chest heaving in turmoil. "This is going to kill Ma." He lifts his eyes to each of us.

"Not to mention, screw up my fucking wedding!" Con snaps like one of those bride-zillas on the show Sky watches on TV.

"We need to tell her." Finn looks toward Cal, as if offering him up as the sacrificial lamb for a very shitty job.

I turn back toward Oscar. "How did he die? When?"

"So, I did a lot of digging with the information Da had. Teddy was handed over to a family unable to have children. He was brought up in what appears to be a loving household as an only child. Around the age of seven, the house was broken into, his parents were murdered, and the house was set on fire, with him inside."

Our mouths drop open.

Jesus, that's fucked up. What sort of monster does that to a kid, to a family?

"Do they know who did it? What for?" Finn's fists open and close in rage. Quite surprising, considering the ass wanted nothing to do with Teddy in the first place, purely based on how the poor kid was conceived.

"According to the authorities, it was a theft gone wrong." Oscar eyes us all, and my eyebrows furrow at his tone.

"You don't agree?"

"No. I'd say our dearly departed uncle's last words were confirmation in itself as to who killed them."

I recall his words in my mind, the ones that have haunted our family for months now, particularly my poor mother. "Tell your ma I know. Tell her I have a surprise for her."

Yeah, the sick fuck offed his own goddamn kid just to get one up on us. On Ma. I scrub a hand over my face in frustration at how fucked up this shit is.

"So, keep the details from her and tell her it was an accident?" I suggest.

We all nod and mumble agreements. "Cal, you got this?" I raise a brow at my brother in question. He sighs dramatically at being the brother to have to break the news. To be fair, out of us all, he's the most compassionate. Mostly because he wears his heart on his sleeve and isn't afraid to show it. I'm missing that compassionate part. The only compassion I feel is toward my girl and baby. Finn would want to show his emotions in blood. Oscar is basically fucking incapable, and Con is mentally unstable after the stunt he pulled not so long ago.

Yep, Cal is definitely the better option.

"Yeah, I got it."

"Anything else?" I query, desperate to get home to my girl.

Everyone shakes their heads.

Thank Christ for that. One issue at a motherfucking time.

SKY

I've spent the past few weeks catching up with the women and family, because that's what they are. They've made sure of that.

Angel has been distant, and I'm guessing it's because she didn't agree with Bren sending me away. Not that I can blame her. I went from feeling utterly destroyed to bordering on hating Bren. I've since had time to reflect, and as much as I don't want to agree with his decision, I can understand why he made it.

He wanted to offer me a new life, to be able to do and achieve things I won't be able to while in his world. Offering me anonymity and a chance to lead a normal life I never got the chance to lead. Throw in the fact that my age freaked him the hell out, and I can see why he made the decision he made.

He did it for me.

We've been living in a happy bubble all week. I've played the good little housewife I enjoy playing, making Bren his dinner for when he gets home, sorting the laundry and cleaning. He bathes Seb every night. I give him his last feed, and then, as soon as the door to his nursery closes, Bren turns into an animal. He fucks me like his life depends on it, sucking my skin and leaving bruises in his frenzy, all the while whispering dirty words and making me come so hard, I'm convinced each time is harder than the last.

Bren appears in the doorway as I tidy away Seb's baby toys. He's home early tonight and his eagerness to get home thrills me. A shiver rushes down my spine at his lazy approach. He scans the room, looking for Seb. "He's in his crib," I confirm, while peering up at him through my lashes.

He stands stoically still, glaring lustfully down at me with such intensity I can feel the wetness pool between my legs. I lick my lips and his eyes track the movement. He flicks open his belt, pops open his button, pulls down his zipper, and tugs his boxers down ever so slightly to release his cock. He briefly closes his eyes on his own touch, as I kneel at his feet, watching him use his large hand to pump his thick cock up and down, up and down. He holds it out to me. "Kiss."

My lips meet his salty stickiness, I open slightly, knowing how Bren likes to feed his cock into my mouth. "Mmm, lick away my cum, baby." He takes in a sharp breath when I accept the swollen head and suck on it, gently swirling my tongue around it. He hisses out a curse before taking my hand and pressing it to his cock, encouraging me to take control.

My hand meets the softness of his erection, a contrast to the rough man in front of me now pumping in and out of my mouth. I work my hand up and down while only accepting the head of his cock in my mouth, a continuation of pushing my tongue into the slit to lick it clean and then swirling it around the head as though toying with it. "Such a good girl," he coos appreciatively. "Letting me fuck this little mouth." His hands weave into my hair, roughly gripping it to a point of stinging, causing me to wince.

I lightly play with his balls with my free hand, cupping and tugging them, causing his hips to drive into my face faster on each tug.

He braces his hands on the side of my head and shoves his cock deep into my mouth, making me gag. "Fuck, yes. Fuck. Don't stop, Sky. Don't fucking stop." His cock hits the back of my throat, and his head drops forward. His mouth opens in a choke when his cock pulsates in my mouth.

I continue to lick him through his orgasm, taking everything from him, draining him before doing as he requests and cleaning his cock up for him.

He pulls his pants up and tucks himself away, offers a hand to help me from the floor, pushes my hair behind my ear with a loving tenderness, a far cry from the dominating brute only a few moments ago. "I missed you, baby." He nuzzles down my neck and rocks his hips into my stomach, letting me feel his already erect penis.

I giggle at his eagerness. "You have some stamina for an old man." I nibble on my lip to stifle my laugh.

"Mmm, I'll give you a fucking old man." He picks me up on a squeal and my ass lands on the kitchen counter, causing him to laugh into my hair.

I startle at the sound of an unfamiliar voice, cutting through the air like a deadly weapon.

"Can you put the mistress down and welcome your fiancée home, Bren?"

CHAPTER 46

Bren

"Can you put the mistress down, and welcome your fiancée home, Bren?" Her voice cuts through our laughter, her words a slice through my veins, and her fucking glare toward Sky boils my temper to the point of near eruption.

I back away from Sky without meaning to, in complete shock that she's here and my worst nightmare has come true.

Sky's bare feet land on the floor in front of me, her eyes flick back and forth between us both, before landing on Marianne's finger, the one with the engagement ring on it, the ring she chose, months before I agreed to this arrangement.

Sky's eyes narrow in confusion, then she darts her eyes over toward mine in explanation. Her face falls when she reads the look of guilt marring my features I'm now unable to contain.

She licks her lips nervously. "Br-Bren?" She keeps looking from me, back to Marianne, and back to me in hopes of an explanation. I sigh in disappointment in myself, in Marianne, in the fucking situation. But worse, in Sky finding out. Like this.

The click of Marianne's heels makes me snap my gaze to her, she stands beside me with her fake red hair sitting in chunky waves over her shoulders, her notorious bright-red lipstick and her curvaceous body in a tight-fitting red dress with red pumps to match. She looks like an escort, okay, a high-class escort because you can tell the woman comes from money, if only by the look of her pure distaste in Sky's direction, as though my girl is nothing compared to her.

Yet, in reality, she's everything. Every. Fucking. Thing.

Her long, red fingernails graze over my chest and snap me out of my stupor. I grasp her wrist in disgust. "Don't fucking touch me." My words sound deadly, making her raise her chin in defiance, she clenches her jaw.

Sky's tear-filled eyes watch the interaction. My heart hammers out of my chest at the look of hurt on her face.

"Oh, Bren," Marianne drones sarcastically, with a cluck of her tongue. "Have you not explained that we're getting married soon?" She oozes fake sympathy in Sky's direction, and I want to take her eyes out with a fucking fork for even looking at my girl.

Sky's eyes bug out at her words and I close mine to will away the look of pain in hers.

"Now, that her"—she waves her manicured nails toward Sky—"and your son are fine. One can only assume that you'll come back home, and you can leave them to it."

BREN

My eyes flare open at her words. *Just what the hell is she doing?* I warned her to stay the fuck away. To leave shit to me. That I'd sort it in my own fucking time. Preferably getting rid of her before the need to tell Sky anything. My fists clench in annoyance at how the bitch has made sure to cause shit here, between us. She knows full well my family come first and she sure as shit means to destroy it.

My nostrils flare, every muscle in my body tightens. "Get the fuck out." I don't even turn in her direction, my words deadly and low.

The bitch sighs dramatically for effect. She spins on her heels. "I'll expect you home for dinner."

"Fucking out!" I scream, making both her and Sky jump in the process.

The door clicks shut and Sky exhales loudly. I move toward my girl, but she puts her hands out to stop me.

My heart shatters at her rejection. "Is it true?" Her tears flow freely down her face, and all I want to do is wipe them away, take away her pain, comfort her, hold her. "Is it?" she prompts when my mouth opens, but nothing comes out.

Because what is there to say? Yes, it's true. I'm engaged to be married. I let you go and went to another woman while you were carrying our child. I promised you forever when, in reality, it never stretched past tomorrow.

"Yo-you pro-promised me forever." Her words come out on a heartbreaking stutter, her lip trembling. "You promised!" She raises her voice, and my throat goes dry at the hurt I've caused.

I scrub a hand over my head, frustration pouring out of me. "Fuck, Sky I can explain." *Can I though? Can anything I say be enough for her? Am I about to lose her?* My stomach drops, an overwhelming urge to vomit at the thought of losing her again. My hands shake. "Sky, listen to me, baby." I edge toward her, but she steps back, causing me to stop in my step.

"You made me your mistress?" she queries. "Is that what you did?" Her eyebrows rise. "Wow, you really did make me your whore, right? Because that's what I am. The girl that sleeps with the taken man."

My jaw ticks at her words, her crude analysis of the situation. She gasps, her trembling hand goes to her heart. "Oh my god, you slept with her?"

Fuck, my heart crumbles at her expression, her eyes searching mine, unable to hide the guilt. She finds what she was searching for and darts them away, swallowing past the lump in her throat. "Of course you did. You slept with her." Her voice a broken whisper.

"You slept with her, you bastard!" her voice raises and she surges forward. I stand stoically still as her small fists hammer at my chest, her whimpers and screams not even a tenth of her pain but heartbreaking, nonetheless. I've destroyed her, and I hate myself for it. Fucking hate myself.

"I'm sorry." My eyes fill with tears. I move to tug her toward me, but she jumps back as if I burned her.

"Don't you fucking touch me." Her eyes now alight with a fire, an inferno of emotions, a depth of hurt, hate, and passion thrown into one furnace of pain.

A crushing sense of loss makes my throat clog. I've lost her. I've destroyed everything we ever had.

Everything I ever needed.

Forever.

SKY

Bren stands stoically still while my chest heaves up and down. I feel sick. *He's engaged to another woman? Loves another woman? He's been having sex with another woman? While promising me forever.*

Was it all lies? Does he not want me? Is it because I'm young? Does he feel a sense of duty to me because of Seb? My eyes close at the thought of our baby, my baby, not being around his daddy every day. It'll be me bathing him in the evenings, me rocking him back to sleep, all the while he's going to be with his fiancée. His wife.

My heart hurts, so I rub my palm over the top of it to ease the pain. It won't ease, it won't go. I don't think it ever will. My body quivers, and my voice feels trapped in my throat. "Please leave." I can't look at him, so I stare at the floor. "Please, just go."

He exhales loudly, the familiar sound of his hand brushing over his head. His voice wavers, "Sky, listen, I can explain."

I snap my eyes up toward him, anger taking over once again. *Explain?* "Explain what? You're engaged, Bren! You slept with another woman!" My words repeat in my head. "Oh god," I gasp. "Did you... did you use protection?" *I've been sleeping with him and he's been screwing someone else?*

He sucks in a breath. "Sky, fuck." His hand goes through his hair again. "I haven't slept with her since you came back, and of course I used fucking protection. I haven't gone bare with anyone but you." He stares at me, trying to drill his truth into my eyes, but I won't allow it. I glance away, unwilling to listen to his excuses.

"I don't want you here." I lift my chin in defiance and he clamps his jaw shut in annoyance.

He doesn't get to be mad at me, not after this. "Get out. Get the hell out." I point at the door, but he doesn't budge.

"Sky, please. We can sort this shit out."

"Out!" I scream at the top of my lungs. "I don't want you here, I don't want you. Leave us alone, Bren."

At the sound of my voice, Seb begins to whimper on the baby monitor. My eyes squeeze shut at the sound, his whimpers a reminder of our baby and what we're losing as a family. The thought curdles my stomach further. I start to hyperventilate. "Please leave us alone." I shake my head from side to side when he tries to approach me. "Please. Just go."

"Sky, baby. Please." His face is distressed, riddled with guilt, sadness. "Please, don't do this."

"I never want to see you again, Bren." My heart aches at my own words.

He drops his head and turns on his heel. Striding toward the door, he flings it open and slams it behind him.

A shout comes from the corridor outside, followed by a loud commotion, before I crumble to the floor at the sound of Seb's whimpers, his soft toy elephant sitting in front of me tauntingly. My eyes become blurry and the ache in my heart increases. I squeeze my eyes closed, the agonizing pain of rejection breaking through me bit by bit. Lifting my head, I scream. I scream until my throat is raw and my head throbs, emotion barreling out of me. I hate it. I hate what they've done. The mess they've caused. But worse of all, I hate him.

My body goes limp, giving into my heartbreak. I choke on my sob, I'm useless without him. So useless.

A feeling of worthlessness I've never felt before hovers over me. Not even in the compound did I feel so unimportant, so disposable, so destroyed.

He promised me forever, but in reality, he couldn't even promise tomorrow.

BREN

I hear her whimpers in the corridor, followed by a gut-wrenching scream. I turn to go back in there but stop myself, knowing it'll do no good. She needs time, then hopefully she'll come to her senses and hear me out. Let me back in.

I spin around, eyeing the glass sideboard in the corridor. I overturn it with ease, sending it shattering into a thousand pieces, but still, I don't feel relief. Still, I need more. I need her. I need her satin, soft hair on my fingers. I need her delicate skin on my hands, and I need her innocent, loving heart to need me. To give me reason other than being the head of the family.

My hands shake as I pull my phone from my pocket. My fingers struggle to press the call button. "Cal?"

"Yeah, is everything okay?" He rustles around in the background, no doubt leaving the room.

I sigh exaggeratively. "No..." My heart hurts, struggling to say the words, I stare up at the ceiling, trying to compose myself.

"Bren, what the fuck's happened? What's wrong?"

My lip quivers. "She knows. She knows man." My heart plummets on my own words. "She knows." My voice a broken whisper.

I can hear him swallow over the line, understanding what a mess I've created. Even when he warned me, when they all warned me. "Shall I ask Lily to go over to her?" His voice is low and unsure, full of disappointment. Fuck, I'm such a failure at things.

"Yeah." It's all I manage to say. The only words I can get out without breaking down completely.

"Come over to our house, and I'll send Lily straight to yours, okay?"

"Thanks." I end the call.

My legs feeling heavy as I reluctantly walk down the corridor.

Away from them both.

CHAPTER 47

Sky

The soft creak of the bedroom door draws my attention away from the little bundle in my arms. Tears stream down my face as I feed Seb. His large hand resting on my breast, a reminder of Bren.

Lily comes into the room, her eyes trained on me as she approaches the bed like a deer in the headlights, unsure of the reception she's going to get.

"Are you okay?" Her voice is soft, a reminder of how caring she is.

I shake my head from side to side, my voice a whisper, "No." I glance down and stroke Seb's hair. A tear drips onto my hand and guilt hits me hard. I shouldn't be feeding my baby while crying, he deserves better than this. All of this.

But he was ready for a feed. He needed settling; he needs his bath, his daddy. I choke on a sob.

"Sky, honey, why don't you give me Seb, and I'll try to settle him?"

I shake my head and hold him tighter. My blurry eyes meet hers. "It's okay, thank you. I want to feed him and care for him." His lip quivers. *Can I do this? Can I do it on my own?*

Lily nods her head and darts her eyes away. But I don't mistake the look of guilt lying there when she does it, not after learning to read people on the compound.

My spine straightens at the thought. "Did you know?" My voice comes out clipped.

Lily's eyes bug out.

"Did you?" I accuse.

Her own eyes fill with tears. "Of course you did. You all did, right? You're family." I raise my chin in disgust. Clearly, I'm not family. All this time I thought they were welcoming me with open arms, being supportive and loyal, when in reality, the only person they're loyal to is Bren.

"Get out," I snap at her.

"Sky, please," Lily pleads.

"I said get out. I don't want you here. Out!" I scream, startling Seb into a cry.

Lily jumps to her feet and turns. "I'm sorry," she whispers as the door closes.

I sit back against the headboard.

"It's just you and me, Sebbie. That's all we need, right?" I kiss his soft head and continue feeding him.

BREN

I wait anxiously in Cal's living room for news of Sky. Lily only left half an hour ago, but it feels like a lifetime.

The door swings open and Angel comes storming in, Finn hot on her heels but not quick enough since he has Prince in his arms.

I don't feel the slap across my face because nothing can hurt me when the sobs of my girl killed every feeling I ever had.

"You bastard! I told you this would happen, I warned you! You broke her heart again, Bren. Again!" My jaw clenches at her words.

Finn tugs her back.

"You need to leave her the hell alone before you completely destroy her."

I stand tall, determined to fight for my woman. For us.

"You don't know what the fuck you're talking about, Angel."

She laughs at me mockingly, pissing me off even more. "Sure, you promise one girl forever. You just put a ring on another woman's finger and drop your dick in to her hole, but I don't know what I'm talking about?"

My jaw ticks. "I did that shit for this family!" I sneer, pointing my finger in her direction.

She smirks at me. "Sure, you did."

Finn pulls on Angel's arm, but she brushes him off, refusing to budge.

"If you fucking cared enough, perhaps you should ask why the fuck I did what I did."

"Go on then, Bren. Hit me with it," the little shit mocks.

I sigh, rubbing at my temple.

"Bren," Finn warns, and my eyes dart to his. Fuck him, I'm done being the one to protect this family, the one that sacrifices and gets fuck all in return. The only thing I ever wanted and asked for gets taken from me. Worse? She hates me.

"Your man, Finn, right here." I wave a hand in his direction, his body slumping in defeat. "With the information Marianne has, he'll go down for life."

Angel jolts, her eyes flick from mine to Finn's, looking for confirmation. He gives her a subtle nod. "What… what'd you do?"

I laugh mockingly now. "What the fuck didn't he do? I'd say the last one of chopping up and spreading the remains of one of Dimitriev's men in the Hudson River, only for them to be discovered with his DNA on it, was the latest of his fuck-ups, wouldn't you?"

Angel's eyes bulge in disbelief as she scans Finn up and down. Finn winces under her scrutiny and his arm tightens on Prince as though Angel is going to swoop in and steal him away.

"Yo-you did that?" she stutters her words out.

He raises his chin in pride and glares at her head-on,

giving a firm nod. She shakes her head in shock before returning her eyes to mine. My cold, emotionless gaze penetrating into hers, letting her know just how much we really are monsters.

She swallows deeply. "Okay, so." Her hands shake uncontrollably. "She knows things." She winces at the words but stares at me for clarity. I dip my head in agreement. "And she's, what? Blackmailing you?"

Cal cuts in, "Her father's the chief of police, so between them both, they know shit. We upset her, we upset her father. She's got it in her head that if we join an allegiance, we'll be a force to be reckoned with amongst the crime underworld and within the five Mafia families."

Before we can elaborate further, Lily walks into the room looking heartbroken. She waves her hand toward me. "She knows we all knew, and she hates us all." Tears flow down her face. "We were supposed to protect her, Bren."

My heart skips a beat and I breathe deeper, my chest rising with stress and anxiety at the situation.

"Great." Angel sighs. "Just fucking great, we're leaving." Her tone comes out clipped toward Finn, who follows her toward the door like a lapdog. *At least he has his woman*, a voice echoes in my head.

"Maybe we should send Sam over?" Cal asks, caution in his voice. My body tightens at his suggestion, but the thought of Sky being alone right now... *fuck.*

"You owe her that much," Angel adds.

I nod at Cal in agreement.

After Sam took his beating down in the basement, we all agreed to give him light duties in the warehouse under close supervision.

For some reason, his connection to Sky and what he's

lost through his brother's actions made me show compassion in circumstances I normally wouldn't have shown any at all.

"Oh, and Bren…" I meet Angel's eyes. "You didn't have to sleep with her."

My stomach drops, but I don't acknowledge her words.

She's wrong, I did have to sleep with her. I had to prove to myself I could get over Sky, like I thought she'd gotten over me.

The day I drove away from that campus and never went back when I thought she'd moved on, was the day I went home determined to move on too. Determined to fuck any thoughts of Sky right out of my mind. Like a disease consuming my body, she was everywhere, covering everything, every thought, every minute of every hour. And even when I closed my eyes and fucked the bitch that's screwing us over, I thought of her. When I spilled my cum into the rubber, it only temporarily eased the pain. Because the moment I'd opened my eyes and it wasn't Sky looking back at me, I'd long for her all over again.

Forever.

CHAPTER 48

Bren

I slam the door so hard it vibrates the walls, but I don't fucking care. Not a single bit.

In fact, I'd smash the whole fucking place to pieces given the chance. I turn to pick up the porcelain vase she's so fond of and launch it at the marble floor.

Her shoes clatter against the tiles as she comes into view, tottering on the ridiculous stilettoes. "Was that necessary?" She raises a brow with a smirk on her face.

My nostrils flare at her nonchalance. The conniving little bitch, enjoying the hell she's created.

"You had to fucking do it, didn't you? You spiteful little cunt." I approach her with my fists clutched at my sides, determined not to lash out at a woman, no matter how much I want to inflict pain on her.

"You weren't going to tell her, Bren. I did it for you."

She shrugs as if it's nothing. As if she didn't just hurt the woman I love and take both her and my son from me in the process.

I keep my distance from her, knowing I won't be able to keep my hands from going around her neck and stopping myself from finishing the job, causing a million other issues if I do.

"You'll pay for this Marianne," I spit down at her.

She sighs dramatically. "You need to get over it. You know what we have is the right thing to do. For business," she tacks on at the end.

I shake my head at the woman, she's deluded and so completely money oriented it makes me pissed with rage.

I turn, unwilling to give her another second of my time, not when I have planning to do.

"Where the hell are you going?" she screeches like a banshee.

I keep walking toward the door.

"Bren, where are you going?"

I turn my head over my shoulder and latch my eyes onto hers, mine cold and deadly. "To organize your demise, Marianne. Where else?"

Panic coats her face before she tries to quickly mask it.

See you in hell, bitch.
I'll be waiting.

I drop into my office chair, my brothers already here after I called a meeting, determined to get to the bottom of this fucked-up situation. Determined to get my family back.

"Is this about Marianne?" Oscar finally has the balls to say something.

I narrow my eyes at him. "Of course it fucking is. I need it sorting." I stub my finger on the table for emphasis.

He shuffles uncomfortably on the spot. My brothers also watch him with uncertainty. "She knows shit, Bren." He laughs, but it doesn't hold mirth. "She knows a lot of shit." He glares at me pointedly. A warning in his eyes.

I shrug nonchalantly, undeterred by his warning. "Let her bring it."

Oscar sighs in disappointment.

"We could just knock her off?" My eyes snap up to Finn's, his suggestion appealing.

Oscar scoffs. "Her daddy is the chief of police. He has eyes every fucking where, including the goddamn morgue her body would show up at."

"Then let's not give them a body," Con throws in.

I graze my hand over my stubbled jaw in thought. *Could we do it? Get rid of her and her flapping mouth without consequences?*

Cal moves forward in his chair. "You really think the chief of police is going to be happy to let his one and only child disappear off the face of the earth? He's not going to leave any stone unturned."

He's right, of course. The man thinks his daughter shits rainbows. Glittery ones.

"Knock him off too." Finn shrugs.

"His Deputy, Anderson. He's quite eager to take his spot," Oscar replies, deep in thought, as if giving it some consideration.

"Look into it and hurry the fuck up." Because I can't wait much longer.

I can't wait forever.

SKY

It's been five days since Bren left, and I haven't heard anything from him. I blocked his number on the cell phone he gave me. I'm sure Oscar could unlock it if he tried, but at least they're leaving me alone.

Bren sent Sam over to me, and as much as I didn't want to admit it, I was grateful. I needed someone here. For no other reason than just being here.

"Have you heard from him?" Sam queries while placing his mug on the counter.

"No." Kneeling on the floor, I button Seb's onesie back together after changing him. Our little man is just almost four months old now and trying to roll, all while shoving his fist in his mouth, making me grin down at him. It's the longest Bren has gone without seeing him, and it hurts my heart, the wound gaping and open.

I shake my head before my thoughts once again become consumed by the man who destroyed me. The man I gave my heart to, and he ruined me, betrayed me in the worse possible way.

"What are your plans?" Sam asks. His eyes tracking my movement of picking Seb up.

"What do you mean?" I sit on the couch and gently rock Seb in my arms.

Sam shrugs. "I don't know. I mean, are you going to talk to him?" I sigh at his words, not wanting to go there again. "He had reasons, Sky. Maybe hear him out?" he suggests with a shrug.

Annoyance bubbles inside me, *reasons*? "What plausible reason could he have for putting his dick in another woman?"

Sam straightens at my words, licks his lips, and dips his head. "Agreed." I nod at him, pleased he's not about to argue any further.

"Listen, I best get going. But I'll be back in the morning. Perhaps take you shopping?" I scrunch my nose up at his suggestion, making him laugh. "Okay, maybe the park?" I glance down at Seb. The fresh air will do us both good.

"Yes, please."

Sam pulls on his jacket.

"Okay, you take care." He bends down and kisses the top of my head like a brother would. "Night little man." He grins in Seb's direction before closing the door on us both.

I slump back against the couch in defeat.

Seb coos at me, as if reminding me he's there. Reminding me I'm needed and someone depends on me. I raise my head, determined to do this, alone.

"Come on, little man, bath time."

CHAPTER 49

Bren

The door closes and her feeling surrounds me like a blanket would for a child. Offering warmth and security. Love.

It's been five days since I saw them both and I've barely slept. I'm pretty fucking sure my prick of a brother slipped me a sleeping pill at some point because I woke this afternoon not even remembering shutting my eyes. Thoughts of Sky and Seb have consumed me, a sheer determination to win them both back and make her understand that it's only ever been her. Always will be. My throat goes dry, and I struggle to swallow past the lump in my throat, already feeling a tsunami of emotions.

Watching her on the apartment camera does not live up to seeing her in person, breathing her in.

I glance around the room, it's immaculate as always, she always keeps it looking so tidy. Pride fills me.

I catch sight of the low lighting shining from underneath the bedroom door and head toward it.

My hand trembles slightly as I gently open the door and step inside. *Please fucking hear me out.*

Sky sits in the middle of the bed, gazing down at Seb who's feeding. My little man has fucking grown and the thought of him growing daily without me seeing it happen makes me choke on emotion.

Her beautiful bright-blue eyes dart up to mine, making my heart still in my chest. Her lips part to speak, but nothing comes out. I stand frozen in place. Silently pleading with her not to push me away. My cock swells at her perusal of me. It's been almost a week since I've had her, and my cock is suffering from withdrawal symptoms.

She tugs a blanket over her chest covering Seb, and annoyance riles me. *She's covering herself from me?* My jaw tics, pissed.

"Sky, put the blanket fucking down." I glare at her from under my lashes.

"No." She shakes her head at me. Her defiance makes my chest vibrate with both rage and terror. *Have I truly lost her?* My innocent, submissive girl.

"Sky," I warn again. Surely, she'll listen this time.

She glares at me head on, hate in her eyes, and it kills me. Fucking kills me.

"No."

My jaw clenches tight and my knuckles hurt at the force of my fists clamping shut.

I fight the urge to wreak havoc on the room and make her do as she's fucking told, like she always does.

I move toward the chair at the end of the bed and drop

down, seething in a silent rage, grasping both sides of the arm to force myself to stay seated. I watch her as she tends lovingly toward our son. A glimmer of jealously courses through me at her tender look toward him and not me, before I knock that shit right out of my head. My son always comes first to both of us.

It feels like fucking days before she stands in her little pajama shorts and camisole top, teasing me without realizing. Sky walks Seb over to his room and I hear her kiss him goodnight, mumbling loving words. My eyes squeeze shut at the pain.

She walks back through the door, about to pass the chair, and a fresh scent hits my nostrils: vanilla; not me.

I throw my arm out and grip her wrist tightly. Still staring at the bed and not her, because, right now, with how angry I am, I can't look at her. I can't see the rejection in her eyes. "Kneel," I clip the words out cold and uncaring. A contrast to how I want to feel around her.

I feel a tremor work through her body, but she doesn't move; she doesn't drop to her knees like I requested. Like I demanded.

"No." Her response is a whisper, but I hear it loud and fucking clear. I hear it. My heart hammers in my chest, my veins pulsate in my body, and every muscle is coiled tight to the point of breaking.

"Fucking kneel!" I bark and gaze up at her. Her eyes trained on me. I scan her body, all the way past her glorious tits. She isn't wearing the necklace I gave her, my heart hammers. *Did she throw it away? Does she not see I was giving her a piece of me? Something she gets to keep, cherish.*

With a small shake of her head, she says, "No."

I explode.

Jumping to my feet and grabbing her by her waist, I

throw her down on the bed, face first. Before she even has a chance to protest, I tear her shorts from her body, tugging them off her feet.

"You don't fucking get to tell me no, Sky! Do you understand me?" I bite my lip to rein in my temper, almost puncturing it. I smack her ass hard, the flesh turning bright red in an instant.

"Ah," she screeches while struggling to pull herself up on the sheets, but I'm quicker, stronger, more prepared for her fight. I smack her ass hard again, leaving a tingle to my own palm, the force of my action knocking her into the mattress.

I pull on her ankles to tug her toward the edge of the bed.

I make quick work of undoing my jeans and dragging my cock out of my boxers. Pre-cum glistens from the slit, leaving a trail on my hand.

"Bren, wait," she warns and I halt my movements, I need reassurance she wants this.

Soothing my palm over her reddened globe. "Fuck baby, I missed you."

She whimpers into the mattress when two of my fingers enter her slick pussy, her body jolts at the sudden intrusion. "Oh god,"

"You want my cock, don't you?"

She shakes her head, and I vibrate in temper at her refusal to say what she clearly so eagerly wants, judging by the humping of my fingers. I'd say I'm damn sure she wants my cock. She just doesn't want to admit it.

I withdraw my fingers before she enjoys it too much, not when she refuses to accept my cock.

Sky scurries up the bed and my jaw tics in aggravation. In quick succession, I clamber onto the bed, now on my knees. I swiftly drag her down the bed and position her ass up in the air.

Positioning my cock at her entrance, I demand, "Say you fucking want it!" My temper is wearing thin, but I need her to want me.

I rub my finger over her clit, eliciting a moan from her. A desperate, needy moan. She pushes her hips back toward me and begins a rocking motion, back and forth.

I take that as my cue and slam into her. Instantly feeling her warmth surrounding me like a blanket, my shoulders relax and the tension slips away. I'm fucking home.

"Bre… nnn," she screeches into the mattress,

It's about time my girl remembers who owns this pussy. I use a palm and press onto the top of her back, effectively pushing her head into the sheets. She fists the sheets in her hands as I pick up speed. One hand tight on her hip and the other holding her in position, her whimpers and moans muffled by her position.

The feeling of her pussy encompassing my cock once again is overwhelming. I'm where I belong. Where I want to be, nothing else will ever compare. I slam into her over and over. Glancing down to where we're joined, I relish in the sight before me, my slick cock working in and out of her tight hole, stretching to accommodate me, made possible by me, made for me. "Fuck yes!"

"Oh god, yes." She groans into the sheets and her pussy clenches tight around me.

"This is my pussy. Mine!" I deliver one, final slam and my cock pulsates. My head drops back in pure euphoria and my mouth opens on a groan.

Wow, absolute motherfucking bliss. I continue pushing myself in and out of her, even though my cock has been milked dry, before I finally give in and withdraw, feeling her loss immediately. My eyes lock onto her pussy dripping with my cum and it's fucking beautiful. I use two fingers to shove some back inside. Sky whimpers and my heart skips a beat.

"Sky?" I flip her onto her back, her face dripping with tears, and my heart sinks. Shit, I fucked up.

My voice wavers with uncertainty. "Sky?" I reach for her, but she turns her head away.

"Please, just go."

My throat goes dry. This was not what I intended. I was supposed to fuck her good, then hold her close to me. Cherish her.

"I don't wanna leave you." I wave my hand up and down her body. She remains unmoved in a fetal position, mirroring how I found her all those months ago. "Like this," I add on.

"Please," I practically beg, my throat feeling raw with emotion, choking on my words.

She turns her head to face me, her eyes telling me a thousand things and none of them what I want to hear. "No."

My stomach sinks, my throat clogs, and my heart shatters.

I walk toward the door. I fucked up.

CHAPTER 50

Sky

I'm grateful for the fresh air today. I needed to get out of the apartment, away from the memories.

When Bren fucked me last night, it was about him asserting his power back, the power I normally freely give him. But not anymore, and that's why he fucked me like a wild animal, not caring to consider what I felt or thought. I wanted to exert some form of authority over him, show him that I can be in control too. He wasn't prepared to hear me say no; he didn't want to hear it, so he shoved my face so far into the mattress he wouldn't have to deal with the consequences.

Given normal circumstances, I'd have probably enjoyed the punishing sex, in fact in some sick, twisted way I actually did. But I just wanted to reject him, to hurt him like he hurt me. I wanted to be strong.

What I wasn't prepared for was when I turned over and saw the broken expression on his face. He knew he'd pushed me too far and probably realized he'd pushed me further away.

"Do you want an ice cream cone or something?" Sam cuts into my thoughts as I take a seat on the bench and park Seb's stroller beside me.

"Sure, thank you." He nods at my words and wonders off toward the stall.

Staring over the lake at the boats, I can't help but reminisce about the time me and Bren went to the Pier. It was, without a doubt, the best night of my entire life. My stomach has butterflies dancing around in it at the mere thought.

A shadow crosses over my path and I turn my head up with a smile, assuming it's Sam. My smile soon slips when a condescending sneer aimed in my direction eyes me up and down.

"Fancy seeing you here," Marianne gloats.

I'm sure it's no coincidence she's here too. She certainly doesn't look like the type of woman to be walking around a park filled with families and people participating in sports. Not with her stilettoes on and her fitted dress showing off ample amounts of her breasts.

I ignore her and face the lake once again.

She clicks her tongue in disapproval at my blatant ignorance. If there's anything that the compound taught us, it was how to be well-mannered and submissive. Right now, I'm neither of those things.

"Me and Bren are due to marry next weekend. Of course he'll want the boy there." She turns her nose up in Seb's direction. My spine straightens at her insinuation of my baby being at their wedding. *Absolutely not.* I clutch his stroller handle tighter.

"We'll start custody proceeding straight after the wedding."

My eyes snap up to hers, my heart ricocheting against my chest, panic bubbling inside me. *They're going to take Seb away? Is that their plan?* My throat goes dry and tears threaten to fall, my mind floating with possibilities of losing my son.

"I mean, I'm not mother material." She drags her manicured hand over her body as she continues on, "The boy can go to boarding school for all I care. But he will be my son, so I will have some say in his upbringing." She smirks at me, no doubt seeing my panic.

Her son? He's my baby. I tighten my hand on the stroller to the point of pain.

"Of course, you could aways disappear, take the little bastard with you." She steps forward and drops a heavy envelope in my lap. My eyes dart down toward it. "Best decide fast, Sky... or is it Jenny?" I glance up toward her in confusion. She mock pouts, "Ah, did Bren not tell you? That's your real name, not the fake one they made for you." A heaviness fills my chest. Sadness, disappointment, and confusion. The name isn't familiar to me and no matter how much I quickly flick through memories, nothing comes to me. The clicking of her heels snaps me back to the present. "So many secrets, Sky. So many lies."

She turns and begins to walk away. "You best hurry. Starting next week, the brat will be mine."

She disappears as quick as she came, and if it wasn't for the heavy envelope in my lap, I'd really question my sanity right now. After everything that has happened recently, I wouldn't be surprised if I was having some sort of mental breakdown.

I open the large envelope with shaky fingers. Wads and wads of cash are stuffed in there.

"Sky?" I fumble quickly to shove the envelope into Seb's stroller. "Sky, was that Marianne?" Sam approaches with two ice cream cones in hand.

I nod.

"She shouldn't fucking be here. She shouldn't be around you." He gazes down at Seb protectively. "I'll call, Bren. He'll blow his fucking stack at this." *What will happen when Bren finds out? Will she tell him I'm aware of their plan?*

I panic the words out, "No, please don't." I hold on to his wrist. "Please, Sam, I don't want any more trouble. She didn't say anything bad." I try to sound convincing, but Sam continues to eye me skeptically. I try again, "Please, Sam. I trust you."

Sam's eyes soften at my words. He finally concedes on a nod. "Okay."

"Thank you."

He sits beside me and hands me the ice cream. The one I no longer want, but take anyway, determined to act normal.

Determined to act like I'm not planning an escape.

A new life.

SKY

I sit on the couch scrolling through my phone as Seb lays cooing at his toys on his blanket. My fingers shake as I try to desperately search for any legal information regarding the marriage of spouses and if the newlyweds can take custody of the child.

What little I do learn leaves a pool of dread deep in my gut as several things go against me. I'm a young single mother, essentially homeless with no real name, trafficked. A desperate whimper escapes my lips.

Bren and Marianne will be an established professional couple, with multiple businesses, and her father is the chief of police? I don't stand a chance. I slink back into the cushions, completely despondent. If it wasn't for the adorable sounds of my Seb, I'd be bawling my eyes out right now. But instead, I need to be strong. I need a plan.

The doorbell rings, startling me.

If it were Bren, he'd literally just walk in, but at the same time if it was someone I didn't know, they wouldn't get as far as the elevator, so whoever it is isn't a threat, not initially anyway. I nibble my lip as I approach the door, feeling like a chained bear being poked for a reaction.

I scan the security screen with my palm and Angel's face appears on the screen. Without even having to think, I unlock the door.

Pushing herself inside before I open it completely, she flings her arms around me. Hugging me so tight it almost hurts. She sobs into my hair, and I find myself stroking her back, easing her pain.

"I'm sorry, Sky." I draw back and stare into her blurry green eyes. "I told him I didn't agree with how he was doing things."

My thought process on Angel keeping her distance is confirmed. She's been pissed at Bren and so chose to stay away. I take hold of her hand and lead her to the couch. She slumps down beside me and stares directly at Seb, a faint smile crossing her lips. "I swear he looks just like Prince did when he was a few months." Prince is now eight months old and twice the size of Seb. I glance down at my boy, shoving his elephant into his mouth. "Is he teething?"

I sigh dramatically. "God, yes."

Angel chuckles. "I know, right?! Hurts like a bitch on your tit, doesn't it?"

I choke at her crudeness, but yes, she's right; I nod at her.

She moves to face me, stroking my hair to behind my ears in a loving gesture. "I'm sorry I wasn't here for you."

"It's okay," I whisper, desperate to take away the pain in her eyes.

She shakes her head. "No, it's not. I'm here now, Sky. When you think you have no one else, you have me." *Can she read my thoughts right now? Does she know how desperate I am to have her, trust her? But can I?*

"You can trust me," she says, as if reading my thoughts.

I stare into her eyes and she stares back with sincerity. "Thank you." I swallow harshly.

"Have you ever considered restarting again?" She eyes me skeptically. *Does she know my thoughts?*

She shrugs off the suggestion. "I mean, you wanted to be a teacher, Sky. I know that can't exactly happen, but you could lead a fairly normal life." She watches me closely for a reaction, no doubt seeing the hope in my eyes. "Away from here." My eyes flare with hope. "I'll help you. If that's what you want."

I nod in agreement as we begin to formulate a plan.

My new forever.

CHAPTER 51

Bren

I slam my phone down on the desk.

"You need to calm the fuck down." Cal's voice cuts through the room as he stares down at the plans for Con's wedding but still manages to spit the words in my direction somehow.

"Oscar said he unblocked my number, she isn't answering any calls or texts."

Cal ignores me and continues to stare at the plans on the table. "Remind me why the fuck we need all this security." He waves his hand over the paperwork.

Con sits forward and an annoyed expression on his face. "We have the other four families coming. We need security top fucking notch. We have Storm Enterprise helping out, we'll be fine."

Cal sighs and rubs his temple before meeting Con's

eyes. "Is this a good idea, inviting every Mafia royalty to your wedding?"

Con's jaw ticks. "It's the wedding of Will's dreams. I'm just making it a reality." He shrugs.

I scoff at his analogy. What a bunch of fucking shit. Con is the biggest fucking show off known on earth and wants to make a dumb ass show of marrying Will. Even at the financial detriment of the family. "Besides, Ma's looking forward to it." He sits forward with a gleam in his eye. The cocky little shit is pulling out the big guns mentioning Ma.

Cal proceeds to flick through the endless plans and pamphlets. "A license for a fucking Helter Skelter?" His eyebrows furrow in confusion.

"I know, right? Who knew you needed a license for something like that?" Con chides as though the planning consent office are the insane ones.

I shake my head and try to call Sky again. At the same time, Cal's phone rings. "Fucking great, Reece." He glares at me as though it's my fault his son is a fucking pest.

"What?" he snaps out.

Reece's voice can be heard throughout the office. "I might need you and Oscar to do a bit of damage control at school."

Cal tenses, before scrubbing his hand through his messy hair. "Why?"

"I might have accidentally mixed up the chlorine in the school pool for the cheerleading squad's pink dye, once they got in the pool and everyone has come out looking… well, pink." Apparently at Reece's school, all the girls dye the tips of their hair pink during football season and that's an okay thing because the school supports sports. Or some shit like that Cal droned on about recently.

"Accidentally?" Cal's voice is cutthroat, lethal. We all

BREN

know Reece doesn't do anything by accident, so he sure as shit wouldn't have accidentally done anything.

Reece scoffs in protest. "Fine, fuck. I broke into the janitors' office and swapped the chemicals over."

Cal jolts, then exhales loudly. "And why the fuck would you do that?"

"They kicked Verity off the team." He's silent for a minute before adding, "Okay, so they didn't kick her off the team, they suspended her."

"They suspended her?" Cal asks, his voice sounding distant as though in shock. Yep, the little shit dyed a bunch of kids pink because his favorite girl, Verity, got suspended.

"Until Saturday," he tacks on.

It's now fucking Tuesday, and if she's suspended until Saturday, it means the girl will still probably cheer. *What the fuck was he thinking?*

"It's Tuesday," Cal cuts in.

"Right? She's gutted." Yeah, the dumb ass isn't getting it.

Cal visibly shakes himself. "Okay, so what do I have to do?"

"Sweet talk the principal."

His face laces with confusion. "Why the principal?"

"Because his wife is the swim teacher, and she's allergic to the dye."

Cal's eyes bug out. "What? What the fuck, Reece?" He jumps to his feet.

Reece breaks out in a chuckle. The little shit sounds sadistic. "I know totally worth it to see her face. But I swear the principal is out to get me."

"Where are you? Are you at school? Are you in a lesson? Oh shit, did they suspend you? I can't fucking homeschool you Reece!" Cal storms toward the door, completely ignoring his role as second in command and doesn't even give us a backward glance when he slams the door behind him.

I raise my eyebrows at his nonchalant attitude toward business, pissed that I've been left with the mess once again while he walks out the door to his family.

While mine is in fucking shambles and I'm sacrificing myself and their happiness for this, the Mafia.

"Just fucking go to her, man." Con's voice snaps me out of my mind, and it's then I realize I voiced all that shit out loud. I scrub a hand down my face.

"Go," he repeats.

He's right. I need to make her understand, make her realize it's her and me.

Forever.

―――

I open the door and step into the apartment, trepidation filling my veins, my throat dry with nerves, completely unlike me but that's how I feel around Sky at the moment, a bag of fucking nerves, desperate to get her to love me back as much as I love her. I'm not sure what I'm going to say or do any differently, but I refuse to leave here until she agrees to listen, agrees to love me.

The apartment is silent.

I flick my gaze around the room, something feeling off when I see pots on the counter, completely unlike the immaculately tidy Sky I know. I feel a sliver of panic as I make my way toward the bedroom. "Sky?"

I push open the door and find an unmade bed, dresser

drawers wide open, and clothes strewn everywhere. *What the fuck?*

I move toward Seb's nursery, his room much the same. Stepping inside, I can see his drawers are empty from his changing station too.

My knees buckle and my heart sinks. *She's left me?* I struggle to stay upright as my chest tightens. I can't fucking breathe. *They're gone.*

Seb's toy cart is overturned as though she was searching for something, probably his stuffed elephant. She's taken him, taken my little boy.

Oh fuck, I scrub at the pain in my chest.

My lips part to scream, but nothing comes out. I drop to my knees, the pain too much to bear. They're fucking gone.

All of this for nothing.

Nothing.

I hammer my fist into the floor as wail after wail leaves my chest. I scream my tears into the carpet, my fucking pain, hurt, anger, all of it, fucking take it all.

My chest feels raw, as if my heart is bleeding and my mind is broken. I only ever wanted her, even if it wasn't forever.

CHAPTER 52

Bren

"Did you find anything yet?" I snap in Oscar's direction.

All my brothers are gathered at Finn's apartment for an impromptu meeting about Sky disappearing without any of our knowledge. Oscar taps away on that fucking tablet and the noise grates on me as I pace back and forth.

"Okay, so I have an idea."

I spin to face him.

"Her phone searches are all centered around laws about custody, married couples, who can get custody of a child and how." He gives me his full attention from over the top of his glasses. His eyes give away a look of sympathy.

My heart dips. "She thought I was going to take Seb from her?" My throat fills with emotion. *My poor girl thought I was going to rip away our baby? And what? Play happy fucking families with that bitch?* The thought turns my insides.

"It appears that way, yes."

"Jesus." I scrub a hand over my head.

"Fuck, man, if Angel thought I was gonna take Prince, she wouldn't think twice about running," Finn cuts in and I glare at him in shock. *Is he for fucking real?* This is the shit I have to deal with. He shrugs nonchalantly at his words.

"So where the hell is she?"

"I'm working on it."

"Work fucking faster," I snap at him.

Cal hands me another whiskey and I throw it back, swallowing it in one gulp.

The door to the apartment opens and Angel walks inside with her hands full of bags. Her eyes scan over us all, a glimmer of concern on her face before she raises her chin and continues to walk toward her bedroom. *What the hell? Why would she not ask what we're all doing here? Unless…*

"Hold. The. Fuck. Up!" My words are cold and deadly, slicing through the air and stopping her in her tracks. Finn's eyes flick back and forth between the both of us, before his shoulders sag with the realization that Angel knows something.

Anger intensifies in me, takes over my body, and in a split second I stride toward her. "You fucking bitch. You couldn't leave it alone, could you?" My hands go toward her throat, but I'm stopped in my tracks by a sharp pain stinging my neck.

"Move another fucking inch and I'll slice you, brother or not. Now, back the fuck up." Finn's voice is deadly, full of intent. My jaw clenches in frustration, desperate to get answers. He digs the knife in farther and I can feel the warmth of my blood trailing down my neck. Angel gasps and her hand goes to her mouth.

Her voice quivers. "Fi... Finn."

I duck my head in understanding before taking a large step back. All our shoulders seem to relax at once.

Con now standing beside me and Cal on the other side of Angel as though ready to move her out of the way if need be.

I concede and step back again.

Finn nods, seemingly happy with the distance I'm putting between us.

His tone is clipped. "What do you know, Angel?"

She raises her chin in defiance, and I don't know whether to be proud of her solidarity or pissed at her petulance.

"I asked you a fucking question!" he barks at her, making her jump and causing her lip to tremble. I don't miss the flicker of guilt crossing his face at her reaction.

"I... I wanted to help her because I let her down before." She wrings her hands in front of her nervously. She swallows back the tears threatening to spill. "I wanted her to have the life you promised her before you hurt her." She glares at me, and this time I don't blame her. She wanted what was best for my girl. I nod at her, understanding her thought process, a silent appreciation of the fact she stepped up for my girl and stood against the family, both fill me with gratitude I wasn't prepared for.

"Daddy, what's wrong?" Charlie's sweet voice fills the room. Her eyes filled with worry as they dart around us all, only just entering the apartment with Sam hot on her heels. The kid runs the poor guy ragged.

He calculates the tension and encourages Charlie to take her shopping bags to her room. As soon as her door closes, I inform him, "Sky's missing. She's taken Seb and left." *Left me.* I drop my head, devastation rearing its ugly head once again.

"Sir." I snap my head up. "Marianne approached Sky at the park yesterday."

My shoulders bunch tight. "What?" My fists throb.

"Sky didn't want me to tell you. She said she was worried it would cause trouble."

"Shit," I breathe out low. "She scared her, said some shit about us taking Seb from her."

"What? She thinks that?" Angel steps forward, her face pale. "I think I know where she might be."

I turn toward her, hope blossoming in my chest.

My eyes plead with hers. "Martin, the guy from the campus. He has a house in the mountains. I think she might have gone there."

Relief fills me. Absolute fucking relief.

"She was only going for a breakaway, Bren. I told her you needed her, and she needs you too. I can see that." I nod at her words. Too little, too fucking late, but right now, I don't care. All I want is my fucking family back.

"Guys!" Oscar shouts toward us, making us all turn in unison. "We have a big problem. I'm tracking Marianne's car, it's heading toward this Martin's house."

My stomach sinks and my hands shake.

"What? You don't think?" Angel splutters. "Finn? She wouldn't hurt her, right?"

Finn stares at Angel, unwilling to confirm or deny, his silence answer enough.

Too fucking right she'd hurt her.

But not if I get there first.

I check the clip on my weapon and tuck it into my jeans.

"I'm coming too," Sam states. I nod in his direction.

"Get us a fucking plan together." I point at Oscar and make toward the door.

"Bre-Bren? Bring her back safely, won't you? Both of them, please," Angel whispers.

I walk over to her and kiss the top of her head with both determination and reassurance of the situation. "I will, darlin, it's what I'm good at."

I stride toward the door with a confidence I don't quite feel.

I'm coming for you, baby.

You and my boy.

CHAPTER 53

Sky

"Wow, the little guy sure knows how to shit, doesn't he?" Martin laughs as he plonks himself down on the couch with a beer in his hand.

"He does. Don't you, little Sebbie?" I coo at my boy and nuzzle into his neck, making him wiggle in glee. "All nice and clean now, little guy." I button up the last of his onesie buttons and give him his teether before dropping back against the couch.

"So, how are you feeling?" Martin eyes me skeptically.

I push my hair over my shoulder. "Honestly? Exhausted, shocked, worried, but most importantly, I feel free." It's the first time in what feels like so long that I feel I have constraints lifted. I was feeling worn down in the apartment. The stress and worry of Bren coming over at any moment and another argument ensuing was mentally crushing. Not to mention the fact that I feel like I've lost friends in the process of them standing alongside Bren and not me, nor Seb.

"You look exhausted. In fact, you look like shit." He exhales loudly and I can't help but giggle at his synopsis of me. "What you need, miss blondie, is chocolate. Lots and lots of chocolate." Martin stands up and approaches the kitchen cupboards, but a loud knock interrupts his path. "I'm not expecting any—" He opens the door but doesn't get a chance to finish his sentence because a loud bang slices through the air, followed abruptly by a thud.

Sebastian begins to scream at the sound. I jump up on instinct and my legs almost buckle when the pool of blood expands around Martin's lifeless body, a hole in his head. My heart drops and I struggle to breathe, but I don't get the chance to so much as move toward him because the sound of clicking heels enters the room.

She stands there like a vision. All dressed in red, like some sort of model, a red scarlet with splatters of my friend's blood on her arm and a gun aimed in my direction. Her demeanor is calm and collected in complete control, but her eyes are manic like a psychopath, alight with glee. Probably reveling in my sheer terror.

"Oh, were you fond of him?" She mock pouts making my eyes bug out at the nonchalance. She just killed a man for God's sake. A good man. My friend. I swallow hard, willing away the emotions.

Sebastian whimpers and my eyes flick over to his but immediately lock back on Marianne's. She sneers in his direction, her lip curling at the edges. *How can this woman claim to want to be a stepmother?* A thought suddenly occurs to me. *Is she here to harm him? Get rid of him? Of us?* So she has Bren all to herself.

"You think you can take everything from me because you spawned that?" She flicks the gun in Sebastian's direction, and I move to stand in front of him, but her arm darts, aiming the gun at me. *Good, aim the gun in my direction, away from my baby.*

My words come out nervously, stuttered, scared, "Marianne, ple-please don't hurt him. I was leaving. Leaving Bren, you can have him. I don't want him." I shake my head from side to side, saying the words but not believing them myself.

There's nothing more I want than Bren and our little family. But not at the detriment of Sebastian being in the firing line, not at the risk of getting hurt both physically and mentally.

"I've been watching you. Waiting for you to leave so I can make my move. Waiting for you to walk away from all your guards, protection. Silly little girl." She clucks her tongue at me and sneers down her nose. This woman hates me, it's clear and that makes me nervous because, no doubt, she hates my baby too. "You think he wasn't going to come running after you? Do you think the Mafia Don wouldn't want the heir to his throne?" Her voice gets louder. "He won't let you leave!" she screams at me, making me jolt. Sebastian's wails fill the room and I wince, willing him to stay quiet, to not aggravate her more.

She holds her chin high as though she's about to give a speech. "I won't let you take him from me, do you hear me? We're going to rule this city!" This woman is insane.

The door hits the floor making us both startle. I take the opportunity to move closer to Sebastian, desperate to protect him.

BREN

We traveled by helicopter, all of us, including Oscar, who normally prefers to hang back and take a role in the background.

A plan of attack has been discussed, and because we don't know if Marianne is going alone, we're bringing reinforcements.

Oscar will inform us with heat technology how many people are on the property once we arrive.

We land just on the outskirts of the property line. Cal and Oscar take off together, they're going around the back.

Con and Finn are hitting the roof and coming in from above.

Me and Sam are going in the front door. During our discussion, Oscar was opposed to this, but I don't give a shit. I'm no coward, and I want my girl and baby back so I'm going in all guns fucking blazing.

Oscar's voice fills the earpiece. "It appears to be Sebastian, Marianne and Sky in the living area, no one else. I repeat, no one else." My shoulders relax at his words. "Follow through as planned." I nod, even though he can't see me. "Bren, do not go in drawing a gun. You might scare her into doing something."

My hands clutch the weapon tightly before bowing my head and conceding he's right. *Fuck. How the hell do you handle a delusional psychotic bitch?*

Sam glares at me as if to cooperate and I side-eye him with a sneer, making him chuckle. The kid has grown on me, that's for sure, and his need to protect Sky has proved his loyalty, therefore, gained my respect.

"I'll go first." Sam nods at the door. A sliver of uncertainty flows through me. I clench my teeth, not liking taking a back seat but also knowing it's probably for the best. The deranged nutter inside might shoot before thinking.

"Fine," I snipe the words out and with one hefty kick, I bust the door in.

Sam enters and in quick succession he begins to lower as if seeing a target. A gun is fired making me raise my own in the sound's direction. Sam drops to the floor, but I ignore him for now, my mind trained on my target.

"Marianne, lower the fucking gun!" I shout from outside the door, my back tightly against the wall.

"Throw your gun in and put your hands behind your head," she screeches back, her voice cutting through me.

I'm going to kill the bitch. One way or another, she isn't leaving here alive.

I do as she asks and throw my gun into the room; I hear it skitter across the wooden floor. "Come in slowly, otherwise the bitch gets it."

My heart drops at the thought of Sky being hurt.

Slowly, I enter the room. I have to stand over Sam's body, the poor kid's eyes staring into nothing. A gaping neck wound bleeds onto the floor. My fists tighten behind my head, realizing the wound is no doubt deadly.

Another body is laid out beside him. *Fucking Jesus, what the hell has she done?*

I scan the room; Sky's terrified eyes meet mine and I nod at her and hope she can see the reassurance in my gaze. She looks down to the mumbles of our little boy on the floor, as though silently pleading with me to do something. To save him. My Adam's apple bobs, suddenly feeling a nervousness I've never felt before.

A desperation to keep my family out of harm's way.

I meet the deranged eyes of Marianne.

How the fuck I could ever have screwed her is beyond me.

What an absolute and utterly desperate shit head.

Her gun is locked on Sky.

"Marianne, lower the fucking gun." My voice comes out low and gruff. I'm trying to rein in my temper, but given the situation, it's a bit fucking difficult.

She laughs, but it's fake and mocking. "You are not in control here. I am!" Her voice rises. "Now come over here and kneel beside the brat."

I clench my jaw at her words. My legs feel like fucking lead, but reluctantly, I do as she's asked, desperate to be nearer to both Sky and Seb.

"You, sit on the couch." She waves the gun at Sky.

Sky's eyes meet mine for reassurance and I tip my head slightly, encouraging her to do as she's been told.

I kneel beside Seb, and my heart dips when I take in my little guy's red face. He's stuffing his fist in his mouth, his face is covered in tears, his little chest heaving up and down.

"Now. Here's what's going to happen…"

She doesn't get a chance to finish the sentence because one of my brothers can be heard on the roof. I wince.

Marianne's eyes narrow. "Oh, you brought the brothers? Of course you fucking did!" Her eyes scream panicked and her hand shakes slightly. *This isn't fucking good. Not good at all.* I dart my eyes around the room, desperate for a solution.

"Well, if I can't have you..." Before I know what's happening, she turns the gun on me, tightens her finger on the trigger. Sky sees it too. She leaps up from the couch and throws herself in front of me as Oscar bursts into the room behind Marianne. The gun goes off and Sky stumbles to the floor.

My eyes meet Oscar's crazed ones. He swings a fucking ax through the air just as Marianne turns. The sound of the ax smacking into her makes me wince, one thud, then another hits the floor.

Oscar startles, his face paling, his eyes taking in Marianne's head rolling toward him. He jumps back and instantly, maniacally starts stripping himself of his clothes and kicking off his shoes, both of which are covered in her blood. He's going into a complete frenzy.

"Holy fucking shit, you took her head off, man. Fucking epic!" Con barreling into the room like an excited child. "Jesus, why the fuck are you stripping?" His eyes knit together in confusion.

"He's having a meltdown at the mess," Finn drawls.

It all happens around me and I can hear it, but I don't take it in, the chaos of my brothers and their appraisal of Oscar saving the day.

I gently scoop Sky into my arms, the only thing I see is

her, my beautiful girl, bleeding profusely from her stomach. I stroke her hair and cradle her.

She jumped in front of the gun to save me.

A tear rolls down my face and lands on her cheek.

My heart cracks, my mouth moves to tell her all the things I've wanted to say but nothing comes out. *I love you. I'm sorry. It's only ever been you. You're my forever. You're my everything. I need you.*

Her eyes empty.

Gone.

Forever.

CHAPTER 54

Bren

The synchronized beeping of the machine changes, making my head dart up from the bed.

"Bre...Bren." Her weak voice sends a flutter to my stomach. *Thank fuck. Thank fuck she's here.*

"Seb." Her chest heaves in a panic and the machine goes wild.

I stroke her cheek and follow it up with a gentle kiss. "Shhh, Seb's fine, baby. You're both fucking fine," I tell her, not only reassuring her but myself too. She's fucking fine.

She relaxes against the pillow and closes her eyes.

I rest my head next to her. I'll be the first thing she sees when she opens those blue eyes again.

My back aches at the position I'm in, hunched over her bed, but I don't intend on moving, not a fucking muscle.

I'm where I need to be.

The door opens, but I don't lift my head.

"Has she woken yet?" Angel's voice drifts through the room.

"Yeah, she was asking about Seb."

"What are you going to do, Bren?"

I raise my head slightly to study her. She's concerned about Sky, and she should be. From now on, Sky comes first.

No other family.

No Mafia.

She's going to be free.

"I'll let her go if that's what she wants." I swallow thickly and rest my head back down, stroking my fingers through the tendrils of her satin hair.

"She won't want to." Will's voice is low, but I hear her.

I only hope she's right.

SKY

My head pounds, and my throat is dry. I open my eyes to find Bren's head resting in an awkward position on my pillow. His eyes closed, I take in his face, the scruff on his chin is longer than normal. I trace the age lines on his face with the tip of my finger and his blue eyes dart open. His whole body relaxes against my touch, and he gifts me with a soft, tight smile.

Before he slowly draws back. I watch the movement, a slight feeling of unease swirls in my stomach.

"Baby." He scrubs a hand over his head. "I got something to talk to you about." He blows out a deep breath, but I already know what he's going to say. I close my eyes, then quickly open them, determined to be strong.

I gulp. "It's Sam, isn't it?"

His jaw locks, and he ducks his head slightly with a solemn nod. "He's not good, baby."

I lick my dry lips, my vision blurry.

"There's err…" Bren fidgets uncomfortably. "There's something else…"

I watch his face carefully. He glances away from me, making me nervous.

"I fucked up." I nod at his words in agreement, *boy did he screw up*. "Really fucked up." He looks at me pointedly. He exhales. "I fucked another baby into you." His eyes dart to my stomach. "Doc, says its early stages yet but everything's going okay." He gulps and my eyes dart to his throat. Taken aback by his words, *a baby?*

I dip my hand to feel for a bump, but nothing, only a sharp pain that makes me wince. The gun shot.

"Don't fucking touch it, not yet," Bren snaps at me then breathes out in deep annoyance at himself.

"I know you don't want this life, Sky." He swallows thickly, his eyes locked on my hand, over my stomach. "I'll give you anything you want. You hear me? Anything?" His eyes come back to mine, the truth seeping from them. My heart tightens at his words.

"You want to be free?" Tears glisten and his throat clogs. "Then, you got that too."

My heart thumps in understanding. He's prepared to let me go, let me lead a life without him. Where I can be a teacher, be free.

With my babies.

Our babies.

But without him, I'd never be free because he has my heart, my body, my soul, my everything. He's all I ever wanted and more, *how could I possibly ask for anything else?*

"Bre… Bren?" Tears fill my eyes. "Forever?"

He chokes and glances away, refusing to look at me. His voice low, faraway. "Yeah, forever."

I shake my head from side to side because he misunderstands me. "Bren. Look at me. Please."

He turns toward me, showing his lip wobble and tears streaming down his cheeks.

"I meant, us. Forever, because without you, there isn't one."

His mouth drops open and his face crumples. He clears his throat. "Yeah?"

"Forever?" I ask him again.

"Fuck yeah." He darts toward the bed, his lips meeting mine, he peppers kisses over me, breathes in my hair, stroking and touching before kissing me again.

He whispers the words, "Forever. So much. For. Fucking. Ever."

CHAPTER 55

Bren

It's been three weeks since Sky came home, and I still can't believe she's mine. She chose me. She had all the fucking options in the world, and she chose me. Us.

The women have rallied around once again to help with Seb, while Sky takes it easy. They've been incredible, and the kids are hands-on with little Sebbie too.

I couldn't be fucking happier.

Con throws a chip at my head. "Are you playing this fucking game or daydreaming again?"

I glare at him, then down at the poker table. The games are getting less frequent, but we still manage one every month. This month it's at my apartment.

I take another pull of my beer just as Sky walks into the room, looking like a vision in one of my shirts and some leggings. She has the smallest of bumps now, and it gets my cock solid just knowing I put that on her. I adjust my dick under the table, and she lifts her eyebrow knowingly.

"Baby, you go have a bath while I finish this game, okay?"

She brings over some more chips and drops them on the table. I can't help but tug her onto my knee. "Be a good girl and do as I say, okay?"

She nibbles on her lip and gives me a coy smile. I move her hair behind her ear and nip at the flesh there. Her fingers find the back of my neck and I all but fucking melt into her.

"I have a date Friday," Oscar announces, making all our heads turn in his direction. The room falls silent.

"With who?" Sky asks. I love how at ease my brother is around her. Growing up, I protected Oscar from a lot of shit, we have some sort of a silent bond that I'm proud of, and now my girl has a connection with him too, it's almost like it's his way of thanking me for saving him, he lets Sky in closer than any of the other women.

"A woman I'm seeing," Oscar replies, dry and cold.

I roll my eyes. He's so fucking straight to the point and vague. *Why the hell mention it in the first place?*

"You're nervous," Sky states, not asking it as a question. I squeeze her thighs, both thanking her and reassuring her for opening him up more.

Oscar nods once. "I don't know what to do." He exhales loudly in annoyance with himself. "How to fucking act." He glares at the wall, not making eye contact with anyone.

"Do you know where you're taking her?" Sky continues on as though it's just them having the conversation.

"No." He winces and squeezes his eyes shut.

"She a hooker too?" Con queries and I tense up by how fucking dumb he is.

Oscar's head snaps in Con's direction. "She's not a fucking hooker."

Con glances over at me, his face marred with confusion. "Not anymore," Oscar tacks on at the end.

Sky rises as though taking a cue to change the subject. "I'm going to have a bath. Oscar, we'll talk about this tomorrow, okay?" He nods back at her.

She bends and pecks my lips, causing tingles to break out over my body. Fuck, I have it bad for her.

The door clicks shut and Finn leans forward. "Have we heard anything more about Chief Flemming?"

"He's off, sick, mourning the loss of his daughter who was in a road collision." He smirks at the end of his words. Sick fuck. I swear Oscar has some grim shit hidden inside him. I dread to think what the hell this girl is like he's so obsessed with. I mean, Reece said he's been fucking stalking her. *Fuck*, I scrub a hand over my head. *This is not what we need.*

"You think we can make a move and get rid of him while he's off sick? Maybe knock him off? You know the poor man did himself in?" Finn suggests.

Oscar nods, musing over Finn's words. "Could work. I have men keeping an eye on him."

Con claps his hands together completely out of the blue. "Anyway, my wedding is twelve weeks and one day away, motherfuckers."

We all groan. Because let's face it, it's been the longest time coming.

"I swear it's going to be epic!"

Here we fucking go a-fucking-gain.

EPILOGUE

S ky

"It's you (I've been looking for) – Lewis Brice"

The music begins, and the words drift around us. It's the song from the bar, the one that tells me I'm the one he's been looking for.

The sun setting warms my bare arms, my hair blows in the shallow breeze, and everyone stands with their eyes transfixed on me and Seb.

My eyes fill with tears. I take in the lanterns lit all the way up to the water's edge, where Bren's tall, muscular body turns, his eyes widen when he meets mine and his throat bobs. Slowly, his eyes drift down my flowy white wedding dress, taking in my swollen stomach before gazing lovingly down at Sebastian, who is cooing in my arms. His blond hair blows in the breeze too. He looks adorable in his little white linen shirt and navy pants, same as his daddy, but Seb also has on little suspenders holding his pants up.

As if being pulled by a magnet, I slowly walk barefooted through the sand toward my soon-to-be husband.

When my feet meet the wet sand, I stare up at Bren. His eyes are filled with tears too. He mouths the ending of the song to me, telling me, *it's you I've been searching for*. I choke on emotion.

He lifts Seb into his arms as the Officiant begins the ceremony.

BREN

A vision. She looks an utter fucking vision.

Seeing my girl standing here with my little boy, filled with my other son, makes my throat catch on a lump with pride. Her necklace hangs gracefully from her delicate neck, the sun catching on it with each movement, beaming as though a reminder of our love and connection.

I wanted to give her the wedding of her dreams.

I want to give her the world.

But all she wants is me.

Forever.

I utter the words the Officiant says, but don't really take them in. I'm as transfixed on my girl's bright-blue eyes as she is on mine.

The love seeps between us, like a love of no other.

Con steps up and takes Seb from me, Sky's eyebrows narrow in confusion as I untuck the small white note I wrote to her when I sent her to away college.

I clear my throat. "Sky, the first time I saw you, I realized you were that special someone that people talk about. The one you never want to leave." I rub over my heart, remembering the physical pain of losing her. "You were the one I was searching for, without realizing I was even looking. The one that hurts my heart just to look at. The one that makes me want to give you the world, even if that means breaking my heart to set you free. You're that one girl that will be in my heart forever." I nod at her and she smiles back, tears streaming down her face in the understanding of our word.

"I may have let you go, but know it's not forever, because you have my heart, Sky. You've taken it from me, made it yours, and I'll let you keep it for as long as you want it. Hoping it's forever." I finish the words but add the question I have to ask.

"What do you say?" I bite into my lip, waiting for her response.

Her smile widens, and she throws her arms around me. "I do."

"You may now kiss the bride."

I bend, my lips move down to hers, and as if in slow motion hers meet mine, tingles spread over my body at our contact.

My family cheer, hoot, and holler.

But I hear her whispered words above them, "I love you."

My body vibrates with happiness, my smile encompassing my face. "Love you too, baby."

"Forever."

THE END.

AFTERWORD

Want a little more?

Would you like more of Bren and Sky?
Come and sign up to BJ Alpha's newsletter for an exclusive extra scene and be the first to hear about the up-and-coming events and book news.

Use the link to get your copy of Bren and Sky's extended epilogue now: BREN Extended Epilogue

ACKNOWLEDGMENTS

Tee the lady that started it all for me. Thank you for an eternity.

I must start with where it all began, TL Swan. When I started reading your books, I never realized I was in a place I needed pulling out of. Your stories brought me back to myself.

With your constant support and the network created as 'Cygnet Inkers' I was able to create something I never realized was possible, I genuinely thought I'd had my day. You made me realize tomorrow is just the beginning.

To some special friends.

Kate, Emma and Heather. Ladies you da best. Thank you for keeping me sane on a daily basis, for all your support and love. I feel truly honored to have you in my life.

To Sadie Kincaid, thank you for putting up with me. I'm so grateful of your support, thank you for answering dumb questions and not blocking me.

Martina Dale, thank you for lifting me up when I need it and pushing me on. I can't wait to see what's in store for your future, you got this!

My girls at Kinks&Chaos, thank you ladies for accepting my crazy.

My D lovers, Tash and Jenn. You're incredible, supportive and always there for me. Thank you.

To the ladies in Cygnets, thank you for all your support. There's so many amazing authors in this group and lots of new ladies starting out. You've totally got this girls. It's amazing to see and be a part of. Thank you for having me.

Swan Squad
I don't know where to start with you ladies, your support is unbelievable, and I feel choked up just writing this. With the help of Tee and the Swan Squad my life has changed so very much. Not only because of writing but because of the friendships this group has brought into my life.

Bren, Patricia, Caroline, Claire, Anita, Sue, Mary-Anne and Sharon a special thank you.

Beta Readers
Thank you to my Beta Readers love you so much, thank you for your continual support and bringing me back when I'm on the edge.

Jaclyn, Kate, Heather, Rhi and Libby.

ARC Team
To my ARC readers thank you. I really don't know what I would do without you all. I now have so many

group chats I never knew I needed in my life. You go above and beyond with your support. My group is growing so much that I'd need a book to list you all! Your reviews, graphics, videos, wow!

I just want you to know I appreciate each and every one of you.

To my world.

To my boys, thank you for everything. I know you find my writing embarrassing, but I hope you realise I don't care what you do in your life as long as you're a good person and are happy, that's everything. If that means you write porn, so be it, I can help with that. Ha ha.

To my hubby, the J in my BJ. Thank you for listening to my filth, I know you benefit from it so really you should be thanking me. But in all seriousness, I wouldn't be doing this without you, so thank you. Without you I wouldn't be BJ Alpha. Love you trillions!

And finally…

Thank you to you, my readers. Thank you for help making my dreams a reality.

ABOUT THE AUTHOR

BJ Alpha lives in the UK with her hubby, two teenage sons and three fur babies.

She loves to read and write about hot, alpha males and feisty females.

Follow me on my social media pages:
Facebook: BJ Alpha
My readers group: BJ's Reckless Readers
Instagram: BJ Alpha

ALSO BY B J ALPHA

Secrets and Lies Series

CAL Book 1

CON Book 2

FINN Book 3

BREN Book 4

OSCAR BOOK 5

CON'S WEDDING NOVELLA

Born Series

Born Reckless

The Brutal Duet

Hidden In Brutal Devotion

Love In Brutal Devotion

STORM ENTERPRISES

SHAW Book 1

Printed in Great Britain
by Amazon